A Cold Dark Heart

Stephen Puleston

ABOUT THE AUTHOR

Stephen Puleston was born and educated in Anglesey, North Wales. He graduated in theology before training as a lawyer. A Cold Dark Heart is his eigth novel in the Inspector Drake series

www.stephenpuleston.co.uk
Facebook:stephenpulestoncrimewriter

OTHER NOVELS

Inspector Drake Mysteries

Brass in Pocket
Worse than Dead
Against the Tide
Dead on your Feet
A Time to Kill
Written in Blood
Nowhere to Hide
Prequel Novella– Ebook only - Devil's Kitchen

Inspector Marco Novels

Speechless
Another Good Killing
Somebody Told Me
Prequel Novella– Ebook only -Dead Smart

Copyright © 2020 Stephen Puleston
All rights reserved.

ISBN: 9798623002792

In memory of my mother
Gwenno Puleston

Chapter 1

The moon's pallid glow filled the cloudless sky barely illuminating the figure hugging the field boundary. Avoiding the ditches and keeping near to the thick hedgerows involved laborious progress. Walking over the damp surface meant socks moistened inside trainers.

After negotiating the first gate, progress was slow and deliberate. Stopping occasionally to register for signs of activity before reaching a dilapidated stone post on which a rickety wooden gate hung, the visitor paused. A gloved hand shook it. It creaked in protest.

Then voices broke the silence.

Despair now as two, no three, figures strolled up the field. Head torches crisscrossed the darkness. Another at knee height swung around.

Youngsters lamping.

A hiding place was needed urgently. Running for a gate nearby was the only option. But the ground was soggy, and progress was laboured, breathing heavy and ribs rattling against a thumping heart. Pausing by the gate and glancing left, the lights were closer now, bobbing up and down, piercing the darkness.

Cursing silently at the heavy chain keeping the gate locked in place; it meant clambering over it as slowly and as silently as possible, praying the gate wouldn't groan or creak.

Falling into a ditch on the other side, panting lungs pulling in deep mouthfuls of breath before focusing for the sound of approaching voices. Silence encouraging a few short steps back to the gate. The backs of the three men walking down the field meant muscles weak with relief. They would return to their homes at some point, but they would probably be out for at least another two or three hours.

More than enough time.

Skirting around the edge of the field heading away from the other lampers now.

Wasting time only heightened the unease dominating the visitor's thoughts.

Two more gates leading into a smaller field and in the distance, the outline of the estate of bungalows. Pausing by a galvanised water trough there was time to scan the surroundings. Squinting into the darkness the gloom and solitude were reassuring.

Ahead, all the properties were well maintained, had manicured lawns and well-tended flower beds. A post and wire fence lined the field side of the estate, the rest of which was bounded by a low, stone boundary wall. Apart from one bungalow at the end, which held no interest, all the lights had been extinguished, the homes in darkness.

Exactly as expected.

Chapter 2

Detective Inspector Ian Drake sat in the room reserved for police officers and prosecution lawyers at Caernarfon Crown Court. He grimaced as he sipped on a plastic cup of insipid, stale coffee. Having to attend court that morning was an unwelcome distraction from the mountain of paperwork needing his attention. One of the first cases he had dealt with after returning from a holiday in Disneyland Paris with Annie and his daughters had been a domestic incident. A woman had called in the early hours and a uniformed officer and a community support officer had attended. But the situation had deteriorated when both had been badly assaulted.

The defendant had a string of previous convictions over several years and an abusive and violent relationship with the victim. He was well overdue a long prison sentence.

Drake had managed a few squares of the medium sudoku puzzle in the newspaper but three tricky squares were proving problematic. He didn't notice Andy Thorsen, one of the senior Crown Prosecution Service lawyers, approaching until he had put his drink on the table next to Drake's.

Drake looked up. 'Andy, good morning. I didn't expect to see you here.'

Thorsen sat down and sighed. 'I know, the prosecution counsel spoke to me last night suggesting it might be best if I attend. It is Judge Hawkins after all.'

It was the nearest he had ever seen to Thorsen expressing emotion. Drake hoped for some facial expression but Thorsen didn't oblige. The presiding judge had a disagreeable temperament that every lawyer who appeared in the Crown Court dreaded.

'How did your holiday go?'

Thorsen's interest in his personal life wrongfooted Drake. The lawyer had never enquired about Drake's family before. Drake paused and looked over and met Thorsen's gaze. 'It was great thank you. My daughters had a wonderful time. It was nice to have a family holiday.'

Thorsen nodded. 'I've been thinking of going myself.'

It made Drake realise how little he knew about Thorsen. He had no idea if he was even married. Asking if Thorsen's children might enjoy Disneyland Paris implied a lack of knowledge but not doing so seemed impolite. Thorsen was a professional colleague so Drake ignored the potential embarrassment. 'How old are your kids?'

'Twelve and fourteen. They've been complaining to their mother that their friends have been. But the idea of going to an amusement park for a holiday doesn't come top of my list.'

'The kids will enjoy it.'

'Yes, I know. My wife keeps telling me that.'

Small talk never came easily to Drake, and Thorsen barely understood the meaning of the word. Drake pondered discussing the details of the case, but the pre-trial management meetings had already done that. They couldn't plan for every twist and turn, especially when Judge Hawkins was presiding.

'Have you heard the rumour that Judge Hawkins might be retiring next year?' Thorsen said and then lowered his voice. 'Apparently there have been complaints.'

Drake raised an eyebrow. It encouraged Thorsen to continue. 'Some members of the Crown Court staff have complained about his bullying behaviour and there was even a whiff of a complaint about inappropriate conduct.'

'It doesn't surprise me. I know he can be… bombastic.'

'That's one word for it. I don't think I've spoken to any lawyer who has a good word to say for him. He treats everyone before him with complete contempt.'

'I had a case involving him some years ago.'

Thorsen frowned at Drake as though he were struggling to remember the facts. Drake helped out. 'The case of the fisherman who was impaled with his own fork.'

Thorsen nodded his recollection. 'Of course.'

Idly they mulled over the details of the prosecution. Thorsen mentioned the name of the prosecuting barrister who wasn't familiar to Drake. There were always strengths and weaknesses in every case and provided the case reached the threshold of being in the public interest, and more likely than not to succeed, a prosecution would follow. As a witness Drake couldn't enter the courtroom until he was called to give evidence, so he had a morning, perhaps longer, to spend in this room, killing time. Wasting his time in this way annoyed Drake, especially as it was a racing certainty the jury would convict. Once Thorsen had been called into court Drake would turn his attention to the paperwork he had brought with him, but not before he had worked through the rest of his sudoku.

Drake was still struggling with some tricky squares when Thorsen returned, a pleased look on his face.

'Good news. He's changed his plea.'

'Good.' Drake stood up, gratified he wouldn't be at court all day.

'Aren't you going to wait for the sentencing?'

Drake glanced at his watch as Thorsen added ominously. 'Judge Hawkins will expect it. He's going to deal with another case first, but you should be clear by lunchtime.'

Drake doubted if there was any point returning to headquarters. He could work from home that afternoon and Annie might be home already after her early morning departmental meeting at the university. These meetings were a recent development by a new head of department, who had been Drake's tutor when he was at university. He hadn't met his old teacher yet although Annie kept threatening to arrange a get-together.

'Yes, I don't want to annoy Judge Hawkins.'

Drake fumbled for his mobile before texting Annie.

Looks like I'll be home early XX.

The liaison officer returned, offering them more coffee and Drake and Thorsen both nodded. Thorsen settled into making calls and Drake overhead him telling his office that the trial had collapsed. The same court official returned with two coffees and cellophane-wrapped digestive biscuits.

Drake took a sip of his drink and immediately regretted doing so. Perhaps he should have asked for water. Just then, his telephone bleeped a message and, assuming it was Annie replying, he scooped up the handset to answer.

Urgent. Please contact operational control.

Drake stiffened and called the number. 'Detective Inspector Drake.'

'We've had reports of a suspicious death. You've been asked to attend.'

'When did this happen?'

'The body was found this morning. We'll send you the postcode.'

'And the CSI team?'

'I've just been asked to contact you.' The line went dead.

Drake turned to face Thorsen. 'I've got to leave.'

'Judge Hawkins won't be happy,' Thorsen replied.

But Drake was already out the door before he'd finished speaking.

Chapter 3

Drake crunched his Mondeo into first gear and shot out of the side street near the Crown Court building. At a junction he indicated left and sped out of Caernarfon. The postcode punched into the satnav gave him an address on the outskirts of Menai Bridge: a journey of no more than a few minutes. Once he was onto the road that bypassed the village of Y Felinheli the speedometer registered over eighty miles an hour. After joining the A55 dual carriageway that stretched over the North Wales coast, he took the short drive over the Britannia Bridge.

The satnav directed him towards Maes yr Haf and Drake noticed the black lettering on the white street sign at the beginning of an estate of bungalows. A marked police car had drawn its passenger side wheels onto the pavement.

As Drake parked up, he noticed a blue Mini was parked in the drive of number six, and in front of the garage door Drake spotted an ageing 3 Series BMW. Two paramedics sat in an ambulance, and there was another in a first responder car. They each gave Drake an expectant glance.

The front door was ajar and Drake pushed it open and entered. He was met in the hallway by a uniformed officer.

'You got here quick, sir.'

'I was in the Crown Court in Caernarfon. What's happened?'

'Emyr Isaac was found by his carer this morning. His head has been smashed in.'

'When do you expect the pathologist?'

'Should be here any minute. And the CSI team should arrive any time.'

'Why is an ambulance and a paramedic vehicle outside?'

'The carer called them. She's in quite a state.'

'You had better show me the body.'

'One other thing, sir. There's a sign of a break in.'

They detoured into the kitchen where broken glass

littered the floor underneath the back door. 'Don't touch anything and when the CSIs arrive make certain you tell them about this.'

Drake followed the officer through into the bedroom. He stood for a moment taking in the room. A large UPVC window offered a view over a lawned garden at the rear with an ornamental pond and carefully cultivated plants and shrubs. An elderly man lay on a thick pile carpet below a gas fire that was screwed to the wall. Blood smeared its metal casing, and there was more over the carpet and all over the man's expensive-looking pyjamas.

A wound was evident on the man's head and blood had caked all over his face. The eyes peered upwards, empty and lifeless. A walking frame was pushed against a radiator and through the open door in the far corner the smell of urine and bleach tickled Drake's nostrils from what he assumed was an en suite bathroom. Fitted wardrobes filled another corner and the rest of the furniture looked expensive. The sheets and duvet didn't look slept in.

Had the man disturbed a burglar?

Or had the old man fallen and cracked his head on the gas fire?

Drake heard the sound of the front door creaking open and the voice of the uniformed officer. 'Come through this way, sir.'

Dr Lee Kings, the pathologist, joined Drake. He was about five foot eight, a couple of inches shorter than Drake and hadn't aged well, judging by the ruddy complexion.

'Good morning, Ian.'

Drake stood back, allowing Kings to enter. 'I thought you were on secondment in Manchester.'

'Started back this week. What have we got?'

'He was found by his carer this morning.' Drake tipped his head towards the body.

'Any sign of foul play? Murder weapon left on the kitchen table with a written confession?'

'Very funny. I'll leave you to it.'

Drake left the bedroom and joined the uniformed officer in the hallway. 'Rachel, the carer who found him, is in one of bedrooms, sir.'

Drake raised a challenging eyebrow.

'The lounge is a mess and I assumed you'd want to talk to her.'

'What do you mean *mess*?'

The officer opened a door in the hallway and waved Drake in. Inside crockery and plates were strewn in angular fragments all over the floor. Heaped in one corner were empty drawers, their papers and stationery piled nearby.

Drake heard vehicles slowing and parking. He left the room and, leaving the house, saw the scientific support vehicle arriving and behind it Sara emerging from her car. Mike Foulds, the crime scene manager, was the first to approach Drake.

'I suppose you're going to tell me that the crime scene has been contaminated by dozens of people.' Foulds sounded harassed.

Drake shrugged. 'I've just got here. Carer found the owner dead this morning. I haven't spoken to her yet.'

Foulds nodded, stepped into the house and after acknowledging the uniformed officer disappeared down the hallway. By then Sara had joined Drake and he gave her a brief summary.

'We need to talk to the carer.' Drake headed for the door.

A woman with vibrant bottle blonde hair sat nursing a handkerchief on a single bed pushed against one wall. It was the only furniture in the room.

'Rachel, I'm Detective Inspector Ian Drake and this is Detective Sergeant Sara Morgan. I understand that you found Emyr Isaac this morning. It must have been a shock, but I'd like you to tell me everything you can remember.'

'I was later than usual. I got delayed by one of my early

appointments. They never give us enough time to do all the work with everybody. I could have been here sooner had Mrs Thomas not kept me. She's a nice old dear but she can talk the hind legs off a donkey.' Drake couldn't place Rachel's accent – Northern Irish maybe or Scots even.

'I called the office and told them I might be late. They usually ring ahead and warn the next appointment on my list if I'm delayed. But nobody answered. I didn't think anything of it, I thought he might have been sleeping in. He can be a grumpy old bugger. Some of the girls never liked coming here and there was one girl who refused point-blank because he'd assaulted her.'

Sara was sitting alongside Rachel and leant forward slightly. 'Did you see anybody else when you got here?' Rachel shook her head.

'Did you hear anything unusual or out of the ordinary?'

Another shake. 'I'm not in any trouble, am I? Just because I was late. I mean I couldn't have saved him, could I?'

Sara shot Drake a glance, suggesting he reassure Rachel.

'I think Mr Isaac has been dead for several hours…'

Rachel let out a long slow breath as though Drake's reassurance allowed her to release the tension bottling up inside her.

Once Drake and Sara had established Rachel's home address and contact number, as well as the details of her employers, they told her she could leave and followed her out onto the drive. As she reached to open the door of the blue Mini, Drake spoke. 'Do you know if he had any family?'

'His wife died a few years ago. He didn't have any children. I didn't hear him talk about family.'

Drake thanked Rachel and once the paramedic had moved his vehicle she drove away. Drake gestured for the two paramedics in the ambulance to join him.

'Do you know anything about Mr Isaac?' Drake asked both men.

'We've been here a few times. He became quite a regular.' The older of the two paramedics spoke first, his younger colleague nodding agreement. They were joined by the third who trotted over after parking his car.

'Another one of our old fogeys kicking the bucket then,' the man said.

'I've been here a couple of times,' the younger paramedic from the ambulance piped up. 'He could be a right awkward customer. We could do nothing right for him and he kept suggesting we weren't properly trained.'

Behind him Drake heard his name being called as the pathologist emerged. He turned to the paramedics, a more detailed conversation about Isaac would have to wait. 'We'll need to speak to you all again in due course. But for now, you can go.'

He made his way back to the property as the ambulance and paramedic vehicle left Maes yr Haf. Lee Kings put his bag on the tarmac by his feet. 'I'll be able to give you a better explanation once I've done the post-mortem, but I can't rule out an accidental fall. I'll see you first thing in the morning.'

Drake nodded. Another post-mortem to attend. Another long day.

Valerie Picton-Davies had sunken cheeks, a thin skeletal figure and short cropped hair that made Drake think she was a regular marathon runner. She sat behind a desk at the offices of Caring Wales piled high with paperwork and three handle-less mugs for pencils and ballpoints as well as two old coffee mugs. There was a film of dust in between the piles on her desk that made Drake feel queasy. How could anyone work in such disorder and chaos?

She had sounded shocked when they explained about Emyr Isaac.

'I don't think he's got any relatives.' Valerie was from Anglesey judging by her accent. She flicked through the file of papers. 'I don't know how much of this information I can really disclose. It's confidential after all.'

'Mr Isaac is dead.' Drake managed to get enough irritation into his voice to earn him a sharp glare from Valerie.

She returned her attention to the documents in front of her. 'Just as I thought,' she sounded relieved. 'We don't have a next of kin for him. I can tell you who his GP was.'

Sara jotted down the details in her notebook.

'What care were you providing for him?'

'He was getting three calls a day. But he could be difficult. Because he'd been so awkward and, frankly, aggressive with several of our team members, particularly the girls, we were running short of staff who were prepared to go there.'

'Was he ever violent towards your staff?'

Valerie sat back in her chair. 'Providing home care facilities is the Cinderella service. We get paid peanuts by the local authority. We're supposed to provide calls that last no more than twenty minutes.' She raised her hands, showed her palms in desperation. 'And what can you do in twenty minutes? After we've spoken with the patient, found out how they are and boiled the kettle for them to have a *paned.*' She used the Welsh word for a cup of tea. 'What else can we do? A lot of our patients have complex needs. And then there's Brexit, well don't start me on that.'

Drake exchanged an exasperated glance with Sara that Valerie didn't pick up.

'The staff we usually get from Europe have completely dried up. Before long we simply won't be able to recruit carers. The system will grind to a standstill.'

Drake raised his voice enough to get Valerie's attention. 'It is important for us to establish if any of the carers had been threatened or assaulted by Emyr Isaac. We met Rachel at the property – she was the one who found his body.'

Valerie nodded energetically. 'He got on well with Rachel. She didn't take any of his nonsense. I mean... She was caring and thoughtful... The government and the county council are expecting us to do miracles. And every year the budget gets tighter and tighter. Pretty soon there won't be anybody left to do this work. And what's going to happen to us then?'

Sara cut across her. 'We'll need full details of all the carers who called at Mr Isaac's over the past few months.'

Valerie fixed Drake with a serious gaze. 'Surely you don't suspect one of the carers might have...'

Now Drake responded. 'It will be to eliminate them from our inquiry of course.'

Valerie darted a glance between Drake and Sara, obviously not satisfied by Drake's response. He added, 'At this stage we can't be certain that Emyr Isaac was murdered.'

'This is terrible... I shall need to speak to the director of the company in Cardiff... He can be—'

'I'm sure that he'd want you to cooperate fully. And your file of papers would really be helpful, so I hope you won't have any objection if we take that with us now.' Drake made it sound the most reasonable thing in the world.

Valerie hesitated. 'There's nothing in it apart from his personal details and the older records of the work completed by the carers each day.'

She closed the folder.

'How do the carers record what they do?' Sara said.

'There's a blue folder in the house where they can record their comments,' Valerie replied.

'We'll need to recover that,' Drake said and made to stand up. He reached over for the folder Valerie still clutched tightly, before she reluctantly handed it over. In exchange Drake gave his card. 'Please email us the full rota of your staff for the last month who called at Emyr Isaac's home.'

Valerie nodded unconvincingly and they left.

Outside Drake made for the car with Sara. Who would have a motive to kill an old man? Although he was paid to be suspicious, perhaps it had just been a burglary that had gone wrong. But an unexplained death always meant digging into the victim's life and Drake wondered what they would find.

He unlocked the car as his mobile rang. He didn't recognise the number.

'Detective Inspector Drake.'

'It's Constable Mowbray. I am at Emyr Isaac's house.' Drake recognised the young officer's voice. 'One of Isaac's neighbours has turned up. She's very distressed. I think you should get back here.'

Chapter 4

Three elderly men were passing the time of day on the pavement in Maes yr Haf. Each wore a heavy jacket as though they were expecting snow imminently. They gave Drake's Mondeo an inquisitive stare as he drove towards number six. Constable Mowbray emerged from the property and appeared relieved to see Drake and Sara.

'A neighbour has been insisting she speaks to you. She's in quite a state – demanding to see you when I told her she couldn't possibly come into the house.'

'Why would she want to do that?' Drake said.

'She kept on about some of her property being in the bungalow and that she had valuable information.'

'Where does she live?'

Mowbray nodded towards a bungalow over Drake's shoulder. 'In number ten. It's Mrs Field. And she's probably spotted you arriving. So, she'll be expecting you soon.'

Drake turned to Sara. 'Let's talk to Mike Foulds before we speak to Mrs Field.'

Sara followed Drake into the bungalow and, passing the sitting room door, spotted two crime scene investigators hard at work, another busy in the kitchen. Mike Foulds was finishing in the bedroom.

'We should be finished by this evening,' Foulds sounded pleased and relieved in equal measure.

'Any preliminary results?'

Foulds shook his head. 'There are numerous fingerprint traces.'

'Probably the carers and the paramedics and visitors to the house,' Drake said. 'There should be a folder the carers use to keep notes about each visit.'

'In the kitchen,' Foulds said. 'Did he have any family?'

Drake shook his head. 'We don't believe so.'

'How sad. It must have been lonely.'

Drake turned on his heels. 'We're going to talk to a neighbour. Send me the report as soon as.'

Drake detoured out of the rear door from the kitchen into the garden. Weed free lawns abutted bark-laden beds where everything had been prepared for winter. The grass was well tended and a little longer; maybe it would need one more mow this year. Beyond the boundary, fields stretched out into the distance. Thin post and wire fencing provided the only protection against livestock entering the garden.

Had the killer traipsed over the fields to reach the property?

Or had he – or she, Drake wasn't going to rule out a woman having been responsible – taken a risk and boldly walked up Maes yr Haf before breaking a window and entering?

'It's a lovely garden,' Sara said.

'If it was a break in the burglar took a risk smashing a window.'

'All the other residents of the estate would have been fast asleep,' Sara said.

Drake nodded. 'We'll have to wait until we get Mike Foulds' report.'

They left the garden and found Mowbray talking to another serious looking individual by the front gate.

The man turned to Drake. A well-honed, upper crust English accent and his question suggested he regretted the end of the colonial era. 'Are you the local inspector in charge of this inquiry?'

'And who exactly are you, sir?'

'Now look, don't get evasive with me. I asked you a straight question.'

Mowbray gave Sara a helpless sort of look. Drake nodded to Sara before turning to the man who had succeeded in getting under his skin. 'I'm sure if you contact Northern Division headquarters someone will be able to help you.'

'I'm not used to this sort of rank insubordination. It's totally uncalled for. What's your name again?'

Drake was already walking away and didn't turn back

to acknowledge or reply.

'Who the hell does he think he is,' Drake said under his breath.

Sara chuckled.

They walked up to the front door of number ten Maes yr Haf. The doorbell sounded a sombre greeting inside the property. A woman in her eighties with a heavily made up face and a full head of glistening white hair, tightly permed, opened the door and scrutinised Drake and Sara with clear confident eyes.

'Are you the police?' Her accent was a couple of notches down from the far back version Drake had encountered moments earlier.

'Detective Inspector Ian Drake and Detective Sergeant Sara Morgan,' Drake said after holding up his warrant card. 'Mrs Field?'

The woman nodded, pushed the door open in a gesture inviting both officers in. 'Agnes Field. Do come in.'

The hallway of the bungalow was wide and comfortable. For the second time that day Drake strolled over an expensive Axminster carpet. Photographs of three healthy-looking graduates in a cap and gown had pride of place along one wall. Several different coats hung on an antique coat stand tucked against another. Field led them into the sitting room, its window overlooking the estate road. Drake caught a glimpse of Mowbray, still deep in conversation.

A wood burner filled the room with a warm reassuring heat. Agnes Field pointed to a sofa and sat down on a chair allowing her skirt to drape over her knees.

'Constable Mowbray said you had some important information. How well did you know Emyr Isaac?' Drake said.

Field let her gaze drift out through the window, the realisation that a neighbour had died clearly painful. 'My late husband and Emyr were good friends.' Her pronunciation of Emyr was possible. In Drake's experience most English people pronounced the Welsh 'y' as an elongated 'e'.

Field continued after a pause. 'We've lived here for fifteen years. My husband retired after thirty-five years in banking. He had family connections to Anglesey, so we bought this place.'

'Mrs Field. What can you tell us about Emyr Isaac?'

'That constable was very rude.'

Drake tipped his head inviting her to continue.

'He told me I couldn't go into the house, but I had to check whether anything had been stolen.'

'Stolen?'

'Yes, of course. Emyr had some antique crockery and china as well as several original Sir Kyffin Williams paintings. And then there were the first editions he owned. I even lent him some of my late husband's books. They are extremely valuable, Inspector. After all, my husband had collected the books over a lifetime.'

'We'll need full details of the books – names of the authors and titles.'

'And what about Emyr's personal possessions. I can check. I knew exactly what he owned. And then there was his cash.' She let the last sentence hang in the air.

'Cash?' Drake said.

Field nodded briskly. 'He would boast about having cash in the house. I told him not to broadcast it to all and sundry. He always kept several hundred pounds in his bedroom.'

Sara made her first contribution. 'I'm afraid it will be impossible for you to go into the property as it is an ongoing crime scene.' She added a brief smile that Field reciprocated with an understanding nod.

'It still doesn't justify that constable talking to me as he did.'

'We'll have a word with him.' Sara said, managing a

warm tone.

Field carried on undeterred. 'When will it be possible for me to go around the property. I'm sure I can tell you if things are missing. After all he didn't have anybody else. No family.'

'We cannot allow anyone inside who isn't part of the investigation as it could lead to contamination of evidence,' Drake said.

Field nodded energetically. 'But this is hardly the same, surely. You know who I am. I was one of his friends. Patrick, my former husband, was in the Freemasons with him. Both were terribly keen. They went to all these fancy dinners.' Her enthusiasm for reminiscing died away.

Drake took the opportunity to enquire about Isaac's circumstances. 'Did Emyr ever mention any family?'

Drake's question refocused Field's attention as she looked over at him. 'He didn't have any children if that's what you mean. I think there are some distant cousins who live in London, but I don't think he was in regular contact with them.'

'One of my officers will be in contact with you in due course but perhaps you could make a list of your possessions that could be in the property.'

'I would much prefer to talk to you, Detective Inspector,' Field used her best ingratiating tone. 'After all this is a murder inquiry.'

'I appreciate that, Mrs Field, but all the detectives on my team are—'

'Have you spoken with that awful woman Rachel?'

Drake paused. 'Do you mean the carer who called this morning?'

'I couldn't abide the woman myself. Emyr thought she was wonderful because she spent more time with him. She used to call to see him even after she finished her shift – can you believe that?' Field lowered her voice conspiratorially. 'He had intended leaving her a large legacy.'

'How much was Emyr Isaac going to leave her?' Sara asked what Drake was thinking. Money always made for motive.

'Nothing,' Field sounded irritated.

'Mrs Field, I don't understand,' Sara said.

'He changed his will after he found out about her husband. He'd been doing the garden and odd jobs around the place, but when Emyr found out that he had been inside for fraud he was determined to change his will.'

Sara shared a glance with Drake, both realising that they couldn't ignore Mrs Field's comments.

Drake trying to sound as casual as he could. 'You don't happen to know the name of the solicitor who prepared Emyr Isaac's will do you?'

'Of course.'

Field shared the name of a firm in Bangor that Sara noted down in her pocketbook.

After thanking Agnes they left and returned to Isaac's property. Drake found his mobile and tapped out a message to Annie – *New inquiry this morning. Late home x*

Two hours later Drake stood in front of the hastily erected board in the Incident Room. En route to headquarters he had called at the GP practice where Emyr Isaac had been a patient. It had taken a significant amount of persuasion and cajoling to get the practice manager to find time to consult with a partner for authority to release Isaac's medical records. Now they sat in a folder near Sara.

The solicitor that had prepared Emyr Isaac's will was out of his office and wasn't expected to return until the following morning. No amount of coaxing could persuade the receptionist in the office to find Emyr Isaac's file.

Gareth Winder pushed open the Incident Room door which crashed with a loud bang against the wall behind it. He entered holding a tray of four coffee mugs. Shorter than

Drake and wearing a tie permanently undone gave him a dishevelled appearance which wasn't helped by the extra pounds he carried. He distributed the coffee around the table. Sara nodded her thanks at Gareth, who moved over to deposit a mug in front of Luned Thomas, the other detective constable on Drake's team. She was the serious one, the one who could focus on being thorough and meticulous when Gareth Winder was untidy and uncoordinated. She didn't have his immediate warm personality but since joining Drake's team she had become an invaluable member.

Emyr Isaac's driving licence photograph had been printed out and was now pinned to the board.

'Emyr Isaac's body was found this morning. He was eighty-nine years of age and in poor health. It looks like a suspected break in: glass had been broken in the rear door and the property had been trashed. His body was found in the bedroom lying on the floor.'

'Who found the body?' Winder said.

'A carer called Rachel Ackroyd. We've also spoken to the care company who organised carers that called on Isaac every day. There is a suggestion from a neighbour that Rachel and her husband had been ingratiating themselves with the victim in the hope of benefiting from his will. Apparently, Isaac changed his mind when he found out about Rachel's husband's criminal record. The neighbour told us she knew Isaac kept a large amount of cash in the house.'

Winder and Luned nodded. Money always meant a motive.

'What's the husband's name, boss?' Winder said.

Drake glanced over at Sara who dictated the full name – Peter Ackroyd.

'Get a PNC check done,' Drake said to Winder. A search of the police national computer would give them full details of any convictions against Peter Ackroyd. 'And do the same against Rachel Ackroyd too.'

'When's the post-mortem being held?' Luned asked.

'First thing in the morning. We should get the results from the forensics tomorrow. We need to do house-to-house in the local area and after the post-mortem Sara and I will call at the solicitors who prepared his will.'

'The press have been in touch,' Luned added.

'What! That was bloody quick.'

Winder piped up. 'And I've had this English toff on the phone complaining like mad about you, boss. Demanding to know who is really in charge.'

Perhaps it had been unwise to be quite as dismissive with the man talking with Constable Mowbray.

'If he calls again – tell him I'm the senior investigating officer. And get his full name address and contact number. In the meantime, let's work out if this was an accident or whether we've got a killer to catch.'

Chapter 5

Sara arrived promptly outside the mortuary and, after parking, waited for Drake. During the previous inquiry Drake had attended post-mortems without her and at the time it had troubled her, but she had dismissed her concerns as being oversensitive. A fellow officer had also dismissed her concerns as something she should ignore, saying something like 'it is Ian Drake after all' – which Sara thought was a little unfair. She had got to know Ian Drake reasonably well and she had certainly seen him change after he had started his relationship with Annie Jenkins.

But since his return from holiday Sara had noticed a greater formality and a heightened impatience. She put all this down to the presence of Superintendent Hobbs and knew it would take time for Drake to become accustomed to his superior officer, just as it had taken time for her to become familiar with Drake's routine.

She spotted Drake's Mondeo as it approached the entrance to the car park. Once he had found a parking slot, she left the car and joined him.

'Morning, boss.'

'Morning Sara. I wonder what Lee Kings will have in store for us this morning.'

The mortuary assistant sitting at a desk in the reception office had two buttons of his shirt undone revealing wisps of dark hair on his chest. His gaze lingered over Sara a second too long and she glared back at him, ignoring his greeting.

'You'll need to sign in.' He pushed over paperwork for Drake and Sara to sign. Sara squiggled quickly; Drake added a more formal signature.

The assistant led them down a corridor towards the main mortuary and on into the post-mortem lab. Inside Dr Kings was humming along to music playing in the pods neatly nestled in his ears. He gave Drake and Sara a warming smile and waved them over.

'Bloody brilliant things,' he removed the pods from his ears and the sound of an orchestra leaked out. 'I can be in my own little world and nobody would know anything about it. That was a Shostakovich violin concerto. Absolutely brilliant composer.'

'My father liked his string quartets. I was brought up with them as a child,' Sara said.

'At last,' Kings exclaimed. 'An officer with some taste. I have been wallowing in the belief that all police officers had little appreciation of classical music.'

Kings' assistant busied himself with readying the well-used stainless steel instruments for the post-mortem. He didn't look the sort of person to appreciate classical music: more heavy metal, Sara thought.

When Kings pulled back the sheet covering the corpse, and Sara caught a glimpse of the naked Emyr Isaac, she caught her breath but hid her shock. The old man was literally skin and bones. The shoulder blades jutted out prominently, the skin looked gossamer thin and blotchy.

Kings started with an examination of his head, neck and shoulders, pulling the skin to examine each blemish. The laceration overlying the fracture in his skull remained gaping, although it was now clean.

Kings took time examining the wound, tilting the head and running his hand around the skull then comparing the wound to the photographs the crime scene investigators had provided. After a few minutes he stood back and announced. 'The wound is consistent with a fall against the gas fire that features in these photographs. Whether that would have been enough to cause death is another matter.'

'Could he have bled to death?'

'It's possible. But the location of the wound isn't near any major artery so it would have been a slow process. Having said that, he's an elderly man and scalp wounds can bleed profusely.'

Sara pressed a fist to her mouth. She rued her lack of

experience at post-mortems, blaming Drake for not having given her the opportunity of becoming more familiar with the scene in the mortuary.

Kings continued. 'Let's see what else we can uncover.'

Kings enthusiastically ran his fresh scalpel blade around Isaac's head, then proceeded to meticulously peel at the various layers of tissue until the shiny white bone of the skull was exposed.

'This bit will be noisy' he said as he reached for a reciprocating saw, after donning a pair of safety glasses. The saw sank through the skull and within moments the top of Isaac's skull was removed. Sara couldn't help but feel it reminded her of opening a boiled egg – something she thought she'd never be able to do again.

'Ahh, this is what killed him,' King's pointed to a large clotted mass overlying the bruised brain. 'An extradural haematoma. This blood clot would almost certainly have led to his death.'

He reached for the scalpel and drew it along the chest and abdomen with a Y-shaped incision extending from both shoulders to the navel. Instinctively Sara stepped back and took a series of deep breaths. The ribs came apart with a splitting sound, the chest cavity opening to reveal the organs which had once sustained life. Sara looked away, returning her gaze only when Kings had removed the heart and lungs and started dictating his report.

Kings stood back and looked over at Drake and Sara. 'I checked his medical records before starting. He had high blood pressure and there is a history of heart disease.' Kings pointed towards Isaac's feet. 'Tell-tale sign of heart problems is the pitting oedema around his ankles.' Kings jerked a finger at the swollen areas around Isaac's ankles.

Kings continued with an examination of Isaac's abdominal cavity, then continued with a detailed inspection of the hands, wrists and upper arms. He examined each of the dead man's nails in turn, taking scrapings from each. He concentrated his attention on the left wrist, frowning as he worked carefully.

'There's bruising to the left wrist and arm which suggests he struggled with somebody, perhaps he resisted his attacker. Although eighty-nine-year-olds bruise very easily the evidence suggests a struggle and force being applied. You'd be surprised how strong older people can be. This man seems to have had a healthy lifestyle, but old age has done its worst to his body. I don't like doing post-mortems of older people. It makes you realise what's ahead of us.'

There was an embarrassed silence.

After a few seconds Drake thanked Kings, said nothing to the mortuary assistant and nodded to Sara that it was time to leave. They stepped outside into the autumn sunshine and stood for a moment breathing deeply.

'That's the first time I've heard Lee Kings complain about his job.' Drake said. 'I always thought he loved cutting up dead people.' He looked over at Sara. She was still feeling queasy and uncomfortable. 'Are you all right?'

'I'll be okay,'

'Let's go and see those lawyers about Isaac's will.'

Williams and Evans occupied rooms on the first floor of a building in the nearby town of Bangor and describing them as offices would be complimentary. Everything about the place had a stale, second-hand feel to it. Rickety old chairs filled a small narrow reception area and a woman in her sixties gave Drake an uninterested look through a glass partition.

'We've come to see Richard Evans – it's about a client of his – Emyr Isaac.'

'Take a seat.'

Drake listened as the woman spoke in Welsh into the telephone announcing that he and Sara had arrived. A table in one corner had glossy magazines and Sunday supplements several months old, as well as the local Papur Bro, the Welsh language community newspaper, with its front page adorned with pictures of children from the primary schools.

Drake didn't have to wait long before the door creaked open.

'Good morning. Richard Evans.' The man reached out a hand. Drake reciprocated and Evans gave him a brisk lifeless shake. He did the same with Sara before inviting them to follow him.

Evans jerked a hand at two wooden chairs alongside the large table he used as a desk in his room. At first glance he didn't seem much younger than Emyr Isaac. Wisps of hair dotted his scalp, tufts sprouted from his ears and a down of white fluff covered his neck. Placing his elbows on the arms of the chair exposed the thin worn material of his suit that matched the greying white shirt. No hint of a successful wealthy lawyer here, Drake thought.

'It's very sad about Emyr. I'd known him for years.'

'Were you friends?' Drake said.

'I suppose so.' Evans had a warm Welsh accent that reminded Drake of his father. 'I understand you were Emyr Isaac's solicitor and that you prepared a will for him. We'd like to know some details about his circumstances as he didn't have any immediate family.'

Evans nodded sombrely. 'I think it might be best if I made a record of exactly your interest.' He opened a blue-covered legal pad on his desk. 'Now let me be clear, it's Detective Inspector Ian Drake and Detective Sergeant Morgan.' He paused for a beat. 'Do you have identification?'

A pair of intelligent eyes looked over at Drake.

Drake and Sara fumbled for their warrant cards and Evans jotted down all the relevant details before giving both officers a professional smile.

'Now, where were we?' Evans relaxed.

'You were responsible for writing a will for Mr Isaac,' Drake said.

'Of course. Emyr left most of his estate to three local

charities. He was keen on protecting the environment, so he gave one third to a wildlife trust and the rest to two charities dealing with disadvantaged children.'

'We've spoken with a neighbour who suggested he had been planning to benefit one of his carers. A woman called Rachel Ackroyd.'

'That's correct. He had provided a legacy for Rachel for over £50,000, quite a substantial amount of money. But…' Evans was obviously enjoying his moment in the spotlight, adding as much theatricality to his fifteen minutes of fame. 'He was intending to remove the legacy.'

'Did he say why?'

'No, he didn't and before you ask, I didn't enquire. If a client wants to change his or her will then it's my job to write a will accordingly.'

Sara made her first contribution. 'When you say *intending* do you mean the will was never signed?'

Evans dipped his head in a gesture signifying his agreement. 'I had prepared the draft will and I corresponded with Emyr, sending him a copy through the post.'

'You didn't contact him via email?' Sara said.

Evans gave her a bewildered look. 'The digital world has passed me by, I'm afraid. I'm far too old to start now.'

'So, Rachel Ackroyd benefits from Emyr Isaac's will to the tune of £50,000.'

'That's correct, Detective Sergeant.'

Evans patted a file of papers on his desk. 'We've made copies of the original will and all my correspondence with Emyr, including a draft of the new will. Emyr prepared a detailed inventory of all his chattels. He wrote out clear instructions about what should happen to them.'

Drake reached over and scribbled his signature on the receipt on the top, handing it back to Evans. 'Do you know anything about his background that might help us?'

Evans shook his head. 'I'm sorry I can't be of more assistance.'

Drake picked up the folder and they left the offices of Williams and Evans. Outside the chill of the autumn air cooled his skin. 'Let's get a coffee,' Drake said.

A few minutes later Drake sat at a table in a coffee shop overlooking the bustling high street. Sara returned from the counter with two hot drinks, the thick cream on the surface of Drake's Americano was just as he liked it. He let it cool and took a sip, pleased it was strong and clean tasting. He had already flicked through the file Richard Evans had given them.

'There are several letters from Evans to Emyr Isaac discussing the changes to his will.' Drake said, as Sarah stirred sugar into her latte.

'So, it's perfectly feasible Rachel could have seen the correspondence and realised she was going to lose out on her £50,000.'

'Money, the root of all evil,' Drake said darkly.

'The love of,' Sara corrected him. 'What did you make of her?'

'She struck me as honest, but perhaps she's a good actor. In any event we shall have to talk to her again in due course. As well as building a detailed picture of any other carers that called to help him.'

'How did the carers get access to the property? Did Mr Isaac have to let them in every time?'

'No, there's a key safe near the front door.'

'So anybody who knew the combination could let themselves in to his house.'

Drake nodded his agreement and took another mouthful of coffee.

An email reaching his mobile took his attention and he read the request from Superintendent Hobbs for a preliminary meeting to review and discuss the inquiry later that afternoon. This would be his first full length investigation where he'd be answerable to Hobbs and a sliver of anxiety made Drake feel suddenly uneasy.

Chapter 6

The crime scene investigators at Emyr Isaac's home were hauling bags of equipment to the scientific support vehicle when Drake and Sara walked up the drive. The yellow fluttering perimeter tape around the property the day before had now been removed. Soon normality would return to Maes yr Haf. To the casual observer nothing would appear to have taken place in the quiet cul-de-sac of bungalows.

The intense stares from residents driving past Drake as he arrived told a different story. The lives of the middle-class homeowners had been turned upside down. Locks would be double checked every evening, security systems installed and more attention given to the neighbourhood watch meetings.

They stood waiting as the investigators finished their work. Sara took a moment to look out over the properties. 'How many of them have got any convenient CCTV cameras?'

The availability of CCTV footage often provided crucial evidence in modern police inquiries. Its absence would mean they'd have to rely on old-fashioned evidence gathering. Drake surveyed the dozen or so bungalows. He couldn't see any cameras discreetly placed underneath eaves or tucked under the gable of any property.

'The residents never had any reason to install CCTV cameras.'

Drake guessed the statistics for the number of crimes committed in the area would be low. A suspicious death like this would create worry and distress. Normally the family would provide a picture of the victim's background. In this inquiry Drake's team would need to be doing that themselves. At this stage the break in and the bruising on Isaac's arms meant they had enough to treat the death as suspicious. Isaac may have confronted a burglar who had overpowered him, causing him to fall against the fire. It might not be a murder charge but manslaughter. There would be evidence somewhere, Drake reassured himself.

Drake turned to see Mike Foulds standing on the threshold.

'Good timing,' Foulds said. 'We've just finished.'

Foulds took them into the bedroom where they had spoken to Rachel the day before. 'We've dusted everything, but there are dozens of prints. You'll need to gather fingerprints from everyone for the purposes of elimination.'

'Carers came in to look after Isaac on a regular basis,' Drake said.

Foulds led them through into the kitchen that stretched around the side of the property to the rear.

'We recovered the glass shards from the broken window and fragments of clothing from the handle and the lock.' Foulds pushed open a door nearby. Drake peered into a wet room and toilet and raised his gaze to the narrow oblong window high up near the ceiling.

'It looks like your man tried to get in through the window first. There's a paint-covered metal stepladder outside.'

Drake gazed up at the smashed pane. 'Why would he try and get in through such a narrow gap?'

Foulds shrugged. 'That's your job.'

They retraced their steps into the kitchen where Drake and Sara stood for a moment looking out over the garden and then towards the fields beyond.

If it had been a bungled break in then why had Isaac been targeted? An old man had died in his home and that sickened Drake. Something about the crime scene would give them the answer... it had to.

The doorbell ringing followed by the sound of knuckles being rapped on the door took Drake's attention. He walked through the hallway and opened the front door where he recognised Mrs Field.

'I thought it was you, Inspector. I noticed you arriving earlier and when I saw the crime scene investigator leaving, I thought it would be a good time to come over. May I come in?'

Agnes Field had the manner of a headmistress unaccustomed to anyone challenging her. When Drake hesitated, she added. 'I want to establish if the first editions my husband owned have been stolen. They are of considerable sentimental value to me.'

'Of course, Mrs Field.' Drake eased the door open.

Confidently Agnes Field found her way to the sitting room. She gaped at the empty display cabinets. 'Oh dear.'

Retreating back into the hallway Agnes pushed past Drake into the second reception room on the ground floor. Seeing the table and chairs were still in place she relaxed. 'This is a Queen Anne dining table. It was Emyr's pride and joy, he inherited it from a relative who ran an antiques business.'

The satisfied look on her face was short lived when she cast her gaze around the walls and more glass fronted cabinets. She shook her head morosely and tut-tutted before she examined the contents of a bookcase.

'It might be helpful, Mrs Field, if you were able to tell us the titles of the books your late husband owned.'

'I'll prepare a detailed list. I know from talking with Emyr that he kept them in a box in this bookcase.' She took a step backwards, surveying the shelves in their entirety. 'And as you can see, there's no sign of the box and none of these books,' she wafted a hand towards the various paperbacks and hardback biographies and history tomes, 'are of any value at all. A burglar must've targeted Emyr. It's exactly what Jonathan thought.'

'Jonathan?' Drake said.

'Tremain, Jonathan Tremain. He lives at number three. Terribly nice man and very wise and sensible. He guessed Emyr was killed when he tackled an intruder.'

Sara sounded reassuring. 'It's far too early for us to make any conclusive determination. But we shall want to reassure everybody who lives in Maes yr Haf as soon as we know more details.' Sara continued, even managing to smile at Agnes Field. 'We'll know more once all the forensic tests have been completed.'

Field didn't look convinced. 'And did you discover his iPad and mobile? He loved to read the news on his iPad, but I have no idea why he had a mobile. Poor thing.'

An iPad and mobile hadn't been recovered so Drake assumed they had been stolen too. Aware that he needed to make progress, Drake added, as politely as he could, 'Mrs Field, thank you for your help. Please let us have details of the first edition books Mr Isaac had borrowed. But if you don't mind, we still have a lot of work to do.'

'Yes, of course, I understand.' Agnes made for the hallway and the front door. After stepping outside she turned to face Drake and Sara. 'I shall need to make an insurance claim. There'll be so much paperwork.'

'Do please contact us if you need anything.'

Drake walked back into the sitting room. Spending time understanding the victim's personal circumstances was always valuable. A tall cupboard against one wall was full of china and cranberry glass that had been left undisturbed. They were too delicate and difficult to move. Drake checked the list of possessions Richard Evans had given him and flicked through it trying to match the contents of the cupboard to the items on the sheet in his folder.

Sara opened a writing desk. 'There's nothing much in here,'

'There must be bank and credit card statements, details of investments that sort of thing.'

Sara nodded. 'He doesn't strike me as a person who would have kept digital records.'

Drake studied the list of the chattels again and glanced around the room. 'Do you recognise any of the paintings listed on the solicitor's file?'

Sara nodded at a striking landscape over the fireplace.

'That looks like one of two Kyffin Williamses on the solicitor's list.'

The well-known Welsh artist had a recognisable style and had been the doyen of middle-class Welsh art collectors. It would almost be a surprise if Emyr Isaac didn't have a Kyffin.

Sara made her way out of the room and Drake lingered before following her. Isaac had sat in this room, entertained friends, laughed with his wife, drunk his favourite tipple and watched television. As his world grew smaller, he would have used the room more infrequently, slept more and – from what they knew – he had upset the carers, those who were paid to look after him. Old age was cruel and perhaps Isaac had found it hard to bear.

Drake met Sara as she emerged from one of the rooms. 'It's a bedroom,' Sara retreated allowing Drake inside. A single bed with an old-fashioned eiderdown dominated the floor. Heavy wooden furniture intended to last the entirety of a married life filled the space.

'Who's going to sort all this stuff out?' Sara said.

'I suppose it'll be Richard Evans.'

'It's so sad. That he didn't have any family, I mean.'

Drake walked down the hallway and into another bedroom. Pushed against a wall were two metal filing cabinets. Drake yanked open the first drawer and it squeaked its reluctance.

Papers and correspondence had been stuffed into suspended files hanging off the side rails. Drake lifted one out, identifying circulars from company registrars about dividend payments and company restructuring proposals. Sara started on the second filing cabinet and soon announced. 'I think I've found the bank statements.'

She hauled out of the drawer a folder embossed with the logo of a high street bank. She opened the first and whistled under her breath. 'He had over one hundred thousand pounds in his current account.'

Operational support could organise emptying the house so Drake called the department and, after finishing, turned to Sara. 'Let's go and see some of the neighbours.'

The owners of number one were an elderly couple who knew Emyr Isaac and had been shocked by his death. Drake asked the usual questions about any suspicious activity in the estate recently. They both shook their heads. Sara adopted a kindly tone when she asked if any of their neighbours might have noticed or mentioned something to cause them concern. She was rewarded with a blank look.

'We've never been involved with something like this before.' The wife said to nods of approval from her husband who added. 'This is such a quiet estate.'

Drake didn't expect to see the face of a younger woman when the door of number two was opened. The sound of a baby crying inside was also unexpected. She gave their warrant cards a quick glance.

'I'm in charge of the inquiry into Emyr Isaac's death.'

She nodded but the child sobbing took her attention as she glanced over her shoulder. 'I don't think I can help you. I didn't know him, and I haven't seen anything. Jonathan Tremain next door says Mr Isaac was killed by a burglar. Is that true?'

Drake found a business card and stretched out his hand. 'If you think of anything then do please contact us.'

They retraced their steps down the drive and clicked the gate closed before making their way to number three.

'Mr Tremain sounds like a real know-it-all,' Sara said.

'You'd better get your warrant card ready,' Drake said as they made for Tremain's front door.

After two rings the door opened, and the man Drake had seen on the first afternoon at Maes yr Haf appeared. He gave Drake and Sara a brief, smug look as they held aloft their warrant cards. 'Detective Inspector Ian Drake and this is Detective Sergeant Sara Morgan.'

'I know who you are.' Tremain pushed the door open

Drake frowned and moved uncomfortably in his chair.

Hobbs continued. 'It was a Jonathan Tremain.'

'English accent?'

'I hope you're not prejudiced against our English cousins?'

Drake scrambled to recover. 'Not at all, sir. There was a lot of activity yesterday and I was trying to recall who the gentleman might be.'

Hobbs raised an eyebrow. 'Mr Tremain is a retired local government chief executive from the south-west of England. He name-dropped some of the senior officers he had previously worked with as the chairman of the neighbourhood watch group. And he is involved in local civic and historical societies. He is the sort of person it pays not to alienate.'

'Yes, of course, sir,' Drake said.

'I've spoken to Inspector Jones who oversees the CID work on Anglesey and he's informed me there's a fairly limited pool of possible suspects amongst the usual burglars so it might be constructive if you were to set up a meeting with him.'

Hobbs enjoyed giving him the thinnest of patronising smiles.

Drake replied, a fraction too keenly. 'We have been able to establish that the carer who found Emyr Isaac's body was interviewed on suspicion of abusive behaviour when she worked at a residential home in Northern Ireland several years ago. And her husband has convictions for fraud and one for assault. And she was going to receive fifty thousand pounds from Isaac's will.'

'Really!' Hobbs exclaimed.

'But Isaac planned to change his will and remove the gift.'

Hobbs sat back. 'So that would give her a motive.' He nodded encouragingly.

'We should have a detailed picture of all the carers with

access to Isaac's home tomorrow.'

Hobbs ignored Drake. 'We need to reassure members of the public, bearing in mind the average age of the residents in that estate. And also to the wider general public that we are doing everything to protect their well-being. I propose organising a press conference as soon as possible. I'll need you to be present, of course.'

'Don't you think it's a bit premature, sir?'

Hobbs dismissed the objection as bordering on rebelliousness. 'Not at all. We make a public appeal for anyone with information to come forward. You know full well, Detective Inspector, that so much of police work these days is intelligence driven.'

'What does Susan Howells think?' Drake said referring to the civilian in charge of public relations at Northern Division headquarters.

Hobbs drew himself closer to the desk and glanced over at Drake. 'That'll be all for now. I'll email you the details about the press conference. And one more thing. I shall be assuming the role of senior investigating officer. So I expect regular, comprehensive updates of all progress.'

Chapter 8

The following morning Drake sat around the kitchen table trying – and failing – to enjoy breakfast with Annie. He had woken early, his thoughts dominated by the image of Hobbs' narrow eyes closing to slits as he announced that he would be the senior investigating officer. The superintendent's face had shown little emotion and Drake had found it difficult to fathom out exactly what was going on in Hobbs' mind. He was convinced his superior officer had enjoyed telling him that he wouldn't be the SIO.

Hobbs was entitled to be SIO, he had told himself.

But still it felt wrong. And it unsettled Drake.

When Superintendent Price had been in charge Drake would have been made the SIO. Now he didn't know how to react.

'You haven't listened to a word I've said? Are you still worrying about not being in charge of the inquiry?' Annie raised her voice enough to gain Drake's attention.

Drake managed a lifeless attempt at a reassuring smile. 'I'm sorry. It's difficult with Hobbs in charge. Working with Wyndham Price was easier. I knew where I stood.'

'We need to discuss this birthday party your mother is organising.'

Drake had expected his mother to downsize after his father's death and sell the farmhouse where she lived – his childhood home. The fields of the smallholding were let on a grazing licence, but Drake assumed the tenants might purchase the land if his mother were ever to sell.

Joining various local groups and enjoying day trips expanded her social network; it all meant she was looking forward to the rest of her life, now that her grieving was over. Her self-consciousness was evident when she told Drake that a man she had known for several years, Elfed, himself a widower, had asked her out. The idea his mother might be dating again had amused Drake. Susan, his sister, was less impressed. Mair's birthday was the reason for the party Annie was talking about, but his mother wanted to introduce Elfed to the family, get their approval.

'Has Susan confirmed her plans?' Annie said. 'You really need to talk to her.'

Annie hadn't met Susan yet and he sensed the apprehension in her voice.

'She and her two children are travelling up in the middle of the week before the party as it's the school holiday.'

'Shall I ring your mother and ask if there's anything I can do to help?'

Drake nodded. 'She'd like that.' Organising family occasions was something his mother enjoyed. It gave her an opportunity of entertaining even though they were not a big family. 'Huw and his children will be there too.'

Annie finished her coffee. 'It's a shame I haven't been able to meet Susan before the party.'

'I'm sure things will be fine.' Drake tried reassurance.

'It must have been difficult when you learned about Huw.'

Annie appeared more relaxed about meeting his half-brother and his family than she was about meeting Susan. Perhaps he had portrayed Susan a little too harshly. Discovering the whereabouts of his half-brother had certainly been challenging. More difficult was overcoming Susan's suspicions that Huw had an ulterior motive for wanting to be part of their family. She couldn't accept Huw simply wanted to find his place in the world, know who his family was.

'My mother knew all about Huw and she took his discovery in her stride. Susan was the awkward one. I still feel annoyed with my father that he didn't tell us when he was alive.'

'He probably couldn't face sharing it with you. After all it must have been quite a scandal when he was younger.'

'Even so, I can't help feeling it would have helped had

he told us.'

'This latest case isn't going to be a problem, is it?'

The worry in her voice reminded Drake that Annie's parents were staying that weekend. Annie's father had retired, and it meant her parents were planning to move home from Cardiff to North Wales. Comments from Annie about the opportunities for her promotion in the department suggested she was settled and although they hadn't spoken about marriage, Drake sensed she wanted more permanence to their relationship.

'I'm sure it'll be fine.' Drake hoped Annie didn't sense any uncertainty in his voice.

Once he finished the last of his coffee, he kissed Annie, found his jacket and left the house for his commute to headquarters. He joined the A55 and listened to the morning's news broadcast. The battle between the various contestants for the Democratic party's nomination in the forthcoming presidential elections in the United States was beginning to garner more coverage.

He indicated off the A55 at the first junction for Colwyn Bay and bought a newspaper from the same newsagents he visited when he had lived with Sian in the town. He folded the paper open at the moderate sudoku puzzle and completed a dozen squares, before continuing his drive towards headquarters, his mind settled.

He was the first of his team to arrive although he wasn't alone when he pushed open the door to the Incident Room and faced Inspector Owen Jones. He knew his colleague from training courses and their paths had crossed many times.

'Morning Ian,' Jones said, despite his name there was little trace of a Welsh accent.

'Owen. I was going to contact you later this morning.' Drake managed to make the statement sound questioning.

'Super Hobbs spoke to me yesterday.' Jones laced his voice with mystery.

Drake nodded towards the door to his office and Jones followed him inside.

Drake was uncertain how to interpret Jones' comment. 'He's the SIO on this investigation.'

'SIO?' Jones shared his surprise as his voice raised a pitch. 'I thought you'd be in charge... I mean as the SIO.'

Drake shook his head.

'What do you make of him?'

'He is very different from Wyndham Price.'

'It was a shame he retired. You become accustomed to people, don't you? Comfortable with the way certain officers like to handle things. You always knew where you stood with Wyndham.'

Drake nodded.

Jones continued. 'Do your team know that Hobbs is the SIO?'

Drake shook his head. 'Not yet. I was only told yesterday.'

'Look, Ian, I know you have a good team. Hobbs is poking his nose in because he's recently been appointed.'

Drake sat back in his chair mulling over Jones' comment. It reminded him of a brief conversation he'd had with Detective Inspector John Marco of Southern Division who had warned him that Hobbs would look after himself. It meant he needed to be careful in his dealings with his superior officer, certainly until he was more confident about the way Superintendent Hobbs worked.

'So how can you help?'

'As requested, I've put together a list of the regular south Anglesey burglars. There are only really six habitual candidates.' Jones handed a sheet of paper over the desk to Drake.

He read the unfamiliar names. Their potential involvement in the inquiry would need to be established.

'What can you tell me about the crime scene?' Jones said.

Drake summarised what they knew so far, Jones occasionally interrupted asking for clarification. Once Drake finished Jones added, 'So it could be a burglary that went wrong? If Isaac's an awkward cuss he might have tackled the intruder. Has anything been stolen?'

Drake nodded. 'Some cash: we don't know how much. Isaac's mobile and iPad are missing. And there were some valuable books we can't trace, owned by a neighbour. They could be worth a tidy sum.'

'But difficult to sell.' Jones let the reply hang in the air. A burglar would want to realise the value of anything stolen reasonably quickly. Trying to dispose of a rare book would be tricky and too sophisticated for the average south Anglesey burglar. 'Anything else? Jewellery? Televisions – although even these days you can buy them so cheap it's hardly worth pinching them.'

'One of the neighbours has seen people lamping in the fields nearby in the middle of the night.'

'You could talk to the Bryn y Neuadd estate – their land borders the estate where Isaac lived. Poachers aren't the sort of thing we get involved with.'

Drake returned his attention to Jones' list. 'Should we keep an eye out for any of these names in particular?'

Jones pondered for a moment. 'Mervyn Ostler is a real hooligan. He's always looking for a big chance.'

'Thanks, Owen.'

Jones made to get up and behind him in the Incident Room Drake could hear the team assembling. 'If there's anything I can do, Ian, get in touch. And don't let Hobbs get under your skin.'

Not so easy when he's refused to appoint me SIO without explanation.

'Where do I start?' Foulds gave Drake a world-weary shrug.

'At the beginning?' Drake pulled up a stool alongside Foulds.

'We recovered at least a dozen full and partial fingerprints. As well as fragments of clothing and sand and gravel on the kitchen floor near where the glass had been smashed. The glass fragments don't have any fingerprints – but I wouldn't expect any.'

'Does that include all the glass fragments from the bathroom window?'

Foulds nodded. 'I couldn't work that out. Why would the killer try to get access through a narrow window?'

'It was at the rear of the building. Perhaps he thought there was less chance of the sound of breaking glass being heard.'

Foulds paused. 'Once he realised he couldn't get in through the bathroom window he must have decided to try the kitchen. He got lucky because Isaac had left the key in the door so that's when he smashed the glass. If you trace who did this then you might find some shard or minuscule piece of glass in his clothing. The stuff goes all over the place.'

'It sounds as though he or she was careful.'

Foulds adjusted his position on the stool. 'I ran the fingerprints through the usual database. The only person of interest is Peter Ackroyd. I understand he is married to one of the carers.'

'Where did you find his fingerprints?'

'They were in the kitchen, on the door into the hallway and on the bedroom door.'

'It sounds like he was a regular visitor. And the other fingerprints?'

'Nothing on the PNC. The place felt like a bungalow used by an old man who had regular carers coming in every day. My guess is that the fingerprints and partial we found belong to them. Not very helpful I know, Ian.'

Drake hauled himself off the stool and thanked Foulds. It was only to be expected. The mass of fingerprint and potential DNA material might be confusing, unhelpful and until they had a person of interest or suspects Drake could see the inquiry getting bogged down. As he left the forensic laboratory an email reached his mobile from Superintendent Hobbs notifying him that a press conference had been organised for the following morning. It was premature, too premature for Drake's liking. It was going to be a display for the media that Superintendent Hobbs was in charge, that things were being handled by a senior officer. How many murder inquiries had Hobbs actually supervised?

Back in his office Drake adjusted the photographs of his daughters on his desk before settling down to work.

Chapter 9

Winder was well accustomed to Luned's lack of small talk but driving over to Menai Bridge that morning it surprised him when she commented on Drake's apparent diffidence that she ascribed to Superintendent Hobbs. Winder hadn't noticed any change and he mumbled his agreement when Luned said, 'It must be difficult having to take orders from someone new. The boss knew what to expect with Super Price.'

Winder drove down into the middle of the town and spotted the mobile incident room near the entrance to the library. After parking they walked over, discovering two elderly women deep in conversation with a sergeant whose facial expressions made clear his patience was running thin.

'But we always park here.' The accent sounded local but grand as well.

'As I've said, madam.' The sergeant tipped his head towards Winder and Luned. 'The detectives in charge of the inquiry need to be certain that every member of the public has the opportunity to come forward.' He lowered his voice. 'After all an elderly gentleman died in suspicious circumstances.'

The second woman who had long auburn hair in carefully coiffured folds and wore a deep purple cashmere overcoat sounded concerned, her voice trembled. 'I slept with my lights on last night. It's terrible. I'm old enough to remember that case years ago when that poor woman was slaughtered in her own home.' She paused for breath. 'That monster who killed her took a knife and cut her heart out. Then he drank her blood. Can you believe it. Here on Anglesey.'

The uniformed sergeant gave Winder and Luned a pleading, can-you-help-me look. Luned offered words of comfort. 'That was a long time ago madam and we have dozens of police officers and detectives busy at work on this investigation. I'm sure it'll only be a matter of time before we apprehend the culprit.'

Both women gave Luned startled looks, obviously hearing her but not listening to a word she'd said. Winder contributed. 'We have specialist officers that could give you advice about making your home completely secure.'

They turned and gave him a frightened look. It was difficult to judge whether his and Luned's contribution was helping. He could sympathise with both women's fear and anxiety.

The uniformed sergeant cut in. 'If I could take your names and contact phone numbers, I can make arrangements for officers to call.'

Both women appeared satisfied and after providing their details they left. Winder heard them discussing where they would have coffee.

The sergeant turned to Winder and Luned. 'Thanks, I thought I'd never get rid of them.'

'Have you had anything useful come in?'

The sergeant shook his head. 'All the usual stuff. Older people terrified about the prospect of somebody breaking into their home and killing them.'

'It's amazing how gossip gets around,' Winder said.

Luned struck a concerned tone. 'I can well imagine how an elderly person would feel, especially living on their own.'

The sergeant again. 'I've had a couple of other people mentioning that ritualistic satanic killing. But it was almost twenty years ago when that happened.'

Winder nodded. 'It'll be like yesterday to a lot of people.'

They spent half an hour discussing the house-to-house inquiries in and around Menai Bridge. Every house in every housing estate would be visited by uniformed officers and if promising leads emerged a more detailed statement would be taken. Winder's gaze turned to the area near Maes yr Haf on the outskirts of the town.

Winder knew that every murder had a motive and every

killer left a trace – at least that's what they had to hope. Visiting the householders surrounding Emyr Isaac's home would be more about public relations than in the anticipation of gathering admissible evidence. But it was a task Winder enjoyed nevertheless. Luned had contributed constructively to handling the two elderly women earlier although she couldn't possibly have known anything about the previous murder. He had only learned about it recently from older officers involved in the case.

The uniformed sergeant complained about the allocation of manpower before asking. 'Will there be a press conference?'

Winder shrugged.

'I hear the new super is a bit of a cold fish.'

'He's new.' Winder added abruptly enough to signal that he wasn't going to be dragged into gossiping about Superintendent Hobbs. 'Luned and I will do that estate of bungalows – Hafod Eryri – next to Maes yr Haf.'

'Of course. Let me know how you get on. I'm not going anywhere.'

After leaving the incident room Luned stood outside looking over the road towards the studio used by a television company for a popular Welsh language soap opera. 'I loved *Rownd a Rownd* when I was younger. I wanted to be an actress then.'

'What happened?'

'My father didn't think it was a good career move. He said I needed to think about my pension and career prospects.' Luned turned on her heel and joined Winder walking back to the car.

Winder drove the short distance out of the town, passing a couple of marked police cars and officers doing the rounds of house-to-house inquiries. He pulled in alongside the pavement at Hafod Eryri.

The householders of the first two properties were couples in their seventies who welcomed the opportunity of discussing the recent horrific events in the neighbouring estate. Luned took command of the conversations naturally as both were native Welsh speakers. Winder understood enough to know she made unflattering but good-natured comments about his inability to speak the language. They left once it was clear that neither had anything constructive to add. Two of the properties they visited were empty and Luned scribbled in her notebook the house numbers she would report back to the uniformed sergeant in due course. They tackled another homeowner as he was washing his car on the drive. He complained about the lack of police resources – bemoaning the absence of officers on the beat. It surprised Winder he was old enough to remember that sort of policing.

At the next bungalow a man emerged from a side door. At first, he didn't notice them, turning his attention to replacing a key in the key safe screwed to the wall. He gave them a surprised look as he finished. Winder had his warrant card ready. 'Detective Constable Gareth Winder and this is Detective Constable Luned Thomas. We're part of the team investigating the death of Emyr Isaac—'

'Don't say any more. I don't live here. If you want to speak to the homeowner he's inside. He's quite frail.'

'Are you a relative?'

'No, I'm just a delivery driver for the meals on wheels service. Mr Shepherd isn't too good today.'

'Can we speak to him?' Winder said.

'I'll get the key.' The man turned and punched in the code giving him access to the front door key. He shouted a greeting and entered, leading them into a sitting room at the rear of the property extended to include a conservatory. It was stifling inside, the clinging odour of disinfectant and drying clothes filling the air.

An elderly man sat in an upright armchair, dozing.

'Mr Shepherd,' the man raised his voice slightly. 'The police are here.'

The man opened his eyes and looked up at Winder and Luned quizzically. 'Who?'

Winder kneeled down. 'Mr Shepherd we're investigating the death of Emyr Isaac in Maes yr Haf.'

'Who?'

Winder shared a glance with Luned – both agreeing little could be achieved by speaking with Mr Shepherd.

'He's not usually like this,' the man said. 'A carer calls to organise his meal later. I've left it in the fridge.'

Winder got to his feet as Mr Shepherd's head slumped back, his eyes closed, his breathing shallow. They retreated to the hallway and then outside.

As Winder watched the man walking down the drive it struck him he might be able to help. So he jogged down towards him. 'Before you go,' Winder spoke up to gain the man's attention. 'Did you deliver to Emyr Isaac's property?'

The man shook his head. 'No, I didn't. But Merv went there.'

'Where can I contact him?'

'Try the café.'

Once Winder had the contact number, he turned to Luned. 'Wasn't quite a waste of time.'

It was a short journey to Café Menai where a thick heavy smell of frying food hung in the air. It reminded Winder of the greasy spoon restaurants he'd favoured in his youth and which guiltily he still longed for occasionally. There could be something satisfying about a plate of fatty bacon, fried egg and baked beans. The very thought made him salivate.

Luned was ahead of him as she spoke to a man behind the counter. Winder joined her as he weaved through the various tables, the occupants enjoying a late breakfast or early lunch.

'We'd like to speak to the person who organises the meals on wheels service.' Luned had already flashed a warrant card as discreetly as possible. Winder didn't bother.

The man behind the counter led them to a door leading to the rear of the property and pointed them down the corridor to a door at the far end. 'You'll want to speak to Norman.'

Norman wore a navy butcher's style apron over a thin white T-shirt. The three-day stubble and the smell of second-hand cigarette smoke in his room didn't enhance his image as a clean and tidy cooking professional.

Luned kicked off the conversation. 'We're investigating the death of Emyr Isaac and we understand he was a customer of yours.'

Norman gave her a pained expression.

'What do you do here?' Winder looked around the makeshift office.

Norman squinted at him. 'What do you think? I run a café.'

'What's this got to do with social services and meals on wheels?'

'Nothing. I'm not social services. People pay me. And I get volunteers to deliver the meals to people who want them. I'm not doing this for free.' He checked his watch. 'Can this wait? I have to be in Holyhead in half an hour – I'm supposed to be organising the cooking for an event in the sailing club. I'm already late.'

'It won't take long.' Luned folded her arms adopting a we're-not-going-anywhere stance.

It earned her and Winder another grimace. Then Norman clicked on his mouse and stared at the monitor as it came to life. Winder and Luned stood and waited. Eventually Norman looked over at them. 'Emyr was an awkward bugger. Merv took him his meals. But he was always complaining about the food and he'd never pay on time.'

'Did Merv deliver every day?'

'Yes, usually. Isaac didn't have any family as I recall.'

'Do you have a contact number for Merv and his full

name?' Winder said.

Norman blew out another impatient lungful of air. 'Will you leave after that?'

'The number, please,' Winder said.

Once Luned had written the details in her notebook she and Winder retraced their steps back to his car.

'I'll call in with this name.'

Winder called Inspector Drake. 'Boss, we've traced the identity of a man who delivered meals to Isaac's home – a man called Mervyn Ostler.'

'Who?' Drake exclaimed. 'Get back here – now!'

Chapter 10

Drake stared at the image of Mervyn Ostler printed from the police national computer records. Ostler's string of previous convictions confirmed Inspector Jones' assessment that he could be a potential suspect. The various conversations he had had that morning with local land agents and the Natural Resources Wales officers responsible for prosecuting poachers had proved inconclusive. But Drake wasn't going to dismiss the possibility the culprit had reached Isaac's home by tramping over the adjacent fields.

It had been two days since Emyr Isaac's body had been found and Drake and his team were overdue a formal review. Drake dreaded the prospect of Superintendent Hobbs's press conference being ineffective, and only compounding the sense that the investigation had little to go on.

It troubled Drake why an opportunistic burglar had gone to the trouble of taking rare books unless he already knew of their value. Taking cash and electrical items was to be expected as was ransacking the house, but stealing first editions seemed odd. Documents removed from Isaac's home confirmed he had stocks and shares worth over a quarter of a million pounds. Isaac certainly had no financial problems.

And was there anything in Emyr Isaac's background they had overlooked? Had his killer harboured a grudge over decades? But if so, why kill the old man now? It struck Drake as unlikely, so his mind turned back to the possibility Isaac had disturbed an intruder. And finally, Drake focused on Rachel Ackroyd – did they have enough to arrest her? Being disinherited by Isaac gave her motive. And she had access to the house. But was she a killer?

Winder and Luned talking to Sara in the Incident Room wrestled Drake from his pondering. Various greetings followed as Drake joined them and walked over to the board where he turned to face the team.

'Mervyn Ostler,' Drake announced, turning to focus on

Ostler's face pinned to the board. 'He has a comprehensive record for burglary and theft, but he's kept his nose clean in the last three years.' Drake turned to Winder. 'And now we discover he delivered meals to Emyr Isaac.'

Winder took it as an invitation to respond. 'Café Menai is responsible for a meals on wheels service in the Menai Bridge area. Nothing to do with social services. Mervyn Ostler is one of the volunteers who delivers the meals.'

'Ideal cover if you want to identify a house with rich pickings,' Sara said.

Luned adopted a sceptical tone when she contributed. 'It's a bit obvious though. And a hell of a risk knowing we could discover his record.'

'We can't ignore him, so I want a full background check undertaken. Let's establish some details of any of his known associates. Ostler might be stupid enough to pass information to his mates in the pub about Emyr Isaac.'

Drake paused and moved his attention to the image of Emyr Isaac. 'I still want more details on Isaac's background – work and family, all the usual stuff. I've spoken to forensics this morning and there's nothing in their preliminary report to assist us. But Rachel Ackroyd and her husband's fingerprints are all over the property.'

'Much as we expected,' Sara said.

Drake nodded. 'Have we had the results on the background checks from Scotland and Northern Ireland?' Winder and Luned shook their heads. 'Chase them. I want to know far more about both Rachel and her husband before we decide to speak to them. Potentially losing £50,000 would have given Rachel one hell of a motive.'

Drake turned back to face the board knowing he couldn't put off telling his team about his usual role as the SIO being taken by Superintendent Hobbs. There would be raised eyebrows, or he certainly hoped so, but they would have the good sense not to make any critical comments. He had to seize the initiative.

'Superintendent Hobbs will be organising a press conference tomorrow.' Drake waited for some reaction but didn't get one. 'And you should be aware he has formally assumed the role of the senior investigating officer.'

Sara's widening eyes blinked rapidly and Winder raised his eyebrows and kept them high. Luned gave him a pensive look.

'Will the superintendent be taking regular briefings?' Sara said slowly.

'I haven't been informed yet as to how he wants to deal with matters.'

'Is it because this is his first major inquiry since his promotion?' Winder said.

'Superintendent Hobbs is in command of the investigation. It's a matter for him to determine who assumes the role of SIO.' Drake wasn't convinced he was doing a good job of defending his superior officer. He didn't want to face any more questions. 'So, let's get on. We have a lot to do.' Drake walked back to his office adding. 'And keep checking through the results of house-to-house.'

As he sat down his mobile rang. The number was unfamiliar.

'Detective Inspector Drake,' the voice announced formally. 'My name's David Rockwell. I run an antiquarian book shop in Llandudno. I may have some information of interest to you.'

Drake parked the Mondeo over double yellow lines. Finding a parking space in Llandudno was always difficult, and even though it was October the place hummed with activity. The town's clientele was of a certain age with a disposable income that supported the coffee shops, small hotels and restaurants, making it popular all year round. After Sara left the car Drake fumbled for the 'On Police Business/Heddlu Swyddogol' sign from the glove compartment which he placed on the dashboard. He joined her on the pavement as she scanned the various shops and cafés.

'It is always busy here,' Sara said.

Drake nodded. 'My father liked to visit a fish and chip shop nearby.'

Drake had fond memories of visiting the town with his parents: walking the prom, travelling on the tram to the top of the Great Orme. They had often dragged him around the shops as he had done with his daughters.

Rockwell Antiquarian Books was tucked down a side street a few streets back from the main shopping parade. He could imagine the estates of the well-to-do population of the town provided a lot of its stock. Above the entrance a battered hoarding advertising the name badly needed a coat of paint. The window of the shop itself had framed images of the tourist spots around Llandudno – the Great Orme and the pier being the most popular.

Drake pushed open the door. Tall bookcases filled with hardback books covered the walls. Behind the counter on his left-hand side Drake saw a man peering over at them.

'David Rockwell?' Drake said.

The man stood up. He wasn't tall and his thin frame made him appear weak and emaciated. As Drake neared the counter, he could see that Rockwell's skin was thin, his hair dyed crudely with what looked like boot polish.

'You're Detective Inspector Drake?' Rockwell had a thin reedy sort of voice.

Drake eliminated any doubt in Rockwell's mind by producing his warrant card, as did Sara. 'You said you might be able to help us with our inquiry?'

'Of course,' Rockwell whispered before scanning the rest of the shop as though he were checking for anyone eavesdropping even though the place was empty of customers. 'I hope you don't think me presumptuous, but a person came in recently with two rare first editions asking if I was interested in buying them.' Rockwell paused, took a breath, drew a hand over his lips, cast another glance over

Drake's shoulder. The place was still empty. 'It's what I do, value antiquarian and first edition books. There are always people keen to buy, even in this digital age.'

Rockwell irritated Drake, who worried he might be no more than a time waster, like the dozens of people who would be calling tomorrow after Superintendent Hobbs' press conference.

'Did you know Emyr Isaac?' Drake said.

Sara hurried to add, smiling as she did so, 'We're treating his death as suspicious…'

Rockwell gave her a courteous nod. 'I didn't know Mr Isaac, but I did know a Mr Patrick Field and he was an avid collector of first editions. He had built up quite a library over the years. It was very sad when he died. He was always such a gentleman although I didn't warm to his wife.'

Drake took a moment, indulging Rockwell. 'Mrs Field is most upset. She knew Emyr Isaac well. They were neighbours of course.'

Rockwell took a deep breath. 'A man came in with three books I know belonged to Patrick Field. He had asked me to value them some time ago. So I know definitively they belonged to him.'

'Have you spoken to Mrs Field about this?' Drake said.

Rockwell shook his head. 'I saw the television news last evening and when I realised Mr Isaac lived in the same street as Mrs Field I thought best to call you.' Rockwell gave Drake a serious look as though he were looking for praise.

Drake duly obliged. 'That was most wise.'

Rockwell gave himself a figurative pat on the shoulder, preening as he did so.

'Is it possible that this gentleman could have acquired the books legitimately? After all there are probably more than one of each first edition?' Sara asked.

Rockwell shook his head. 'I had seen the editions Patrick Field owned with my own eyes. Each book is quite unique. Each cover has been used and worn giving them each a distinct look and feel.'

'Even so, Mr Rockwell, there could be dozens of first editions.'

'Inspector, what do you take me for? Some sleazy market trader? I know the books I was presented with belonged to Patrick Field.'

A telephone ringing deep in the bowels of the property interrupted the building tension between Drake and Rockwell. Drake said nothing, Rockwell seemed pained as though he wanted to hurry and answer the telephone while wanting to stay and continue his conversation.

Once it stopped Drake continued. 'Did you take a name?'

'He called himself 'Jeff' and I got his number. I told him I would consider the valuations for the three books and get back to him.'

Sara butted in asking Rockwell what was on Drake's mind. 'Did you make a note of the books in question?'

Rockwell reeled off the names of three of the titles Agnes Field had given Drake and Sara from their initial conversation. Drake stared over at Rockwell. Despite his pretentious and arrogant manner there was something sincere and honest about the man. He could well be their first lead to the burglar and Emyr Isaac's possible killer.

'This could be extremely helpful. I hope you may be able to assist us further,' Drake said.

Rockwell smiled his approval.

'I'd like you to contact this Jeff. Ask him if he can call again with the books as you want to check some details before you can give him a definitive valuation.' Rockwell's eyes opened wide. 'And tell him that you have good news – you think the books may be extremely valuable.'

Rockwell nodded and blinked simultaneously. It was almost comical.

Drake took a step towards him, lowered his voice conspiratorially. 'And once you have spoken to him and arranged a time, call me. Any time, just call me.'

Chapter 11

Drake paired the recently dry-cleaned navy suit with a crisp white shirt the following morning. He slid the knot of a silk tie with discrete burgundy stripes to his collar and drew a comb through his hair as he stared at his image in the mirror in the hallway.

'You look very smart,' Annie smiled as he turned towards her.

'Superintendent Hobbs has organised a press conference.'

Events involving the press, meetings with senior management of the Wales Police Service, or some other occasion when he needed to make a good impression always justified getting his appearance just so. Superintendent Wyndham Price wore his heart on his sleeve, he could be impulsive and quick to anger, but Superintendent Hobbs was a different animal. The small brown, almost piggy eyes, gave him an air that created distrust.

Annie gave him an apprehensive gaze. 'How are you getting on with him?'

'It's difficult.'

Annie drew a hand over his cheek. 'I'm sure things will be okay.'

Drake smiled back.

Annie continued. 'You haven't forgotten that my parents are arriving tonight?'

'Of course not. I'll text you later.'

Drake's thoughts turned to the press release circulated by Superintendent Hobbs the evening before. Price would have invited comments before releasing it, but this was Hobbs and he did things differently. Even the tone of the language Hobbs adopted in the few paragraphs was more strident than Drake would have favoured. He suspected that Susan Howells, in charge of public relations at Northern Division, hadn't approved the content.

The drive to Colwyn Bay gave Drake time to order his

thoughts, identify priorities and occasionally he'd dictate a reminder to himself into his mobile. The first few hours and days after any suspicious death were the most crucial – it gave the investigating team their best opportunity of gathering evidence and identifying suspects. A nagging sense that more progress should have been made dominated his thoughts. At least the possible lead through Rockwell Antiquarian Books looked promising.

Another email had landed in his inbox the night before from Inspector Owen Jones telling him that intelligence from Anglesey and the surrounding area had drawn a blank. None of the usual sources had heard anything about the burglary at Isaac's home.

There would be a small shortlist of the likely candidates. So eliminating them left Drake realising the suspect was someone with prior knowledge of Emyr Isaac's home. Someone who knew he had cash and jewellery and electronic equipment worth stealing.

And of course, the rare first editions.

Drake began constructing a scenario of how the culprit would have broken into the home. Isaac's bungalow must have been approached from the field. Walking into Maes yr Haf, even under the cover of darkness in the early hours of the morning, would have been a risk. And how would the thief embark on removing any valuables unless he knew exactly what to take?

He called at the newsagent in Colwyn Bay and bought the day's edition of *The Guardian* and turned to the sudoku puzzles, ignoring the headlines about the latest factory closures blamed directly on the tariffs imposed on the economy following Brexit. Getting his daily sudoku fix was one of those rituals he wasn't prepared to surrender. It settled his mind, gave him a brief boost of confidence to face the rest of the day.

He turned into the car park at Northern Division headquarters and, after finding a spot to park far enough away from other vehicles to minimise the risk of bumps and scratches, he strode through headquarters to his office. Drake had all morning before the press conference, which gave him time to focus his attention on learning more about Emyr Isaac.

The possibility that something in Isaac's background could point them in the direction of the killer couldn't be discounted. Isaac had worked with one of the major banks all his working life. He had moved around various towns in North and Mid Wales as well as a stint at the Cardiff headquarters. He had been retired for over thirty years, well before Internet banking had resulted in the closures of bank branches up and down the country. Drake recalled his father valuing the advice from his local bank manager. What would Emyr Isaac make of how things had changed? Now there were only regional centres, overdrafts and loans considered by algorithms untouched by humans. It had left the town centres with large old bank buildings decked out with 'For Sale' boards.

A Google search displayed Isaac's smiling face, a chain of office as a Freemason Grand Master around his neck presenting a cheque to a charity in Bangor. Old age had been unkind to Emyr Isaac, confining him to his home when he had clearly loved being part of the community.

Drake trawled through Isaac's personal information and he discovered the contact details for a distant relative and the name of a man in Isaac's telephone book with the words Grand Master alongside it. Several calls later, with Drake's impatience rising, he spoke to the current grandmaster of the lodge to which Isaac belonged. The man listened carefully as Drake asked if he knew anything about Isaac's personal life.

'I don't think I can help. He was ordinary, like most of us. He worked in the bank all his life, when there were town centre branches and bank managers had a certain status.'

Drake thanked him and rang off. Frustration crept into his mind that nothing in Isaac's life suggested anyone bore a grudge against him. But had they been digging deep enough? Was he as scandal-free as their enquires suggested? Mid-morning arrived and Drake trooped off to the kitchen where he followed his ritual of making coffee, carefully measuring the ground beans, adding hot water just off the boil and waiting the right amount of time for it to brew. Returning to his office Sara raised her head and announced, 'We've had the details on Rachel Ackroyd from the Police Service of Northern Ireland and from Police Scotland. I'm working on it now.'

Winder and Luned gave Drake noncommittal replies assuring him they were making progress with the task of building a background to Mervyn Ostler and Isaac's carers, respectively.

Before getting back to Emyr Isaac, Drake finished a few more squares of his sudoku as he drank his coffee. He spent some time tracking down some of Isaac's relations. None was helpful and a distant nephew wasn't complimentary about Isaac, suggesting that boasting about money had been the one pleasure in his life.

By lunchtime Drake was satisfied that nothing in Isaac's private life pointed in the direction of a motive for a killer. He glanced at his watch. He had enough time for a hurried lunch and a brisk walk around the parkland surrounding headquarters before his meeting with Superintendent Hobbs.

Once Drake was back in his office, he trawled through the emails that cluttered his inbox before printing off the press release and reading it thoroughly. He found a notepad and jotted bullet points on the first page as an aide-memoir for the meeting. He trundled through headquarters to the senior management suite and joined Susan Howells sitting on one of the sofas. She smiled and her body language relaxed once she saw Drake.

'Have you seen the press release?' Howells asked.

Before Drake could reply the telephone rang on Hannah's desk. Hobbs' secretary used a formal tone, very different from the conversational style she'd adopted when Superintendent Price had been in charge. 'He'll see you now.'

Drake pushed open the door to Hobbs' room and Howells followed him inside.

The superintendent didn't bother standing up from his desk. He gestured to the visitors' chairs and Drake and Howells sat down.

Hobbs' white shirt and regulation black tie looked immaculate. His uniform jacket hung on a wooden hanger on the coat stand in one corner. At least he likes things neat and tidy, Drake thought. Hobbs' short back and sides had recently been trimmed and noticed the merest glint of hair gel. Even Superintendent Hobbs wasn't immune to a little vanity.

'I think I've covered all the relevant details in the press release, but I wanted to run through everything. We don't have much time.' Hobbs looked at his watch before nodding at Drake. 'Inspector Drake give me a summary of progress so far.'

Drake opened the notepad on his knee and duly obliged. Hobbs scribbled occasionally but didn't interrupt, he even raised an eyebrow when Drake mentioned the latest thread from the Rockwell antiquarian shop.

Hobbs looked over at Susan Howells. 'Have all the press been briefed?'

'Yes. They will have been sent the usual pack. A couple of the journalists are regulars and they know Detective Inspector Drake well.'

The last sentence earned her a look of mild rebuke which she ignored. Howells wasn't part of the hierarchical chain of command. She didn't need to call Hobbs 'sir', even though he was her boss.

'I've set out the table in the conference room with place

names for the three of us.'

Hobbs tapped a ballpoint on the desk. 'That won't be necessary. Give me the names of the journalists primed to ask questions. As the SIO I shall deal with the press conference on my own. Keep it simple.'

Howells' mouth fell open slightly and Drake could see that she wanted to say something, raise an objection, but she obviously thought the better of it. Drake stared at Hobbs trying to fathom out what his superior officer had in mind.

Hobbs read the time again. 'That's all, thanks.'

Drake stood up; Howells reluctantly followed.

In the corridor leading away from the senior management suite Howells whispered to Drake. 'What the hell is he playing at? Did you know it was going to be like this? And I thought you were the SIO?'

Drake shook his head. 'Superintendent Hobbs has his own way of dealing with things.'

'But the journalists will be expecting to see us both.'

Drake reached the staircase and paused for a moment. 'Nothing much we can do.'

Howells squinted over at him. 'You don't think this press conference is a very good idea.'

Drake wasn't going to be dragged into a discussion about the management of the case particularly as it might imply a criticism of Hobbs. 'I'm sure it will be helpful,' Drake added diplomatically.

Chapter 12

Reading the reports from the Police Service of Northern Ireland's investigation into several incidents at a care home near Belfast made Sara realise how easy it was to criticise with the benefit of hindsight. It was clear the allegations against Rachel Ackroyd hadn't been taken seriously. Scepticism seeped from every paragraph and page of the investigating officer's report. It was little wonder no action had been forthcoming.

Several of the residents had accused Rachel of assaulting them, being heavy-handed and ignoring their requests for help. Bruises on arms and shoulders had largely been ignored and blamed on the thin skin of old age.

Statements from relatives complained about their loved ones' health and well-being. Some threatened to involve local politicians in creating adverse publicity but there was nothing to suggest it had been carried out.

Sara turned her attention to the record of the interviews with the employees. They all sounded defensive and mostly evasive. It left Sara with the distinct impression they were hiding something but without talking to them it would be difficult to get a clear picture. The manager used formal management speak and jargon in her statement that only compounded the uneasy feeling for Sara that Rachel Ackroyd was involved.

Police Scotland's intelligence report on Rachel Ackroyd was linked to that of her husband. Peter Ackroyd had initially trained as a nurse, spending ten years working at a local hospital in his native Dumfries. A one-line reference to Peter Ackroyd leaving the nursing profession and starting as a carer in a residential home made Sara wary. The reference to complaints about the conduct of Peter and Rachel Ackroyd when they worked together focused Sara's attention. But the inquiry had stalled. One of the suspected victims died and another's dementia had deteriorated so badly it would have been impossible for her to have given evidence. Neither had relatives to cause a fuss and Peter Ackroyd left of his own accord to retrain as a plumber. Rachel had continued to work at the care home for another few months until they relocated to North Wales, clearly hoping to leave their past behind. For Peter Ackroyd that included two convictions for fraud and theft.

How had he continued with his nursing career with such a criminal history?

What else had the report authors omitted?

Grabbing her phone, she decided there was only one way of finding out.

It took an hour to track down the officer in charge of the investigation.

'I remember Peter,' Sergeant Foyle said once Sara had explained the nature of her enquiry. 'He was a sleazebag. And he had a hell of a temper.'

'I was hoping you might be able to tell me more about the inquiry into the allegations when both Rachel and Peter worked at the Highland View residential home.'

'Peter was dead lucky.'

'I read that one of the residents died.'

Foyle grunted. 'All the other staff there were frightened of Peter and Rachel. So getting them to give evidence against the Ackroyds was difficult.'

'Is there anything else you can tell me about their background?'

Foyle paused. 'There was something rotten about both of them. You should go and check with the PSNI. They might be able to tell you more about Rachel especially.'

She thanked Foyle and, finding the right number for the PSNI, called Belfast.

Drake stood at the back of the room during the press conference sensing Susan Howells becoming more and more uncomfortable. Superintendent Hobbs' confidence grew with each minute as he preened himself in front of the cameras.

When he announced there was a dedicated helpline staffed by specially trained officers who would take calls from anyone with information Howells groaned.

'He never mentioned that.' Howells muttered under her breath.

Drake glanced towards her, but her eyes stared at Hobbs and the fingernail of her right forefinger was firmly planted between her teeth. Occasionally the regular journalists cast a quizzical glance at him and Howells.

When Hobbs referred to the previous case over twenty years earlier that had satanic overtones in the same breath as seeking to reassure the public there were no similarities Drake realised his superior officer might be out of his depth.

Howells hissed. 'What the fuck!'

He shared Howells' indignation. Comments like this could have an unwelcome impact on the case.

After the press conference had finished a reporter from the Welsh language news programme came over to Howells and Drake. 'Are you doing any interviews in Welsh?'

'Superintendent Hobbs is taking all the interviews,' Howells replied making no attempt to hide her sharp tone.

'What was that all about the satanic murder – it happened years ago.'

Howells again. 'As I said, Superintendent Hobbs is dealing with all media requests.'

Drake returned to the Incident Room, his mind on edge. Before he left the conference room Susan Howells had made clear in unequivocal terms what she thought of Hobbs' performance. 'We are going to get so much shit after that. Every swivel-eyed lunatic is going to be calling in.'

Drake wanted to agree, wholeheartedly. But common sense and loyalty to his superior officer got the better of him so he had mumbled platitudes – 'things will work out'. He wasn't at all certain if they would. Winder, Sara and Luned were busy at their desks, presumably oblivious to the car-crash press conference he had just witnessed.

'How did it go, boss?' Sara said.

Drake shrugged. 'I don't like press conferences. You can judge for yourself I guess.'

'That bad?' Winder said.

Winder straying over the invisible line between confidence and arrogance troubled Drake. Hobbs' stubbornness, verging on folly, didn't encourage Drake to defend the superintendent. Even so, the comment was a sign that perhaps Winder had been working in his team a fraction too long. The constable could be dedicated and determined – all qualities Drake valued even if sometimes he could be indiscreet.

Drake stood with his back to the board. 'Let's have some progress reports.'

Sara was the first to reply. 'I spoke with a sergeant in Police Scotland about Rachel and Peter Ackroyd. It doesn't make for attractive reading. He said they were suspected of physically abusing the residents in a nursing home where they worked.'

'Were they prosecuted?' Drake said.

Sara shook her head. 'Peter Ackroyd left to retrain as a plumber.'

'Plumber?' Winder spluttered.

'Soon after that they both moved to North Wales. I'm quite surprised Caring Wales didn't pick up on Rachel's previous history from her time in Scotland and Northern Ireland.'

'Perhaps she lied about where she had previously been employed,' Luned added.

'It's possible or it's the case that Caring Wales are so desperate for carers they cut corners.' Sara said. 'I'm still waiting for details of what happened when she was living in Northern Ireland.'

Drake glanced at Rachel's picture on the board. 'The suspicion she assaulted residents of previous care homes gives us enough, with her financial motive, to make her a significant person of interest. I'll organise a warrant to search her home early next week.'

Drake nodded at Winder who piped up. 'I've got details of Mervyn Ostler's known associates, boss. I need to cross-reference them against the list of carers Luned is finalising.'

Luned took the reference to her name as a prompt. 'Emyr Isaac had eight carers who went there regularly. They'd been employed by Caring Wales for some time. All quite experienced.'

'Have you done PNC and background checks on all of them?' Drake said.

Luned shook her head.

'Get them done.'

Drake took a step back from the board and tilted his head from side to side looking at the image of Emyr Isaac as an elderly man. 'I spent this morning trawling through Isaac's history. Nothing remarkable, he worked for a bank all his life. A distant nephew didn't particularly like him, and he still had friends from his Freemasonry days.'

'So no possibility of a disgruntled customer with a grudge against him,' Sara said.

'It's got to be a botched burglary, boss.' Winder sounded confident. 'A villain thinks the old people in the estate are easy targets and takes a chance breaking into Isaac's home. But Isaac tackles him and then they struggle. And he falls and—'

'That would make it manslaughter,' Luned announced seriously.

Drake nodded before heading back to his office where he tidied the columns of Post-it notes, allowing his mind to dwell on everything they knew. Why had the window to the bathroom been smashed? Perhaps the burglar didn't want to run the risk of being seen and when the window had proved to be an impractical method to access the house, he had been forced to use the door. And why had old books been stolen?

Rockwell would be sure to call him if 'Jeff' made contact so Drake decided against ringing the bookseller.

Drake couldn't identify what was niggling him about the inquiry. Something didn't feel right; it was as though someone had forced together two pieces of a jigsaw that shouldn't fit. Perhaps it was just his reaction to the press conference, so he shook off his unease and texted Annie, telling her he was leaving soon. As her parents were staying that weekend Drake knew she'd be pleased he wouldn't be late and the row of smiley emojis in her reply bought a grin to his face.

Chapter 13

The following morning Drake reached his arm over and threaded it around Annie's waist. She murmured a greeting and turned to face him. Then she ran a hand down his chest, whispering as she squeezed him. 'Good morning, Inspector.' Drake caught his breath and let his hand cup her breasts before caressing a nipple gently.

'Is the door closed?' Annie grinned. 'And you need to be quiet. I don't want to frighten my parents.'

Drake glanced over at the door and then dragged the duvet over them. Skin to skin with Annie made him feel alive, they kissed, and their legs intertwined. A creaking floorboard made her stop, then she giggled before pushing Drake onto his back and straddling him.

Then Drake's mobile lying on the bedside cabinet rang.

They both glanced at it accusingly as though by doing so would make it stop.

But it continued to ring.

Drake reached over a hand as Annie lay by his side.

'It's Hobbs.' Drake announced giving Annie a worried glance.

He straightened up in bed, his passion subsiding and answered the call.

'Good morning, sir.'

'Inspector,' Hobbs dispensed with the usual greetings. 'We've had a number of telephone calls following the public appeal I made yesterday. The team have identified several credible threads and leads. I'd like you to follow up this morning.'

'Yes, sir.' House-hunting with Annie and her parents was out of the question now.

'The officers in charge of the mobile incident room in Menai Bridge have all the details. Get over there as soon as possible.'

Before Drake could say anything else the line went dead.

Drake turned to Annie. He could see the realisation on her face. 'Don't worry, I'll go with my parents. Don't be too late home.'

A murder inquiry would always take priority over a police officer's homelife. Sometimes Drake wished he could say that he wasn't available. The pressures of work as a senior detective had already cost him one marriage, and he often blamed himself for failing to get his work–life balance right and for allowing his obsessions to drive the rituals that could keep him at the office until late in the evening. Annie was very different from his ex-wife and he wanted to make certain he'd value their relationship and protect her as best he could from the demands of his job.

Annie's parents gave him an incredulous look when he explained he had to work. Roland Jenkins' career as a civil servant made him accustomed to having weekends off and a regular nine-to-five activity. Drake worried how they felt about the impact on Annie.

It was a short drive to Menai Bridge and Drake pulled up into the public car park requisitioned by the mobile incident room. Inside, a uniformed sergeant looked pleased to see Drake, the relief evident on his face.

'I'm glad you made it, sir,' the sergeant said. 'We've had a dozen people in yesterday afternoon and evening after the press conference. And they all came back this morning, whingeing and complaining nobody had been to see them.'

Drake sighed. Hobbs' public appeal for assistance had almost sounded desperate, pleading even, triggering a desire amongst the population to assist. After all, Hobbs had invited anyone with any comments or information to come forward – even adding alarmingly 'no matter how insignificant, we welcome the public's support and cooperation'.

'What are the details?'

The sergeant waved a hand at a plastic chair and Drake sat down. After twenty minutes any hope of him finishing by lunchtime had evaporated. Sara arriving as the sergeant commented about the caller who had mentioned aliens landing in the field behind Emyr Isaac's property caught Drake by surprise.

'Aliens?' Sara said.

The sergeant laughed. 'The woman looked respectable enough, she must have been in her fifties but there was a stale smell of cannabis about her.'

'Maybe Gareth would like to visit her?' Sara smiled.

Drake turned to Sara. 'Who contacted you?'

'The superintendent called me.' Sara managed to get surprise and dutiful respect into her voice.

Drake ignored her comment. 'I don't want to be doing this all day. Let's make progress.'

The satnav took Drake and Sara painlessly to the first property and they sat listening to a man in a tweed suit telling them he regularly exercised his dog around the quiet estates of Menai Bridge noting down on his mobile telephone the 'funny comings and goings'. Sara dutifully made a note in her pocketbook and nodded appreciatively as the man spoke. It transpired he hadn't been anywhere near Emyr Isaac's property although he did know where Maes yr Haf was located.

By the middle of the morning Drake and Sara had seen various time-wasters and attention seekers. A woman who was housebound complained about cars pulling up in the drive of her neighbours' property at all hours. Another railed about noisy parties and windows being smashed in the adjacent properties.

A man with protruding eyes and an intense stare was utterly convinced he had seen Emyr Isaac driving his car with a bearded man smoking a cigarette. Drake didn't share with him that Emyr Isaac had been housebound for several years but reassured him they would do everything to check out the information.

Drake and Sara returned to the mobile incident room by

lunchtime. Drake hoped there would be no further pointless leads for him to pursue. After parking, a text reached his mobile from Annie telling him the two properties they had viewed that morning weren't suitable. Drake drafted a reply, suggesting he would meet up with her at the first property they were seeing after lunch, but he delayed sending it. The sergeant still looked flustered, two uniformed officers had joined him, and they were pouring over various pocketbooks.

'Inspector, I'm really glad to see you. Superintendent Hobbs has called. He's going to call this afternoon and wanted to check you'd be here for a formal briefing.'

Formal briefing – about time-wasters and fantasists. Drake mentally counted to ten.

'When did the superintendent say he'd be here?'

'He didn't specify.'

Drake looked over at Sara, she raised an eyebrow.

'Let's get something to eat.' Drake said through gritted teeth as they headed to a small café on the town's high street. Drake settled for a ham and tomato Panini with a side salad, Sara ordered a feta cheese variety.

What did Superintendent Hobbs hope he could achieve by having a formal briefing? The only conclusion was exactly nothing. Hobbs should have known the tone of his press conference would have generated time-wasters. He was making himself feel important, making his officers chase their tails.

Drake found the details the sergeant had given him earlier, calculating he didn't want to give Superintendent Hobbs any reason to criticise his inactivity. When the waitress brought their coffees Drake's telephone rang.

He recognised Rockwell's number.

'Inspector Drake, I thought you might be interested to learn that your man has been in touch.' Rockwell paused theatrically.

'And?' Drake sounded tetchy.

'He's going to call on Monday morning.'

Chapter 14

Sara woke early, energised at the prospect of arresting someone. She dragged on her running gear and left before breakfast for a five-mile run around the country lanes where she lived. Avoiding potholes and the occasional car took her attention, allowing her mind to relax and her body to enjoy the physical exertion. Back at home she felt invigorated and ready for the day ahead.

Luned was organising coffee when Sara arrived at headquarters in good time for the meeting Inspector Drake had requested to coordinate their arrest of the mystery man calling at Rockwell Antiquarian Books. Winder was finishing his customary breakfast sausage roll, the smell of pastry and grease filling the Incident Room. When Inspector Drake breezed in, he turned up his nose. giving Winder a reproachful glance.

He reached the board, where he stood facing the team before reading the time on his watch. 'Let's get on with this.'

Sara drank her coffee listening intently as Drake pointed to a plan of the streets in the immediate vicinity of the bookshop.

'Sara and I will be inside the shop. There is a back entrance which we can use to avoid any possibility that Jeff – not that I expect it to be his real name – sees us arriving. Rockwell has promised to be at the shop by eight-fifteen am.'

Winder stifled a belch with a fist to his mouth and mumbled. 'What time did this Jeff say he might call?'

'Rockwell told him that he would be leaving at about eleven-thirty. So, let's assume Jeff will call before then.'

Drake turned his attention to the map. 'There's a café a little way down the main road from where you can get a good view of the side street. It should be possible to see anybody carrying something that looks like a bag of books easily enough.' Drake tipped his head at Winder and Luned. 'Both of you alternate between drinking coffee and sitting in the car here.' Drake tapped the location. It meant any person heading for Rockwell Antiquarian Books would be spotted. 'Use your phones to get photographs of anyone who might look suspicious.'

Luned had been keeping notes furiously and the excitement made her face flush. 'Did Rockwell give us a description?'

Drake nodded. 'Male, mid-forties, with a mop of unruly dark hair.' Drake paused. 'This is the first positive link connected with the death of Emyr Isaac. It's important we arrest this man.'

Drake scanned the three faces in front of him. Sara had seen the look before many times. It was serious, determined. She was the first to get to her feet and grab her coat. 'We'd better get going, boss.'

They travelled separately to Llandudno. Force of habit made her punch the details into the satnav which told her the journey would take twenty minutes. She found a slot to park in one of the unrestricted roads away from the centre of the town and made for the shop, keeping a surreptitious lookout for Inspector Drake and the others. She slowed as she reached the side street, glancing into the shop window while checking the surrounding pavements and occupants of parked cars. She enjoyed this cloak and dagger activity. It made a change from watching hours of CCTV footage.

No one caught her attention, so she nonchalantly strolled down towards the shop, ducking into the alley as instructed and pushing open the door Rockwell had left ajar. The shop owner appeared and Sara noticed a makeshift kitchen behind him.

'Good morning, sergeant,' Rockwell said formally, reaching out a hand. 'This is all a bit James Bond isn't it?' If there was humour intended, his delivery was utterly deadpan. 'I thought you could trace people from their mobile telephone numbers these days.'

Behind them the door to the alley opened and Drake

entered.

'Good morning, Mr Rockwell,' Drake said.

'Good morning, Inspector. I was just about to tell your sergeant that there is a small kitchen with the usual accoutrements for making tea and coffee et cetera.'

'Thank you.'

'I've organised a desk and some chairs for you in the space I use as an office behind the shop area. Anybody coming in won't be able to see you, but you can hear any activity and so forth. I hope there won't be any unpleasantness.'

It wasn't the sort of comment that would endear him to Inspector Drake, Sara thought. Drake briefly narrowed his eyes and Sara guessed he was composing some sharp reply, but he didn't bother.

'Let's get settled in,' Drake replied.

Rockwell opened the shop promptly at nine am. The sound of his morning routine drifted into the office where Drake and Sara sat. She watched Drake as he focused on completing a sudoku from the newspaper. It had always been one of his habits, and it was almost reassuring to see him jotting down the answers. There had been comments from officers about Drake having a touch of OCD – it was a lot more than that when she had totted up all his little foibles and rituals.

Sara had brought with her a folder with the summary of house-to-house inquiries in the Menai Bridge area. She got to work scanning the notes made by the various officers.

'Was Superintendent Hobbs content with the response after the appeal at the press conference for public assistance?' It had taken time for Sara to craft the question. It was probably two maybe even three questions in one. There had been a lot of gossip in Northern Division about Superintendent Hobbs; what Drake really thought of him intrigued her.

'I don't think he expected quite the extent of crank calls

and hoaxes.' Drake put the newspaper on the desk in front of him and looked over at Sara. 'What do you make of Superintendent Hobbs?'

The directness of his question surprised her. 'He certainly has a different style from Superintendent Price.'

Drake murmured noncommittally and Sara took it as an invitation to comment further. 'I'm not certain we made much progress on Saturday, sir.'

Drake nodded. 'I don't like press conferences. They never achieve very much.'

The sound of the door into the street opening and Rockwell's voice greeting a customer bought their small talk to a swift conclusion. Drake and Sara shared an intense look as they focused on the activity in the adjacent shop area. Both relaxed when they heard a woman's voice and Rockwell's friendly tone. They could hear snippets of conversation about various books and authors Sara didn't recognise. The woman soon left, and Sara could hear Rockwell clicking on his mouse. She idly speculated what sort of income an antiquarian bookseller made and whether it was worth his while running a shop when presumably a lot of his sales came from the Internet.

An hour passed during which time two more customers entered. Neither seemed to be known to Rockwell from the lack of small talk. Only one made a purchase and the shop fell silent again. Sara trooped off into the kitchen to make coffee after asking for Rockwell's preference. She returned with three mugs, knowing that Drake would turn up his nose at the cheap instant. Rockwell collected his drink and went back into the shop.

Another hour dragged by. Sara managed to finish only a small section of the house-to-house reports. Nothing had struck her as needing further attention, but she knew Drake would want every statement checked and rechecked. There might be a nugget of information lying somewhere pointing them to a thread that would crack the case wide open.

A few minutes before the artificial eleven-thirty deadline Rockwell had given Jeff the door into the shop squeaked open. Sara and Drake listened for Rockwell's voice and her pulse spiked when she heard his familiar tone. 'Good morning, Jeff, I'm glad you were able to call.'

Drake jerked his head at Sara. They both stood up together and hurried out into the shop area. Jeff gasped. 'What the fuck?' Drake had his warrant card held aloft. 'I'm arresting you on suspicion of theft and burglary. You do not have to say anything…'

'Fuck off.' Jeff grabbed the supermarket plastic bag he was holding tight to his chest and took three quick steps towards the front door. Before reaching it, he yanked at a bookcase, a good foot taller than he was, sending books spilling over the floor followed by the frame itself blocking the shop.

In a few seconds he was out the door and running down the street.

Drake turned to Sara as he scrambled over the bookcase and its contents. 'Call Gareth and Luned. We need to catch him.'

Sara climbed over the carnage and once she was on the street watching Drake galloping away, no sign of Jeff anywhere, she called Luned and Winder.

Winder was sitting in the café and hadn't seen anybody approach.

'Get down here, Gareth,' Sara demanded.

She had better luck with Luned who answered after a couple of rings. She sounded breathless. 'He's heading towards the promenade. The inspector is chasing him.'

'Stay with him. I'm on my way.'

Seconds later Winder joined Sara and they ran, eventually emerging onto another shopping street. Quickly Sara calculated the easiest way to reach the promenade and jerked a hand over towards another road leading towards the seafront.

Sara's breathing became laboured and she could hear Winder panting by her side as they reached a pedestrian crossing and bolted across. She jumped onto a wooden bench and craned to see them. 'Call Luned again. Find out where she is,' Sara said to Winder who fumbled with his mobile. He pinned it to his ear but shook his head. Eventually his face lit up and he raised an arm pointing at the Great Orme.

Sara squinted into the distance until she saw two running figures.

'Let's go.'

She picked up speed as she ran along the promenade still popular with visitors despite the October chill. She caught the faintest smell of seaweed and salt as the high tide lapped against the shingle beach.

She was nearer to Drake than she first realised. He was at least a hundred yards behind Jeff who appeared fitter and leaner than she recalled from the person she'd seen briefly in the shop. On her left were the hotels and bed-and-breakfast establishments that made Llandudno a popular destination resort. Jeff turned left back into town and Drake was doing the same so Sara followed, Winder hard on her heels.

Jeff took a right up the hill towards the tram station. Sara pressed on, drawing closer to Drake. Then she saw in the distance Luned emerging from a side street. She stopped and Sara could see her taking deep lungfuls of breath. Jeff slowed and it gave Drake an opportunity to close the gap even further.

As Jeff jogged past the entrance to an old chapel and neared some tables and chairs outside an Italian restaurant, Drake finally grabbed hold of his prey. Sara watched as though in slow motion as both men crashed into the furniture. They sent the upright menu card crashing onto the pavement. A startled waiter emerged.

Sara reached the scene in time to hear Drake breathlessly cautioning Jeff. 'I'm arresting you on suspicion of theft from the home of Emyr Isaac. You do not have to say anything…'

Chapter 15

Jeff turned out to be Peter Ackroyd once his identity had been established. Safely delivered to a cell in the area custody suite it gave Drake and his team time to find Rachel and invite her to assist with their inquiries. As well as execute a search of her home.

Drake was sitting in the canteen at the area control centre eating a soggy ham sandwich the bread sticking to the sides of his mouth. Eventually he dislodged a piece with his tongue.

'Do we arrest her boss?' Luned said before slurping noisily on a steaming mug of tea.

Luned appeared dishevelled from her exertions but there was an excited determined glint in her eyes. Chasing a suspect around the streets of Llandudno had done her good, Drake thought, rather than being stuck behind a desk.

Drake nodded. 'Suspicion of handling stolen goods for now.'

He turned to Winder and Luned. 'Get back to headquarters and collect all the background details we have on Peter Ackroyd. Sara and I will track down Rachel and then we'll see what husband and wife have to say.'

Drake left the coffee unfinished, pushed the plate away before standing up. Sara followed suit and they returned to his car. Once they reached the Britannia Bridge Sara called Caring Wales and sounding as nonchalant as possible asked if Rachel was working that afternoon.

Drake listened to the one-sided conversation until Sara finished announcing that Rachel was off until the evening shift. A few minutes later they pulled up outside the terraced property where she lived. The vehicle with a search team parked a little way behind them.

Drake led the way to the front door which Rachel opened after the bell had rung a couple of times. She looked inquisitively at Drake and Sara. Was there a flicker of worry in her eyes? Colour drained from her face when Drake arrested and cautioned her.

'I'm starting my shift later.'

'I'm sure Caring Wales can make other arrangements.'

Rachel turned on her heel and shrugged on her coat announcing she had to call Caring Wales. Judging by the look on Rachel's face the company weren't happy. Drake and Sara waited as Rachel tapped a message on her mobile. Drake guessed it was to Peter. What she didn't know was that his mobile was safely in the possession of the custody sergeant.

They drove back to the custody suite in silence.

Drake deposited Rachel in an interview room before he and Sara went to speak to Winder and Luned. He found both officers exchanging small talk with a rotund sergeant with a loud voice.

'We took a statement from Rockwell, boss,' Winder said. 'And he identified the books Ackroyd had in his possession as Patrick Field's.'

'And we've got Ackroyd's background history,' Luned added.

'Ackroyd's solicitor is here,' Winder said.

'Good, we'll speak to Rachel. I want both of you to interview Peter. Let's see what he has to say for himself.'

Drake took the papers Luned had produced and trooped back with Sara to the interview suite where Rachel fingered a thin plastic cup filled with an insipid looking brown liquid.

After completing the necessary formalities, Drake pushed tapes into the recorder and waited until the machine made a buzzing sound, before turning to look at Rachel. Now he could see despair teetering on the edge of panic. How far did he need to push before she would crack and admit her guilt?

'As you know, I'm investigating the death of Emyr Isaac. How did you get on with Mr Isaac?'

Rachel kept his eye contact direct but now her breathing was laboured.

'Okay, I suppose. He could be awkward and belligerent… but a lot of older people who live on their own and have health problems… Well, it's difficult.'

'How long have you been one of his carers?'

Rachel paused. 'I can't think, it must be a couple of years.'

'And did your husband Peter ever do odd jobs for Mr Isaac?'

'Yes, of course. Peter would help him out all the time fixing this and that. Mow the lawn and do the weeding and tending to the shrubs.'

'And did Mr Isaac pay Peter for that work?'

'Yes, of course he did.'

'Were you aware that Mr Isaac kept a large amount of cash in the house?'

She nodded tentatively.

'Did you know where he stored the money?'

'In a cashbox in the bedroom.' Rachel spluttered the reply.

'Did Peter know where Emyr Isaac kept the cashbox?'

Rachel looked away.

Her reticence exasperated Drake. 'You must have told him.'

'Mr Isaac never kept it a secret. And I never stole his money if that's what you think.'

'Did Peter?'

'You think he's guilty because of his past. But Pete wouldn't do that – he liked Mr Isaac.'

'So we're not going to find the cash box at your home.'

Rachel opened her eyes wide in astonishment when she realised what Drake meant.

'How much did you know about Emyr Isaac's financial position?'

'I don't know what you mean.'

'For example, did he ever tell you about his investments?'

'No, never.'

Drake searched her face and her body language looking for the tell-tale sign of a lie. Everything they knew about Emyr Isaac contradicted her last denial.

'That's not true is it. Mr Isaac regularly boasted about the cash in the house and his wealth.'

Rachel tipped her head, stared at her fingers threaded together tightly on the table in front of her.

'And Mr Isaac had made a will leaving you a legacy. It was quite generous, very generous, some say you stand to inherit £50,000.'

Rachel shared a glance between Sara and Drake. It struck Drake that she realised they knew everything and there was little sense in her prevaricating any longer.

'Yes, he said it was his way of saying thank you for my work. I used to go there after I'd finished my shift and sit and chat with him. It wasn't talking really. I would listen to him spouting on and on about all sorts of different things. He thought he could be so clever asking me about poetry and the history of Wales – things I knew nothing about. I spent hours with him.'

'Did you only do that once you knew about the legacy?' Sara made her first contribution.

Rachel bit down on her bottom lip. 'No, of course not. He was difficult and he treated some of the other carers badly, but he was always okay with me. And Caring Wales – that's a joke – they don't know how to care about anything. Their only interest is in making money. We were supposed to spend twenty minutes with every client but they cut it down to fifteen so we could squeeze in more calls.'

Sara leaned over the table. She kept her voice low. 'We are aware Emyr Isaac was intending to change his will. He was going to remove the legacy to you. If the will had been signed you weren't going to benefit. How did you feel about that?'

Tears ran down Rachel's cheeks. She brushed them

away quickly.

Sara continued. 'It must have been a big disappointment. Were you angry when you realised that Mr Isaac wasn't going to give you £50,000 after his death? Did you confront him?'

'I saw the new will, I admit that,' she mumbled. 'But I never killed him, never.'

'Why did you steal the books, Rachel?'

Her mouth fell open, realisation hitting her like a boxer's blow to the chest, winding her.

Sara continued. 'We arrested Peter this morning as he was trying to sell the books in an antiquarian bookshop.'

Drake added using a dark tone. 'You must have known and that makes you an accomplice.'

Rachel shook her head violently before giving Drake a frightened look.

He continued. 'And that's a very serious matter.' Drake paused allowing his words to strike home.

'When I told Peter the will had been changed, he was mad, really mad. Told me I'd been stupid to spend all that extra time with Mr Isaac. Told me I should have my head examined. He wanted to go there and argue with him. Get him to change his mind, tell him how good I'd been with him.' Rachel paused to gather her breath. 'Being a carer is a shit job. We never had any holidays. And the money Peter got from doing the odd jobs for Emyr was never enough. He said it was what I deserved.'

Drake interrupted her. 'What do you mean… deserved?'

'Pete… He said I'd earned whatever the books were worth.' She gazed at Drake and Sara as though what she was saying was defensible.

'Did Peter take the books?'

She nodded briskly.

'Did Peter go back to the house to steal the money?'

Rachel rocked back and forth.

'Did he argue with Emyr Isaac? Was there a struggle?
Rachel blinked rapidly.
'Did he kill Emyr Isaac?'
'No, no, of course not.'

'Ackroyd denied everything, boss,' Winder announced folding his arms severely. 'He said he'd found the books in a skip.'

Drake stifled a chortle. It always surprised him how absurd criminals could be with their explanations, hoping they'd be believed no matter how ridiculous. Drake sat with the three officers in his team in the duty inspector's room mulling over the day's progress, pondering what decisions could be made about prosecuting Rachel and Peter Ackroyd.

'Rachel implicated Peter in stealing Agnes Field's books. He thought she deserved the money once he knew Isaac was planning to change his will. But she denied vehemently any suggestion Peter might have argued with Isaac.'

'Do you believe her, sir?' Luned said.

Drake was paid to be suspicious. But they needed more than his gut feeling to convict. 'She looked terrified and it's possible Peter went back there but…'

Drake's thoughts turned to evidence and in particular the search team busy going through the Ackroyds' property, removing clothes, identifying anything that could link them directly to the murder of Emyr Isaac. Perhaps a fragment of glass from a broken window that Peter Ackroyd had smashed to create the impression of a break in. Blood from Emyr Isaac's wound would have got everywhere, clinging to Ackroyd's clothes.

'We can't make a decision about charging them until the search team has finished.' Drake announced.

'At the very least, boss,' Sara said. 'We can charge them with burglary.'

A nagging sense the pieces didn't all fit together settled

heavily into Drake's mind. He didn't have long to deliberate, as his mobile rang and he recognised the number of Dr Lee Kings the pathologist.

'Ian, I need to see you – I'm concerned about a death.'

Drake and Sara travelled separately to the hospital, which gave Drake the opportunity of playing a Rolling Stones greatest hits album that iTunes had recommended. He turned up the volume when the opening chords of Start Me Up filled the car. Before leaving headquarters he had texted Annie warning her he would be late home.

Drake met Sara in the mortuary reception as Lee Kings emerged from his office.

'Good evening,' Kings said.

Drake and Sara ambled down the corridor to his office. The room was functional. A monitor sat on the corner of the desk although the keyboard and mouse were on a cupboard behind Kings. A pile of paperwork was stacked on his desk. Two pot plants stood perched on the windowsill. Several certificates in simple black frames hung on one wall and, on another, the image of a lighthouse with a wave crashing over it.

Kings waved at the visitor chairs. Drake and Sara sat down.

'What's this about, Lee?' Drake said.

Kings turned to Drake and Sara.

'Yesterday, the coroner's office called about a death. A Mr David Morris lived in a village on Anglesey, he was in his nineties, was found dead in bed yesterday morning. He had been living at home, he had dementia along with heart failure and deranged liver function. He also suffered from prostate cancer although it wasn't advanced and was unlikely to have caused his death. He had hearing problems and his eyesight was poor.'

'He must have been under the care of the GP?'

'Yes, and I spoke to the doctor and arranged for his

medical records to be sent over.' Kings nodded at the monitor.

'So, what's the problem?'

Kings settled back in his chair. 'Mr Morris' daughter has been on the telephone making wild allegations that her brother was responsible for killing their father and demanding a full post-mortem be undertaken.'

'I see.'

'She was extremely aggressive and used very direct language. It seems her late father was quite wealthy – apparently; he had been a timber merchant who built up a successful business. In view of the allegations his daughter made and emails I received from her brother's solicitor threatening all sorts I took the precaution of discussing the best way to proceed with a colleague. I decided to arrange a computed tomography scan of the body of David Morris.'

'Is that normal procedure?' Sara said.

Kings shook his head. 'Not at all, although the US military do CT scans on autopsies as a matter of course. In the UK it wouldn't be routine.'

Kings paused and shared a look with Drake and Sara allowing the significance of what he had said to sink in.

'The traditional 'body-opening' post-mortem is used to determine the cause of death in most cases. I wouldn't normally justify a CT scan but bearing in mind the circumstances I thought it was a sensible precaution.'

Drake surreptitiously looked at the time. He'd promised Annie he'd be home two hours ago. He tapped out another text – *still in the mortuary. XX.*

Kings paused, his face darkened. 'There's a problem. Let me show you.'

Kings adjusted the monitor on his desk enabling Drake and Sara to see the enlarged image of Morris' skull. 'I want to show you this specific area.' Kings circled a specific part of the brain. 'These images suggest he died from an air embolism, his right ventricle is empty of blood and full of air.'

Drake's gathering sense they had made a significant discovery forced him to ask, 'In layman's terms?'

'It means we can't rule out that he was killed by someone injecting air into a vein, effectively causing an airlock as you have in a radiator at home. The heart can't pump, then bingo, it stops.'

Sara caught her breath. 'So the sister could be right?'

The silence in the room was answer enough.

Kings continued. 'After the CT scan I examined the body more closely. And I found a puncture wound on his arm.'

'What does that mean?' Sara said.

'It could be a puncture wound from a needle, or even an intravenous cannula. It's the piece of kit used to inject fluids or drugs into the body.' Kings stood back. 'It means I need to get a specialist second opinion and you get the basis for a murder investigation.'

Chapter 16

Sleep eluded Drake despite his tiredness. So he got up and left Annie sleeping. In the kitchen he nibbled on a biscuit and drank some orange juice and pondered the day ahead. Protocols set in motion the machinery of an inquiry. First thing that morning a team of crime scene investigators would arrive at the property of David Morris, accompanied by Winder and Luned.

Drake had met Catrin Roach, Morris' daughter, the evening before at a fancy hotel in Anglesey where she was staying. She didn't seem surprised when he broke the news to her and had blamed her brother, Richard, without missing a beat. Describing him as a 'money grabber' with 'wastrel children' made certain Drake realised the depth of her sibling hatred. His brief discussion with Richard Morris was equally depressing.

There were similarities between the deaths of Isaac and Morris he couldn't ignore. Both men were elderly and lived at home with carers who called regularly to visit them. Did his experience as a detective justify the uneasy feeling creeping into his mind? Or was he just seeing connections where none existed? Looking out over the Menai Strait he watched as the moonlight danced over the choppy surface. Yawning he went back to bed and slept fitfully.

Drake left before Annie's parents were awake. They were viewing one more property before travelling back to Cardiff. Annie worried her parents would find it difficult relocating from Cardiff to North Wales, but Drake reassured her that they would settle easily enough to the rhythm of life in North Wales.

After parking at headquarters, a text reached his mobile from Annie confirming the details of another property they hoped to see that afternoon. Drake opened the link and speed-read the estate agent's summary. The bungalow in Beaumaris had pleasant views down over the Menai Strait and on towards the mountains of Snowdonia. He tapped out a reply – *looks lovely, let me know how you get on. X*

In the Incident Room he greeted Sara and told her about his conversation with Morris' children the night before. 'I'll get some background work done on him,' Sara said.

'See if you can find a photograph,' Drake said over his shoulder heading for his office. 'I've got the name of Morris' solicitor too. We'll go and see him before the full post-mortem later.'

He pulled his chair to the desk and booted up his computer. He read the text from Winder confirming he and Luned had arrived at Morris' home. The custody time limit for the Ackroyds was looming, as was his meeting with Hobbs. As the SIO, his superior officer would make the call about the Ackroyds, but Drake didn't want Hobbs to criticise him, find an angle he hadn't covered, spot a loophole.

Drake turned to the emails in his inbox and found the report from the search team supervisor who must have arrived early. The officers had worked late the previous evening at the Ackroyd's home. Drake hoped for a breakthrough, Rachel and Peter Ackroyd had the means, opportunity and motive – the only thing missing was definitive evidence linking them to the assault that had killed Emyr Isaac.

The report was couched in bland terms referring to the belongings, bags of clothes and shoes removed from the property. Drake would have to wait for the forensic department to work its way through each item of clothing.

Peter and Rachel Ackroyd were still in custody and they would have to be released that afternoon unless they could be charged, or the time limits extended. At the moment, the only realistic option Drake could see was releasing them on bail with strict conditions they talk to nobody associated with the case.

Luned had time to spare that morning. Her journey to Morris' home was shorter than Winder's so she sat in her car outside the house pondering what was likely to happen to the Ackroyds and dwelling on Drake's instructions the evening before about the suspicious death of David Morris. He hadn't mentioned that the deaths of Isaac and Morris were connected but intuition told her it would be uppermost in his mind.

Peter Ackroyd's explanation that he had found the books in a skip was clearly a lie and Luned preferred his wife's version of events. It fitted into Ackroyd's profile. She could easily imagine how he would justify stealing the books once Emyr Isaac no longer intended to benefit his wife in his will. But a nagging doubt persisted about the likelihood of Ackroyd's involvement in Isaac's murder. It seemed improbable he would have faked a break in to gain access to a property he knew his wife could visit unrestricted. If it was a clumsy attempt at faking a burglary to implicate a third party then why had he stolen the books?

Luned realised that often there was no logical explanation. Criminals could act foolishly and illogically. And if the evidence pointed to Ackroyd's guilt a prosecution would surely follow. She just wasn't convinced.

Several different threads developed in Luned's mind and she tried to focus on the task Drake had assigned them. Was Richard Morris a person of interest or even a suspect in his own father's death? And was the house a crime scene?

Morris' home was a handsome old property, but the evidence of decline was evident from the patchy external render and the old wooden window frames with their layers of white paint. It was typical, Luned thought, of a property belonging to an elderly person unwilling to spend money on it, believing it would see him out.

Winder arrived at the same time as the scientific support vehicle.

The CSIs would report back once their work was complete. The record of carers looking after David Morris needed to be recovered and preserved. Richard Morris had already told them where his father's financial records and paperwork were kept. Luned doubted their presence and that of the CSIs would achieve anything. There hadn't been a break in, no forced entry or smashed glass and David Morris had died in his sleep.

Winder led the way and unlocked the house. Parquet flooring lined the hallway and the occasional loose section clattered under Winder's footstep as he walked to the rear. A heavy armchair with an electrical cable winding its way from the back to a socket on the wall and a television on a table meant the kitchen they reached doubled up as a living room for David Morris.

Luned soon found the blue folder where the carers kept a log of each visit.

'I'll go in search of the financial records,' Winder said.

Luned drew up a chair in front of the table. It didn't take long to flick to the final few entries. At least Caring Wales were consistent with the paperwork they used. She read the names of the carers and the times they visited in the week before David Morris had died. Some were familiar and the consequences made her shiver.

She flicked back a couple of pages and noticed Rachel Ackroyd's name. She had seen David Morris on the Wednesday morning and Thursday afternoon before he died. Despite the poor handwriting, and the dreadful grammar and spelling the comments were neutral and sometimes complimentary about David Morris – quite a change from the criticisms of Emyr Isaac.

She reached the Saturday morning and noted David Morris had eaten porridge with a generous portion of honey and brown sugar. At his age he doesn't have to worry about his weight, Luned thought. A call at lunchtime recorded that he was in good spirits and about to watch a black-and-white film on television.

It was the evening call that drew Luned's attention.

Rachel Ackroyd's name appeared again. When she left

at seven-thirty pm all was well, David Morris was ready for bed.

Luned bellowed for Winder. 'Gareth, I found something.'

Chapter 17

Drake's telephone gave an insistent ring. He scooped up the handset from his desk.

'Somebody told me you needed a report on the items recovered from the Ackroyd home by this afternoon.' Foulds sounded angry.

'Well—'

'If Super Hobbs thinks we can produce a report that quickly – well he'll have to think again. It's going to be impossible. The clothes and shoes and bags of stuff need to be examined carefully.'

'How long will it take?'

'You know the score, Ian. How long is a piece of string?'

Foulds finished the call abruptly. Drake knew they couldn't justify Rachel and Peter Ackroyd's continued detention without good cause. He found a ballpoint and started a mind map on his notepad. That way he could prepare for his meeting with Hobbs in half an hour.

He wrote the name Emyr Isaac in capitals in the middle and the names of Rachel and Peter Ackroyd to one side. On the opposite side he jotted down 'books' and 'evidence of break in' and then he paused. Proving the Ackroyds had staged the burglary to cover up Isaac's death required evidence.

Evidence they didn't have, yet.

He trooped off to the senior management suite in good time. He didn't have to wait long for Hannah to announce that Hobbs would see him. Hobbs was sorting paperwork on his desk. There was no invitation to sit down.

'Did you speak to Catrin Roach this morning?'

'Last night, sir.'

'Well her brother has arrived in reception, with his solicitor, demanding to see us both. This is the last thing I need today.' It sounded reproachful as though Drake were responsible.

'But first give me a summary of the Ackroyd arrest. Then we'll go and see Richard Morris and his solicitor.'

Drake duly obliged, Hobbs listened intently, not averting his eye contact.

'So as the SIO I need to consider if we can justify extending the custody time limits to await forensic results. Otherwise the Ackroyds walk.'

'Yes, sir.'

Hobbs pressed his lips together tightly. 'Once we have the forensic results we can reconsider everything. At the very least we can charge them with theft – the CPS can make the final decision. For now, tell the custody sergeant to release them on bail.'

Hobbs hadn't asked for his view nor invited him to contribute. Had it been Wyndham Price, Drake may well have butted in with his contribution, but he was only just settling into understanding Superintendent Hobbs. He wasn't *that* confident with his superior officer.

They left the senior management suite for a conference room on the ground floor next to reception.

Richard Morris had thick dark hair and a swarthy complexion. Alongside him sat Colin Nelson who introduced himself as a solicitor, pushing over a fancy embossed card with the name of his firm.

'My client understands a complaint has been made by Mrs Roach that he murdered his father Mr David Morris.'

Hobbs frowned. Drake wasn't certain if he was expected to fill the immediate silence.

'The initial post-mortem has only just been completed,' Hobbs replied slowly. 'We are treating Mr Morris' death as suspicious.'

Nelson had the most annoyingly patronising English accent Drake had heard for some time. 'As I'm sure you understand, Superintendent, my client wishes to vehemently deny any suggestion, any allegation that he harmed his father in any way. My client has done nothing but look after his elderly father over many years, sacrificing his own time and career. You must know what it's like with the recent cutbacks in government spending on social care. It has placed a terrific burden on family members.'

Richard Morris spat out the next sentence. 'And that bitch Catrin was never around. She was in London swanning around with her rich friends. She never lifted a finger to help him.'

'Mr Nelson,' Hobbs regained control of the conversation. 'I'm not entirely certain why you and Mr Morris are here.'

'I expect, Superintendent, no, rather, I demand you be utterly transparent with us and provide us with as much information as you can, bearing in mind our spirit of cooperation today.'

Hobbs bristled.

'The conduct of any police investigation requires the utmost confidentiality—'

Nelson sighed dismissively.

Hobbs ignored him. 'And as a solicitor, and an officer of the court you will know it would be *wholly* inappropriate for me to make any comment about allegations that may or may not have been made to us.'

'It's damn well not good enough.'

Hobbs stood up. Drake followed suit. 'Unless you have something else to add this meeting is over.' Hobbs said to the solicitor.

Nelson and Morris sat where they were for a few seconds, glaring accusingly at Hobbs. Then the superintendent moved away from the table, nodded at Drake and they left. They watched Morris and Nelson leave reception.

Hobbs turned to face Drake spitting out through gritted teeth. 'Make Morris a person of interest in his father's death.'

The offices of David Morris' solicitors, Pugh & Co., were far more salubrious than those Sara and Drake had visited the previous week. Leaflets advertising the solicitor's services were the only thing on the table in the reception area. Sara idly flicked through the outline of conveyancing procedures, divorce litigation and probate work. It all sounded very boring.

A musty smell filled Reginald Pugh's office. After the customary handshake they sat down. Pugh was a neat, punctilious sort of man in his early fifties. He wore a crisp white shirt with a neatly knotted silk tie.

'I've never known such activity around the death of one of my clients.' Pugh announced. 'I've had instructions from Richard Morris and Catrin Roach to cooperate fully with your inquiry. It all sounds terribly exciting.'

'Catrin Roach has made certain... allegations.' Drake said tentatively.

Pugh nodded forcefully. 'Of course, of course. She told me.'

'Did you write a will for Mr Morris?'

'I did indeed. And before you ask, he left a significant legacy to his son Richard. Which I daresay is what is causing Catrin Roach considerable anxiety. She thinks he was leaned on by her brother.'

'And was he?'

Pugh chuckled. 'He hated her.'

'Pardon me.'

'Mr Morris hated his daughter. It grieves me to say so, but he made his views abundantly clear to me. He thought she was a money grabbing bitch with no interest in anybody but herself.' He looked at Drake and Sara with a serious but mischievous edge to his face. 'His words exactly.'

'Is there any basis to Mrs Roach's allegations that her father may not have been of sound mind?' Sara said.

Pugh settled back in his chair and roared with laughter. 'I can happily confirm David Morris was of perfectly sound mind. His GP will tell you the same, particularly as he was a witness to the will and saw him regularly.'

'Thank you, Mr Pugh,' Drake said abruptly getting to his feet.

The solicitor handed him the file of papers sitting on his desk. 'I daresay you will need these.'

'That was a waste of time,' Drake muttered under his breath as they left.

After unlocking the car Drake sat for a moment staring out of the windscreen. He had been more taciturn than usual on their journey from headquarters, which Sara blamed on the inevitable decision to release the Ackroyds on bail. Drake's mood hadn't improved after speaking to Pugh. Nothing linked Isaac and Morris apart from the fact that both men were elderly and lived locally.

Sara knew he was thinking, contemplating.

'It might be sensible to see David Morris's GP,' Sara said.

Drake said nothing, but he drummed the fingers of one hand on the steering wheel.

'You're right,' he started the car engine. 'Give the practice a ring – you know what these GPs are like – don't let the receptionist give you any excuses.'

Sara dialled the number as Drake drove. It had an annoying multiple-choice recorded message. Eventually she got through to a receptionist who made it clear the doctor, a Merfyn Cadwalader, didn't have any spare appointments and could she call back in the morning.

Sara curbed her impatience. 'We should be there in a few minutes. Detective Inspector Drake expects to see Dr Cadwalader once we arrive. Please tell him to expect us.' She finished the call without waiting for a reply.

Drake drove straight into a slot marked 'Doctors Only/Meddygon yn Unig'. A plaque by the front door displayed the names of the GPs: one looked German, another Spanish or Portuguese, but most appeared local – at least the people of Menai Bridge had a surgery, Sara thought, recalling the headlines in the newspapers recently about the spate of GP practice closures.

Drake marched up to the reception window and spoke to the receptionist. '*Dwi yma i weld Dr Cadwalader.*' Then he pushed his warrant card discreetly towards her. Using Welsh was sensible, Sara realised. It was bound to get more cooperation from the staff.

Sara understood when he was told to sit down and wait. None of the other patients paid them any attention. A woman on two crutches hobbled towards the reception and complained she hadn't been able to make an appointment to see the GP and were there any emergency appointments available. She began crying, telling staff she was desperate and in so much pain. She was told to sit down and wait too.

Drake glanced at his watch and Sara knew he was impatient to make progress, get back to headquarters.

A few minutes passed. A nurse called the elderly woman, who almost toppled over as she got to her feet from the chair in reception. Soon after a member of staff came through and asked Drake and Sara to follow her. After walking down a short corridor she stopped by a door before knocking and pushing the door open for Drake and Sara.

Merfyn Cadwalader was the same age and vintage as the solicitor they had seen earlier. Drake guessed he was early fifties although judging by the long hair draping his shoulders he longed for his misspent youth.

'Detective Inspector Drake, good morning,' Cadwalader said jerking a hand at two visitors' chairs.

'This is Detective Sergeant Morgan,' Drake said.

Cadwalader nodded a greeting.

'I understand you'd like to discuss David Morris.'

'We've spoken with Mr Pugh his solicitor this morning who tells us you were Morris' GP and that you were witness to his will. How would you describe Mr Morris?'

'He was a charming old fellow. A lot of elderly people

get very sour and reflective, but he was always upbeat and positive. And he was of perfectly sound mind.'

Merfyn Cadwalader anticipated Drake's next question.

'Mrs Catrin Roach contacted me about her late father asking about his mental capacity and so forth. And I've had a letter from her solicitors telling me they are considering challenging his will and demanding copies of all his medical records.'

'And how have you responded?'

'I haven't yet. But when I do, I'll tell her quite clearly her father was of sound mind when he made the will. There is no suggestion at all in his medical records of any dementia, despite his age. He made clear his... displeasure with his daughter's attitude and lifestyle. He had decided rationally to benefit his son more than his daughter.'

Drake shared an exasperated glance with Sara. The doctor was only confirming what they knew already. Even so it depressed her that families could come to this.

'How long have you been David Morris' doctor?' Sara said.

'Ever since I joined the practice twenty years ago. He was of an older generation. He believed in politeness and courtesy. I suppose he was a bit old-fashioned. He'd been a magistrate and quite an important local figure. He and Emyr Isaac were old friends.'

'Were you Emyr Isaac's doctor too?'

'No, one of my colleagues usually went to see Mr Isaac. We have an excellent team of district nurses who provided treatment for Mr Isaac and Mr Morris.'

'We'll need David Morris's medical records,' Sara said, adding. 'As a precaution.'

Cadwalader clicked on his mouse and the monitor on his desk flickered into life. 'That shouldn't be a problem. Although I don't think we've had the latest reports from the ambulance service.'

'Ambulance service?' Drake said.

Cadwalader looked over at him. 'There have been a couple of occurrences recently where David Morris had fallen and the carers hadn't been able to get him back to his feet. They worried about the possibility he might have suffered a stroke.'

'When was the last incident?'

'The district nurse from the practice saw David on Saturday, the day before he died. And the paramedics were called the evening he died, I believe.'

Drake stared at the medic. Sara had seen the look before. Paramedics had attended the home of Mr Isaac and he was a patient of this surgery, too. But the circumstances were different – Isaac had died from a blood clot to the brain after a struggle with an intruder and Morris had been killed by an embolism. Sara glanced over at Drake and she could see that he was making the same connections. The prospect that Morris' killer was a nurse or paramedic was preposterous, but the idea settled uncomfortably into her thoughts, nonetheless.

Chapter 18

No matter how hard he tried to isolate the circumstances of Isaac's death from Morris' Drake failed. They were looking for a burglar who had broken into Isaac's home but Morris' death was altogether more sinister. But both men were elderly, both had carers and both had been seen regularly by paramedics and district nurses. Was it more than a coincidence? The possibility that paramedics or district nurses were implicated alarmed Drake. He said little as they drove back to headquarters. Luned and Winder jumped to their feet when Drake entered the Incident Room followed closely by Sara.

'There's something you should know about Morris' circumstances,' Winder said.

Luned gripped a blue folder, her eyes a study in concentration.

Drake made for the board. 'Go on.'

'Rachel Ackroyd was one of Morris' carers and she saw him the evening before he died,' Winder said.

Luned fell over her words. 'And we called at the offices of Caring Wales. They gave us details of Morris' care plan. Rachel was one of his regular carers.'

Sara sat at her desk. 'That puts her back in the frame as a person of interest.'

Drake mumbled his agreement as he glanced at the clock on the wall, conscious that he was expected at the full post-mortem later that day. Dr Kings had made it clear that conducting a CT scan had only been justified because of Catrin Roach's conduct. Drake sympathised once he had learned of the legal threats Catrin Roach had made.

Sara continued. 'We spoke to Dr Cadwalader who works in the GP practice that treated Isaac and Morris. Paramedics and district nurses saw them both before they died.'

'But...' Luned started.

'I know the deaths are not directly linked.' Drake

paused and glanced over at the board wondering if two entirely different inquiries were justified.

'It's too much of a coincidence isn't it boss?' Winder said. 'I mean two old blokes and the same carers.'

The constable had been on his team too long, Drake thought – now he could read his mind.

'The inquiries will have to be separate until we determine otherwise. Tomorrow we make progress with identifying names. We need a detailed picture of who saw both men before they died.

Apprehension was etched into every squint and gaze on the faces in front of him.

Denver Watkins wore a different shirt from the night before. He had even shaved and drawn a comb through his hair. The reception to the mortuary was neat and tidy too. Obviously having the Welsh Government's chief forensic pathologist on duty had sharpened Denver's act.

He dispensed with trying to make small talk, but he did insist Drake and Sara sign the necessary health and safety forms. Then he added almost courteously. 'They are waiting to see you.'

He led them through into a conference room Drake had never visited before. It had a well-polished table with comfortable chairs and images flickered on the large screen occupying one wall of what Drake assumed to be David Morris' skull.

Sitting at the table alongside Lee Kings were two other men. Recognition crossed Drake's mind as he saw the older man. A case several years before involving the death of two police officers had involved Dr John Crewe who, at the time, had been the Home Office pathologist.

'Dr Crewe,' Drake said reaching out a hand.

'Detective Inspector Drake, how nice to see you again.' Crewe's rich cultured English accent hadn't changed.

'Dr Crewe is here as the principal Welsh Government

forensic pathologist,' Kings said.

'I much preferred the good old days when I worked for the Home Office. It sounded so much more reassuring then. But, hey ho, nothing stays the same I suppose.'

Kings continued. 'I don't think you've met Dr Penrose. He's one of our Consultant Radiologists. He's been providing valuable advice about the CT scan images.'

Penrose nodded and after shaking hands with Drake and Sara they sat down.

Kings stood by the board. 'We've had the opportunity of examining the CT scan images this morning and we've completed a traditional open post-mortem. I'll let Dr Crewe explain.'

Crewe placed his hands on the table. He was greyer than Drake recalled, a lot flabbier around the gills and less healthy looking. 'After assessing the CT scan most carefully and with the valuable contribution from Dr Penrose it was clear the air found in the RV needed further examination.

'A venous air embolism is a rare cause of death. Entry of air into the circulation can be caused by any number of things – trauma or it could be surgical. But David Morris wasn't in hospital so we've been able to eliminate all these from what we know of his medical records. So that leaves us with the possibility of a criminal intervention. I'm sure that you're interested in knowing whether we can determine this definitively.'

Crewe looked over at Drake who said nothing.

The pathologist continued. 'The detection of air embolism requires special precautions during the post-mortem. This morning we used an aspirometer to detect the nature of the gas in the heart. I shan't bore you with the exact technical details but, once we've gathered that gas, it is analysed. We then compare the results with known criteria that justify the diagnosis of 'air embolism' as gas can form in the deceased from the veritable menagerie of bacteria we host.'

'It sounds complicated,' Drake said.

'The technique is simple but does require care. I have undertaken it several times when there was a suspected case of criminal intervention causing the air embolism. There are several known cases of air embolism being used by serial killers as their modus operandi. I was at a conference once when I spoke to a pathologist from Poland who entertained us at great length about a Catholic priest who knocked off his parishioners.'

'So what are the results in this case?'

Dr Penrose piped up. 'I've had the opportunity this morning of examining the CT scan results. When you have excluded the impossible whatever remains, however improbable, must be the truth. And from a radiological perspective, in the absence of any other explanation, a criminal intervention has to be the reason for these air embolisms.'

'Precisely,' Crewe agreed loudly. 'And when we completed a microscopic examination it was possible to identify intravasal air locks in the lungs.' Crewe managed a triumphant tone.

When Kings spoke he sounded sombre. 'It means, Ian, David Morris didn't die of natural causes. Air was deliberately injected, and a significant volume at that, into his vein which caused an airlock in the heart, causing cardiac arrest and death.'

Drake sat back in his chair. 'Are you certain?' He regretted the question before he had finished asking it from the pained looks on the faces of the doctors in front of him. 'We've been doing some preliminary work on Morris's home circumstances. As well as his son he had various carers who came into the house regularly. It was the same team of carers that cared for Emyr Isaac.'

Drake noticed Crewe raising a quizzical eyebrow.

Kings offered an explanation. 'I completed the post-mortem on Mr Isaac last week. He died from a blood clot to the brain after falling or being thrown against a gas fire in the bedroom.'

Crewe nodded as though the circumstances sounded like an everyday occurrence.

'There's something else you need to know, Ian,' Kings paused, ran two fingers over his lips and then took a deep breath. 'When I was on secondment the health board used various locum pathologists. During the last eight weeks there was a Portuguese doctor in charge. Denver, that's the mortuary assistant,' Kings added for Crewe and Penrose's benefit. 'Reckoned he was half pissed most of the time and that he was no more qualified to be a pathologist than the shop assistants at Tesco.'

Drake wanted Kings to get to the point, quickly.

'I've had a chance of reviewing some of the deaths during my absence – four cases in particular. All were recorded as heart attacks and all were elderly patients with no medical history to suggest cardiovascular disease, although some people do have heart attacks out of the blue.'

An ominous silence filled the room as though everyone was holding their breath: nobody fidgeted, nobody blinked.

'Christ, Lee. Do you have *any* idea what you're suggesting?'

Kings nodded solemnly. 'You may have a serial killer to catch.'

Chapter 19

Drake arrived back at headquarters and shrugged on an overcoat against the autumn evening chill. There was still another half an hour or so until sunset, and at the end of the month the days would get shorter once the clocks changed. Dried copper-coloured leaves shuffled around the edges of the car park. Drake enjoyed the changing seasons; watching the cycle of nature always reminded him of his upbringing in the smallholding his father ran.

His thoughts turned to the potential consequences of Lee Kings' initial conclusion. Could all four deaths be attributed to the same killer? And if the culprit had then killed David Morris it meant his inquiry had taken on a vastly different proportion. How would Superintendent Hobbs react? Wyndham Price would have been determined, resolute in offering unflinching support for the investigating team and Drake hoped that he could expect similar from Superintendent Hobbs.

Thankfully serial killers were rare in Wales and the United Kingdom. And for that Drake was grateful. Police officers in the United States regularly dealt with serial killers, experiencing first-hand the worst of human depravity and it filled Drake with admiration. How did they cope?

He took the lift to the senior management suite and threaded his way along the corridor towards Superintendent Hobbs' office. Hannah had long left for the day, so he rapped his knuckles on the door to Hobbs' room.

After hearing Hobbs' voice, he entered. There was a comfortable warm feel to the room. Two uplighters complemented the expensive-looking desk lamp Hobbs had introduced. The superintendent looked settled, as though he were expecting to be working for another few hours.

He waved a hand at one of the visitors' chairs, said nothing, and gave Drake one of his narrow piggy eyed stares. Hobbs' features were a little disjointed, his eyes too small, his cheeks a little too chubby. As a detective Drake valued his ability to read a face, delve into a person's eyes and fathom out what was going on behind them. Not with Hobbs.

'I've just come back from David Morris' post-mortem.'

'And how was Dr Crewe?'

'I've only met him once before.'

Hobbs nodded. 'He applied for a position with the Home Office in London. He didn't like the pace of devolution and made it abundantly clear to everyone that he wasn't going to stay around living in the sticks.'

Drake raised a quizzical eyebrow, inviting Hobbs to enlighten him. He duly obliged. 'He was turned down. So now he has to face the rest of his career working in Wales.' Hobbs drew himself nearer the desk. Smalltalk was over. 'What are the details?'

'Crewe and Kings completed a detailed post-mortem on David Morris. Their conclusion is that someone injected air into a vein that caused an embolism.'

Hobbs propped his chin on steepled forearms, his face darkening. 'Go on.'

'They believe they can prove his death was as a result of 'criminal intervention'. It's a quaint way of calling it murder.'

'Are they certain?'

Drake nodded. He drew a breath. But before he could continue Hobbs cut across him. 'Is this linked to the death of Emyr Isaac?'

'Dr Crewe has made a preliminary review of Lee Kings' conclusions and he wants to have a CT scan undertaken.'

Hobbs looked mystified. 'But there's already been a post-mortem. Presumably all that's left are…'

'He still thinks it might be constructive.'

Hobbs took on a slightly sickly look.

Drake continued. 'They're going to undertake it tomorrow. There are no next of kin to consult. We'll be seeking permission from the solicitor who acts as his executor.'

'Can we link the two deaths in *any* way?'

'We've established that they had carers in common as well as the same district nurses from the surgery and they were seen by paramedics the evening before they died.' Drake paused. 'There's more, sir.'

Hobbs gave Drake a puzzled glance.

'Lee Kings has been away on secondment and there was a locum pathologist in charge whilst he was away. The mortuary assistant raised some issues with Lee when he returned about the standard of the work involved.'

'And?'

There are concerns about four other deaths during Lee's absence.'

Hobbs' eye contact never wavered. 'So what does Lee suggest we do about these other deaths?'

Drake paused before answering, 'Both pathologists believe that we have sufficient evidence to justify exhumations.'

Hobbs blew out a lungful of breath. Then he reached for a notepad, grabbed his fountain pen and looked over at Drake. 'I'll need all the details.'

Drake woke from a restless sleep the following morning. He spent longer under the shower than usual as his mind filled with the possibility that all six deaths were linked. He shuddered at the thought. Superintendent Hobbs had kept him at headquarters until after seven-thirty the previous evening as he insisted on examining everything in minute detail as though his understanding needed to be reinforced by repetition.

Annie had said little when he arrived home, but Drake sensed she wanted to enquire, sympathise, be supportive. Telling her that within a few hours they would be exhuming four corpses with a view to embarking on a multiple murder inquiry was hardly the stuff for small talk over the breakfast table. He tried his best to be cheerful but when she gave him a lingering kiss before leaving and told him to be careful, he realised he hadn't done a good job.

Striding into the Incident Room that morning he cast off his misgivings and strode up to the board announcing greetings to the three members of his team as he did so. He turned to look at the officers. 'There's been a development.'

The serious tone to his voice changed the relaxed morning faces into hard set jaws. He explained Dr Crewe's conclusions – the technical definitions dissuaded any interruptions.

'Superintendent Hobbs has formally authorised that we seek permission for exhumations.'

Winder whistled under his breath. Luned and Sara nodded seriously.

Drake glanced at the board behind him. 'Get one of the civilian support staff to erect another board. Then get the details of all four individuals together.'

'Are we treating their deaths as suspicious before the post-mortems?' Sara said.

'It might be premature, but I don't want to waste any time.'

Drake folded his arms, pulled them closer to his chest. 'I don't need to spell out the consequences.' Three heads nodded in unison. 'Gareth, I want you to identify the next of kin of the four deceased. Sara and I will concentrate on organising the exhumation licences and the undertakers. Luned get the details of the district nurses who treated Isaac and Morris and the medical records for the other four – see if you can identify *any* common features.'

Gareth struck a serious tone. 'What do we tell the next of kin, sir?'

Drake paused. There wasn't any way of sugar-coating what they were doing. The families needed to be notified. 'As part of an ongoing inquiry certain irregularities have come up relating to post-mortems conducted whilst the regular North Wales pathologist was away on secondment. At this stage it is nothing to worry about but it's necessary for a more complete post-mortem to be undertaken.'

Undertakers needed to be contacted, licences obtained, paperwork signed off. It would take time, but Sara knew Drake well enough to know that if he was serious about something, he would expect results. A further meeting before lunch meant she had to work fast.

She settled down at her desk, ignoring the signs of activity around her. Winder was using his best official-sounding voice trying to track down the family of William Longman, the first name on the list. Sara flicked through the details finding the name of the undertakers. That was the easy part, Sara thought as she reached for the telephone and dialled the number.

Ten minutes later she finished her explanation to the director of the company who sounded surprised when Sara explained that once they had the approval for an exhumation it would have to be undertaken under the cover of darkness.

'I see.' His voice was laced with excitement and exhilaration.

The second name on Sara's list was Michael Capon. He had been buried in the same grave as his wife in a cemetery in Caernarfon. Tracking down his only daughter who lived in Vienna was Luned's task. And from the exasperated look on her face Sara judged it was a frustrating exercise.

Contacting the undertaker was easier.

'I've never been involved with an exhumation,' Maldwyn Pritchard's voice mixed astonishment and intrigue.

'Would you be able to make tentative arrangements for tomorrow evening?'

'I'll... It might be difficult... I'll need to contact the cemetery authorities.'

Sara chose her most officious sounding tone. 'This is an

urgent matter.'

'And arrange for a sexton. Perhaps we should get a mini-digger? Good job he's buried on top of his late wife.'

Funerals and corpses were the day-to-day business of Maldwyn Pritchard but his casual discussion about mini-diggers and who was buried on top of whom made Sara feel queasy.

Pritchard continued. 'There'll be paperwork of course. You'll need licences and consent from the family.'

'Everything is in hand.'

Sara then turned her attention to the last two names – Victoria Rowlands and John Kerr. Both funerals had been organised by the same undertaker in Menai Bridge. She rang the landline number, but there was no reply. She quickly googled the name and found an alternative contact number. It was answered almost immediately.

'Grace Parry.' Sara detected the warm tones of the accent typical of north-west Wales.

Sara ran through the explanation she had used and polished twice already.

'It will take some organising. Exhumations at such short notice could be quite expensive. Will the Wales Police Service be paying the cost?'

'Of course.' Sara replied surprised by Parry's matter-of-fact attitude.

'You'll need all the paperwork and the correct licences in good time.'

'We should be able to get back to you later this afternoon. I suggest you make preliminary arrangements for tomorrow evening.'

Sara sat back in her chair, pleased with progress. She glanced over at the studious, intense faces of Gareth Winder and Luned Thomas. Winder had the handset propped between his shoulder and jaw as he tapped on the keyboard of his computer. Luned was speaking intently down the telephone.

Sara read the time on her watch. She had time enough before their next briefing to make coffee and print out the names of the latest victims. She glanced over her shoulder. Drake stared at the monitor on his desk and she wondered how much progress he had made.

Chapter 20

Drake marched over to the Incident Room board as Sara returned with a tray of three coffees. He had shaken his head when she asked if he'd like one. Coffee could wait, they had to get on, make progress.

'You wouldn't believe the hassle I've had with some civil servant in Cardiff. He had simply no idea about the procedures for requesting an exhumation licence.'

'It's probably all new to them boss.' Sara sat at her desk, a steaming mug on a coaster.

'Even so, I had to get Assistant Chief Constable Neary to call him and threaten all sorts of dire consequences unless he cooperated.'

Nods of approval circulated around the desks.

'We should have the paperwork in less than an hour. So bring me up to date.' Drake invited Sara to start.

Winder and Luned turned to look at her as she straightened in her chair. 'I've spoken with all the undertakers who organised the original funerals. I've given them advance warning to arrange the exhumations for tomorrow evening.'

'Excellent,' Drake said. 'Very good work. We'll each attend one exhumation and we'll make certain that there are uniformed officers present too.'

Drake aimed a brief jerk of his head at Winder and Luned. 'And how did you get on with contacting the relatives?'

Winder was the first to reply. 'I managed to track down William Longman's son. He's a solicitor in one of the big city firms. He didn't sound particularly interested and didn't raise any objections to a more detailed post-mortem.'

'And did you ask about Longman's circumstances before he died?' Drake said.

'Longman's son confirmed that Caring Wales had provided care in the home for him.'

Sara put a mug down on the coaster on the desk.

'Hardly a surprise – they're the biggest care company in the area.'

Drake turned to the second board erected that morning. Longman's name was the first of the four new names and alongside him was Michael Capon.

'I spoke to Ffion Capon who lives in Vienna,' Luned said. 'And she was really shocked. She kept asking me all sorts of questions about what was going on and whether her father had been killed. I reiterated there was nothing to worry about and that it was part of our normal inquiries. She didn't sound convinced, sir.'

'But did she agree for the exhumation to take place?' Drake sounded impatient.

She nodded. 'Eventually. It took some persuading and she rang me back telling me that she'd been having so many crank calls lately from spammers she wanted to be sure it wasn't something dodgy.'

After a mouthful of her drink Luned continued. 'I spoke with Victoria Rowlands' two daughters.' Drake turned to look at the third new name on the board. 'They both live locally in Bangor and they were shocked. They aren't prepared to give their consent until you've been to see them, sir.'

Sara checked the notepad in front of her. 'She's the lady buried on Church Island. And it was the same undertaker who organised John Kerr's funeral. She was matter-of-fact and businesslike when I spoke to her.'

Drake sounded exasperated. 'We'll need to go and see them as soon as we can. Has someone spoken to John Kerr's family?'

'That was me, boss,' Winder responded. 'They have no objection to the exhumation. John Kerr moved to the island a few years ago to run a pub before he opened a café and restaurant.'

'Progress,' Drake looked his watch. 'Sara and I will go and see Victoria Rowlands' daughters. In the meantime,

Gareth, Luned, get organised with recovering any information you can from Caring Wales about William Longman and John Kerr. And get all the paperwork from the care homes where Michael Capon and Victoria Rowlands lived. As well as their complete medical records. There has to be a connection here that we are missing…'

When Drake returned to his office it annoyed him that no email waited for him from the Justice Department of the Welsh Government. So he tapped out a brief message to the civil servant he had spoken to earlier telling him he expected the necessary licences and paperwork within an hour, adding: 'It is imperative this matter is given the highest priority.'

He left his desk and shrugged on his suit jacket. In the Incident Room he joined Sara. 'Let's go.'

Sara fiddled with the heating controls of the car, getting a blast of warm air into her side of the cabin. At least the inside was clean; Drake always kept his Mondeo neat and tidy, hoovering the footwells regularly – he hated the stones and grit and gravel that could collect by the accelerator and the brake pedal.

Sara tapped the postcode into the satnav, but he knew the basic route. It meant driving west along the A55. It was only when they reached the city of Bangor itself that the satnav would kick in and take them around the streets towards the address they needed.

Drake listened as Sara called ahead, speaking with one of the sisters, telling her they were en route. After the conversation Sara turned to Drake. 'They sound very worried.'

'It's hardly a common occurrence, so I can understand how they feel.'

'I wonder, boss, if it might be sensible if I were to take the lead? After all they've spoken with Luned and myself already and…'

'Female touch?'

'Something like that.'

Sara had been with Drake for over a year and after a tentative start she was confident with her own abilities and implicitly critical of his. Not a bad thing, Drake thought. He could be cranky and rude, and he decided he didn't have any objection to Sara handling what sounded like a potentially awkward situation.

'Of course. But we can't be too long.'

The satnav directed Drake off the dual carriageway and over in the direction of the hospital. He had travelled this section of the route frequently when his father visited the outpatients department. Losing his father at a relatively young age still hurt, and time had been a reluctant healer. But the satnav bleeped instructions for him to turn away from the hospital towards a new housing estate, and Drake slowed before indicating left.

Sara pointed to the house number and Drake pulled the car into the paved drive.

A woman in her mid-forties opened the door to them. She had thin, bloodless lips and hair permed into long thick locks draped over her shoulders. Sara had her warrant card ready and Drake dug into a jacket pocket for his own.

They were shown into a sitting room at the front of the property where a second woman got to her feet. She had inherited the same mouth and lips as her sister, but her hair was short and cut neatly around her head.

The first woman reached out a hand. 'I'm Nest and this is my sister Llinos. We don't understand what's happening and we're very worried indeed.' There was an angry edge to the last few words and Drake wasn't certain if it was intentional.

'May we sit down?' Sara smiled.

Nest reacted. 'Yes, of course, I'm sorry.'

'We were shocked,' Llinos added. 'When you rang about Mam's post-mortem.'

Sara sat at the edge of the sofa and tilted her head at Llinos. 'I can really sympathise. It must have been quite a surprise when Detective Constable Thomas called about our request. You see sometimes these things do come up within inquiries. We must look at everything, make certain all the threads are followed up. Otherwise we wouldn't be doing our job properly.'

Llinos was warming to Sara's charm offensive.

'Is there any suggestion that Mam might have been...?' Nest was unable to finish her sentence – was she hoping to use 'killed' or 'murdered'?

'All we can tell you is that your mother's post-mortem was completed by a locum pathologist who has since returned to Portugal.'

Nest and Llinos rolled their eyes, as though the non-British identity of the doctor responsible was somehow to blame.

Sara continued. 'Certain irregularities cropped up once the usual North Wales pathologist was able to review the paperwork,' Sara managed a comforting tone now. 'He has decided it would be sensible to undertake some tests – just to be on the safe side.'

'Does this have anything to do with the death of Emyr Isaac?' Nest asked.

'We are responsible for investigating his murder,' Sara said. 'but there is no link at the moment.' Nest and Llinos looked unconvinced.

It mirrored exactly how Drake felt.

'We are hoping you will consent to an exhumation.'

'I don't know. I really don't know,' Llinos said. 'It strikes me as very odd and I'm extremely uncomfortable. Mam has gone after all. Another post-mortem isn't going to change anything.'

She was right about that, Drake thought, even wondering if he might interject but Sara beat him to it.

'What I can tell you is that we have contacted other

families.'

Llinos' and Nest's mouths fell open.

'There are others?' Nest said.

'I'm sure you can appreciate the confidentiality involved and it is a matter of great sensitivity. I'd like to be able to share with you more details, but it wouldn't be right to do so.' Sara tipped her head, sharing a serious I-know-best look with both women. 'Your consent will greatly assist the Wales Police Service in its inquiry.'

There was a moment of silence as both women stared at Sara and then at Drake.

Then they looked at each other before nodding slowly.

Chapter 21

Luned arrived at the Afon Menai Medical Centre in good time for her meeting the following morning with the practice manager. He had explained that he could spare her fifteen minutes at the start of his day.

Learning about the care Emyr Isaac and David Morris had needed made sobering reading and Luned worried what the NHS would be like when her parents were in their eighties. Her parents had complained recently how difficult it was getting an appointment to see the GP. The practice where they were patients had been taken over by the health board and some days there were no GPs at all.

A man in his mid-forties, grey suit, black brogues, a blue striped shirt with a tie loosely knotted flashed the remote at a compact SUV before hurrying towards the surgery. Luned guessed he was Bill Jones, the practice manager.

Once the main entrance was open Luned joined the queue of patients threading its way into the building. The woman at the reception desk told her Mr Jones was expecting her. Luned sat down and waited. A young child, no more than five or six ran around coughing and spluttering, ignoring the attempts by his mother at scolding. Luckily Luned didn't have to wait long and Jones gestured for her to follow him through a door. After the usual greetings he led Luned up a staircase to the first floor, explaining this was the administrative centre of the practice. Luned caught a glimpse of members of staff already peering at monitors.

Jones' room at the end of the corridor had a window looking out over the car park. The glossy leaves of an indoor palm plant dominated one corner and above it was a whiteboard with black, red and green writing with different names that Luned assumed to be staff rotas.

'We are investigating the deaths of Emyr Isaac and David Morris.' Luned chose her words carefully. 'Dr

Cadwalader was kind enough to provide Detective Inspector Drake with Mr Morris' medical records. We need details of all the members of your staff who came into contact with both Mr Morris and Mr Isaac.' Luned took a beat to assess the reaction to her request. Jones blinked nervously – just as Luned expected. 'It's a matter of routine of course. We need to be able to identify and eliminate, where appropriate, people who had contact with both Mr Morris and Mr Isaac.'

Jones ran a hand over his lips. 'I understand.'

Luned reinforced her message. 'I'm sure I can rely on your professionalism to keep this request strictly between ourselves.'

Jones lowered his voice conspiratorially. 'No need to say any more.'

Luned turned to the staff list she had printed out from the surgery's website. 'I need the employment records and history of all your staff and in particular the district nurses who visited Mr Isaac and Mr Morris.'

Preliminaries dealt with Jones relaxed. 'There are two district nurses. Elaine Boxford has been with us for twelve months and Mandy Price has been attached to the practice for over twenty years. Both have a wealth of experience in general practice and the medical records for Mr Morris and Mr Isaac will tell you which of them visited.'

'One final thing,' Luned said as Jones sat back in his chair. 'The coroner has asked us to deputise as his officer in the case of four other recent deaths. Apparently, they've arisen as a result of an incompetent pathologist, and families are kicking up a bit of a stink.' It all sounded so inconsequential, although Luned had rehearsed it carefully. 'We'll need the medical records of these four individuals.' She handed Jones a list. 'I understand they were patients here too.'

He gave his watch a furtive glance. 'All this might take some time.'

Luned's smile told him she wasn't going without the

paperwork.

An hour had elapsed by the time Luned was sitting back in her car, knowing Bill Jones' fifteen minutes was always going to be completely unrealistic. As soon as she was back at headquarters she'd get preliminary searches done against Elaine Boxford and Mandy Price. In the meantime, she had the records to collect from Caring Wales relating to David Morris, John Kerr and William Longman.

Luned use the same excuse with Victoria Picton-Davies, who did her best to extract information about what was happening in the inquiry. Luned deflected her interest with comments like 'it must be distressing for you as a company' and 'I know you're trying to provide the best possible care for your clients'.

Picton-Davies smiled her cooperation. Luned left clutching the files she needed.

When Luned arrived back at headquarters Winder was busy working his way through a sandwich. An orange coloured bottle of soft drink stood alongside an enormous bag of crisps which he had torn open.

'You won't believe the trouble I've had speaking to William Longman's next of kin. Apparently, he specialises in banking work and he was in Zurich yesterday. And today he only had a window of ten minutes in which he could talk to me.'

'And did he agree to the exhumation?'

Winder mumbled confirmation through a mouthful of BLT sandwich. Then he wiped a tissue over his mouth. 'I haven't been able to speak to the manager of the ambulance service so I'm going there after I finish lunch.'

It meant Luned could have a couple of hours without Winder's presence in the Incident Room.

She got to work examining the details of the district nurses. Initially discounting Mandy Price on the basis, logically, Luned assumed, that as she had been with the practice for over twenty years if she was a serial killer she would have started much sooner. Boxford was an unusual surname for North Wales and it carried an air of mystery.

Luned ordered a preliminary financial search and the result of the Police National Computer search intrigued her. Boxford had a conviction for possession of cannabis. The WPS rarely prosecuted possession of cannabis offences any longer. Four other names appeared on the PNC results as co-defendants with Boxford which suggested there might be more to the background of the offence.

Was there a Mr Boxford? And if so, was he employed in the medical professions? Her curriculum vitae indicated she had worked in a surgery in Liverpool before moving to Anglesey. So she rang the practice and explained to the practice manager that she needed a more complete picture of Elaine Boxford's employment history as part of the coroner's inquiry.

'She was never employed here.' The woman's Scouse accent sounded harsh.

Hurriedly Luned checked the curriculum vitae. 'But I thought she had been with you for four years.'

'She was an agency nurse. Four months more like it.'

'And do you know where she worked before?'

'No idea. You should talk to the agency. What's this about again?'

'What's the name of the agency?'

Luned put the phone down hurriedly once she had the name. An incomplete curriculum vitae raised all sorts of questions. Like why would a district nurse lie about her employment history? What did she have to hide?

Chapter 22

Drake sat by his desk and stared at the photograph of Helen and Megan taken at Disneyland Paris a few weeks earlier when he had been with the girls and Annie for their first holiday together. Things had gone well. He had missed being a family after his divorce from Sian and he warmed to the recollection of how Helen and Megan had enjoyed Annie's company. Looking at the cheerful faces brought a smile to Drake's face. Annie's parents moving from Cardiff to North Wales and the prospect of her promotion in the history department of Bangor University meant a new direction in his life. He reached over and adjusted the photograph a few millimetres. On impulse he picked up the telephone and called Sian.

'Are you still at work?' Sian said recognising his number.

'I'm working late.'

Sian sounded dismissive. 'Nothing new.'

'Can I speak to Helen and Megan?'

'They're busy with homework.'

'I won't be long.'

Sian sighed. Drake heard her call his daughters and he spent time talking to both. He reminded them of the imminent party to celebrate his mother's birthday. They sounded genuine when they asked after Annie and, when Drake rang off, he thought about the future, regretting the past.

Then he dialled Annie. She answered after two rings. He could hear classical music playing in the background.

'I'm going to be late home tonight.'

'Is it about that Menai Bridge murder?'

'It's connected. I can't tell you too much now.'

'I understand, Ian. Text me when you can.'

Sharing with her that they suspected a serial killer was responsible for perhaps six deaths wasn't the sort of detail he could discuss. Seconds after finishing the call his mobile bleeped. *Cymer ofal. Caru chdi X.* Telling him to take care and that she loved him always warmed his spirit.

He paced out to the Incident Room where he drew up a chair and sat by an empty desk. One of the team had organised sandwiches, bags of crisps and bars of chocolate. He snapped open a can of soft drink and surveyed the anxious faces around him. Each had made excuses to family and friends that work commitments meant they wouldn't be home at the usual time – perhaps not even until the early hours. They had a long night ahead of them.

'Updates please.'

Luned seized the initiative and replied first. 'I've got the details of the district nurses who visited Morris and Isaac. One of them has a CV that doesn't check out and she has a conviction for possession of cannabis several years ago.'

Drake nodded. 'Send me the details.'

'And the ambulance service manager won't disclose any information unless he talks to you, boss,' Winder said. 'And I finally got Longman's next of kin to consent to the exhumation.'

'Good.' Drake glanced at the board.

'It means that all the families have consented, sir,' Sara said. 'And all the licences are in place and the undertakers ready to go.'

Drake turned to face the team. 'Let's run through the checklist once again.'

Sara would be present with an exhumation team at the cemetery where John Kerr was buried. She recited the names of the three uniformed officers tasked to accompany her. Two CSIs would be there to erect a tent over the grave. Luned was in charge at the grave of Michael Capon in Caernarfon. And Gareth Winder had been delegated to supervise the exhumation at the Beaumaris town graveyard.

He would be responsible for the exhumation of Victoria Rowlands buried on Ynys Tysilio, known as Church Island, in the Menai Strait.

'All organised then.' Drake finished his drink and got to his feet. 'Let's go.

On the journey from Colwyn Bay to Menai Bridge Drake mentally checked off what the team needed to do tomorrow once the post-mortems had been completed. Four families to be reassured if there was no indication of foul play or be informed their loved ones might have been murdered. It wasn't a prospect he welcomed.

He indicated off the A55 after crossing the Britannia Bridge and skirted down the coast towards Menai Bridge, casting a brief glance over at the floodlights illuminating the original bridge over the Menai Strait built by Thomas Telford in the middle of the 1820s. It was the first important suspension bridge ever built and it still looked majestic.

He pulled into a car park and joined three uniformed police officers milling around by the side of a police van. Seconds later a scientific support vehicle drew up, and behind it an undertaker's hearse.

Undertaker Grace Parry introduced herself to Drake. Sara had already recounted her earlier conversation with Parry which matched exactly the formal businesslike approach she took with him that evening.

Drake knew their access to Ynys Tysilio would be across a narrow causeway that split off from the Belgium Promenade – so called because it had been built by Belgian refugees during the First World War as a thank you for their welcome in the area. St Tysilio's church, after which the island was named, had been built in the fifteenth century and its graveyard covered the whole tiny island.

After Parry unlocked the gate nearby, the scientific support vehicle and the hearse made their way down through the trees. Drake and the uniformed officers followed behind on foot. At the bottom Parry greeted the sexton and his assistant and led everyone onto the island.

The team worked quickly to erect a tent over the grave and Drake stood exchanging small talk with the uniformed officers standing by the gate at the end of the causeway. It was difficult to imagine anyone wanting to visit the island at this time of night, so the officers had little to do apart from relishing the overtime. Occasionally Drake glanced over, but the zip of the tent remained firmly closed. The smell of seaweed drifted in the air and the sound of water lapping against the side of the promenade broke the silence.

Drake walked around the perimeter path, away from the floodlights. The moon cast harsh shadows and Drake sensed movement in the shrubbery. All the activity must have disturbed something. He reached the southern side of the island where the electric lights lit up the entrance of the small church and seeped over the island's perimeter wall, bathing the rocks beneath. If this proved to be a dead end, then he'd caused a lot of anguish for the families who had wanted to grieve without the distress of being involved in an exhumation.

Drake paused and looked down the Strait towards the Britannia Bridge, its deck lined with streetlights reflecting off the water's surface. Trucks sped over the bridge and on for the port at Holyhead and then Ireland. It was a chilly, cloudless evening and Drake drew the collar of his jacket up to his neck.

He found his mobile in a pocket and called Sara.

'They've finished erecting the tent, sir.'

'Same here. Let me know as soon as you've finished.'

Then he called Winder and Luned who both reported similar progress. He read the time – almost nine-thirty pm. He sauntered down the path that threaded its way through the graveyard back towards the tent and the floodlights. Parry gave him a brief nod.

'How much progress are you making?'

She reached for the zip of the tent. 'Judge for yourself.'

Drake peered inside. Two men in thin black boiler suits

were busy heaving soil to either side of the grave. The top of the casket was already in view. Drake could see an engraved brass plaque at its head. He decided against asking how long they might be. He retreated and let Parry rezip the tent.

Another half an hour passed. A walker with a torch hurried briskly along the Belgian promenade, a dog tugging at a lead. There was a buzz of traffic that drifted off both bridges and swirled around the gravestones and small buildings on the island. Was this resting in peace, Drake wondered?

The zip was opened from the inside this time and the sexton emerged, exchanging a few words with Parry who nodded for the driver of the hearse to get ready. Once the front flap of the tent had been moved to one side the sexton and his assistant unceremoniously manhandled the casket onto a trolley which they wheeled down to the hearse. That part of the process was over quickly and Drake watched as the hearse sedately made its way over the causeway and back up towards the middle of Menai Bridge.

The journey to the mortuary would take thirty minutes with the evening roads clear of traffic.

It was another thirty minutes before the sexton was finished and the scientific support team could dismantle the tent. They would have to do the whole process in reverse once Dr Kings and Dr Crewe had completed the post-mortems. Flattening the tent and its metal superstructure took far less than its erection. The scientific support vehicle left the island and Drake followed the uniformed officers back through the trees, mobile at his ear, checking progress with the others in his team. When he reached his car, he had spoken to all three. Hearses from each exhumation were on their way to the mortuary. Drake stood by his car wondering what the morning might bring.

Chapter 23

'Does the Wales Police Service have any comments to make about the exhumations conducted last evening?'

'How the bloody hell did you get my number?' Drake regretted swearing when he realised he was probably talking to a journalist.

'This is John Hopkins of the BBC. I understand there have been four exhumations, two in Menai Bridge, another in Beaumaris and the fourth in Caernarfon. It's highly unusual of course – is it linked to the ongoing investigations into the deaths of Emyr Isaac and David Morris?'

'Contact public relations. And don't ever call me again,' Drake snapped. His mood hadn't improved when he entered the Incident Room. He mumbled darkly to Sara and Winder about 'bloody press' and stalked into his office where he called Susan Howells.

'Calm down, Ian. There's nothing I can do.'

Drake sat back in his chair and rubbed the bridge of his nose. Howells was right.

'It's the last thing we need.'

'I understand that. I'll do what I can to control it. But they won't publish anything unless they have some details to back it up.'

'We'll tell the undertakers and the families not to say anything to the press.'

'Good, that might help.'

Howells rang off and Drake sat for a moment chewing his lip. Somehow the damned journalist had got hold of his mobile number. Involving so many people in the exhumation processes made confidentiality impossible. It rankled even so.

Then he grabbed at the phone and called Lee Kings.

'Good morning, Dr Crewe and I are about to begin the first post-mortem.'

'Any idea how long you'll be?'

'Get here as soon as you can, Ian.' Kings used an

irritated tone.

Technically he wasn't the senior investigating officer. Superintendent Hobbs should have been spending the rest of the day in the mortuary.

Drake stalked into the Incident Room where Luned was talking to the others. Grey skin and tired eyes meant they all looked as jaded as he felt.

'Have they started on the post-mortems?' Sara said.

Drake leaned against a spare desk. 'Not yet. We need to get over there as soon as we can.' He turned to look at Luned and Winder. 'I want you both building a detailed picture of everything that happened in the last week of the lives of each of these four deaths.'

Luned responded. 'What are we looking for?'

'A pattern of activity that cross-references to any of the other victims. If the pathologists confirm their worst fears, then there must be something in common.'

The sugar-dusted plate on Winder's desk alongside his coffee mug was evidence of his early morning doughnut hit. He sounded tired. 'What if the pathologists don't discover any foul play and conclude the deaths are all due to natural causes?'

'Then we can tell four families that their loved ones have been reburied and apologise for any distress.'

Three sets of troubled eyes stared over at Drake sharing his reservation that such an outcome was likely. He got up, nodded to Sara. 'We'll review again later this afternoon.'

Winder's girlfriend had complained vociferously when he had arrived home a little before eleven pm the night before. She had an early start the following morning and if he disturbed her when he came to bed it would ruin her sleep. His mind kept dwelling on the sight of the casket being exhumed from the grave. Standing around the cemetery he had felt chilled and no amount of stamping his feet or clapping his hands together had made him any warmer. The funeral undertaker and his assistant were both formally dressed in black suits, white shirt and black ties. Why the hell had they bothered? There were no grieving relatives, nobody to witness the scene apart from Winder and uniformed officers there to ensure privacy. But the grave was at the far end of a cemetery at the top of a field that sloped to the road. A biting wind had blown up over the tombstones. The scientific support team had struggled erecting the tent. Despite the activity Winder had felt spooked. Being a semi-official undertaker wasn't part of his job description.

Slumping in the sofa he might normally have skipped through the channels on the TV searching for some horror or vampire film, but it seemed oddly out of place, so he had settled on a cheesy romantic comedy. After an hour he had yawned uncontrollably so decided to venture to bed, praying his girlfriend was fast asleep. The sound of her snoring reassured him that he wasn't likely to get an earful of complaints. He managed a few hours' sleep and left before her.

Now he looked down at the empty plate on his desk. He would need a few more sugar hits during the day to counteract what he expected to be creeping exhaustion that afternoon. How could Luned look so fresh and alert?

'Where do you want to start?' Luned said.

Winder looked over at the board and the names of Longman, Capon, Rowlands and Kerr lined up waiting for the space underneath to be populated with details and links. 'I'll do Longman and Capon.'

Luned nodded.

'Let's work up a spreadsheet we can use to impress the boss,' Winder glanced at Luned. She would know full well he would expect her to take the lead.

By lunchtime Winder admired anew Luned's expertise in mastering Excel. The spreadsheet containing the names of the victims with columns for the names of the persons of interest was impressive. They could identify common links between the suspected deaths reasonably quickly. Winder reminded himself that Drake wanted progress by the end of the day, and he was left in little doubt that his superior officer was convinced the pathologists would uncover the evidence they needed.

He turned his attention again to Luned's spreadsheet. Each name had a separate page where the personal details of each could be inputted.

William Longman was eighty-six years of age and had retired to live in the seaside town of Beaumaris after a career working in the City of London. The file from Caring Wales had details of the care plan which outlined his day-to-day needs and how care would be provided. After reading the details for five minutes Winder tired of the jargon and jotted a quick summary into the Longman spreadsheet. Rachel Ackroyd's name drew Winder's attention. There were others, of course, and he quickly typed their names into the spreadsheet, identifying the carers who had been to Longman's home in the twelve hours before his death. He had been seen by paramedics the evening before he died. The initial post-mortem had concluded he died of a heart attack. The next of kin was a son with an address in the suburbs of London.

Winder turned his attention to Michael Capon whose background was quite different. He was a retired GP – Winder wondered if retired doctors realised when they were dying and, if so, what went through their minds? He had lived at home, managing with regular carers but the evening before he died a carer had called an ambulance. She'd stayed with him until the paramedics had checked him out, but the notes were scant on details. However, there were comments about Michael Capon being a lovely old gentleman. The wording of the post-mortem report was practically identical to that for William Longman. Capon's only daughter lived in

Vienna but it could have been Perth or Sydney, Winder thought. She hadn't been able to reach her father in time for one last goodbye.

Luned finished the work on Victoria Rowlands and John Kerr a few minutes after Winder, who returned to the Incident Room with a tray of coffee.

'Have you made any progress?' Winder plonked a mug of coffee on a coaster on Luned's desk.

'The name Rachel Ackroyd appears as one of the carers who was looking after John Kerr.'

Winder took the first sip of his drink. 'Really – she's also one of William Longman's carers. Was she there the day he died?'

Luned nodded.

Winder announced seriously. 'Well that's our first link.'

'There were paramedics there as well,' Luned continued. 'They attended to Victoria Rowlands at the home where she lived. She'd fallen and cracked her nose. She was disorientated and she'd pressed the panic alarm.'

'And paramedics attended at William Longman's house.'

'And they saw John Kerr the night he died. So that gives us paramedics present at three of the deaths. And what about Michael Capon – was he seen by paramedics?'

Winder nodded. 'A carer stayed with him until they arrived. They checked him out and left. And the carer *wasn't* Rachel Ackroyd.'

'And did you check that meals on wheels service?'

He scrambled through the documentation, finding the confirmation he needed. He turned to Luned. 'Dammit, there's another connection. They did provide meals to Longman.'

'And they delivered to John Kerr too.'

'Something else to check out.'

Luned paused for a moment, staring at the monitor. Winder tried to second-guess what she was fathoming out.

Luned clicked on her mouse which activated the printer in the corner of the Incident Room. She stood up and gathered both copies of the printed spreadsheet, giving one to Winder.

'If this becomes a multiple murder inquiry, we will need the names of the meals on wheels delivery drivers as well as all the paramedics.'

Winder stared at the column with paramedics written on the top. 'It'll probably mean a trip to the hospital for someone.'

Chapter 24

Dr Crewe elevated his little finger and sipped from a china cup in the classic English afternoon tea style. Lee Kings nursed a mug and from the inky black colour of its contents Drake assumed it to be instant coffee. He turned his attention away from the monitor on his desk and gave Drake a curt nod.

'Good morning,' Drake said.

Crewe, sitting in front of King's desk, put the cup on the saucer and brushed a hand down his waistcoat. The suit looked expensive, its pinstripe glistened and matched Crewe's neatly trimmed silver-grey hair.

'Good morning to you, Detective Inspector,' Crewe said a little too enthusiastically. 'And Detective Sergeant Morgan, I presume.' He stood up and reached a hand over to Sara. 'I'm sure Denver will organise a coffee or tea for you.' He craned to catch the attention of the mortuary assistant lurking behind Drake and Sara. Denver grunted and scuttled away once Drake and Sara had given him their preferences. Sara pulled over two chairs.

'It's a fine crisp autumn morning don't you think.' Crewe again sounding like a schoolboy on a trip. 'I was staying in Llandudno last evening. At least the Justice Department of the Welsh Government can stretch to a five-star hotel.' There was an edge of incredulity to Crewe's voice as though he couldn't quite believe his last comment. 'I had a wonderful bracing walk along the promenade this morning – just the thing to work up an appetite for breakfast, don't you know.'

Drake hadn't managed to finish a piece of toast that morning, fearing the impact of multiple post-mortems on his stomach.

Denver returned and gave Crewe a suspicious glance. Sara thanked him for her coffee and Drake examined the liquid in his mug warily. Crewe continued. 'You'll be delighted to know that we've made some progress prior to your arrival. The first two CT scans have been completed and Dr Kings here is taking the opportunity of studying the report from the first.' He reached over for the cup and saucer and delicately took another mouthful.

Kings cleared his throat. 'We've postponed all the appointments at the CT clinic this morning. It led to a barrage of complaints from patients.' He continued in the same sober vein. 'It meant substantial overtime for the staff.'

'When are we likely to be finished?' Drake said.

Kings sighed heavily. 'With any luck we'll have the third and fourth CT scans completed this morning. It gives us this afternoon for the post-mortems.'

'Can you give us any preliminary indicators?' Sara said.

Kings gave Crewe the barest of glances and the senior pathologist briefly raised a quizzical eyebrow. 'Too early to say at the moment,' Kings said.

Denver entered without knocking and announced they were ready for the final scans. Sara had finished her tea and Drake was happy enough to leave most of his coffee, having only managed a mouthful or two. They followed both pathologists through the corridors of the hospital to the CT unit where they were met with reproachful glances from staff and orderlies. Drake imagined that soon enough the journalist who had spoken to him earlier that morning would be tracking down the staff to enquire about the post-mortems. Indiscretions would come cheaply, Drake thought, a couple of pints at the local pub probably. He made a mental note to remind Susan Howells.

A radiographer adjusted various settings on a computer screen whilst Denver and some radiography assistants transferred the bagged remains of Victoria Rowlands onto the table of the CT scanner.

Drake and Sara stood inside the control room behind a radiation-proof glass window as the CT scan began its work. Kings and Crewe crowded over the radiographer and the radiologist as images flickered on the screen. They said nothing, didn't react, occasionally crossing and uncrossing their arms. Once the scan of Victoria Rowlands had been completed they moved on to John Kerr. Drake was impressed how well organised Denver had turned out to be. He grudgingly accepted he might have misjudged him. Another half an hour passed until the trolley carrying John Kerr was wheeled out and an orderly assisted Denver in returning the body to the mortuary.

The pathologists exchanged a few words with the radiologist and radiographer. Processing the images would take some time so they all arranged to meet after lunch. Drake wasn't hungry, a glass of water would do just fine. Sara had a pasty look. He recalled her queasiness when she had first attended a post-mortem. It was never easy, seeing a body being ripped apart. The sound and sight of a saw opening a human skull was something Drake would never get accustomed to.

In the event, when they returned to the mortuary Crewe announced, 'Let's get started.' He turned to Denver. 'My particular poison during the post-mortem is a weak tea so perhaps you could organise that once we've done the first.'

'Yeah, sure thing.'

'Thanks awfully.'

William Longman was the first body to appear on the table. It amazed Drake that a look of excitement and scientific curiosity filled the faces of Kings and Crewe when they pulled back the sheet revealing the remains of William Longman. It was gruesome – partly decayed flesh clung to bits of his skull. It was literally skin and bones.

'Let me give you a quick explanation, Detective Inspector,' Crewe said. 'We are looking specifically for evidence of venous air embolism which is a rare cause of death. So we shall be completing that part of the post-mortem first. I shall be using an aspirometer to detect and measure and then store the gas originating from the heart ventricles. Once we've trapped the gas, it is analysed by using gas chromatography. We compare the results with established criteria which will enable us to confirm a diagnosis of air embolism.'

Crewe wasn't looking for confirmation. Drake nodded.

Crewe and Kings worked in silence. Drake and Sara watched spellbound as Crewe undertook the procedure methodically. After completing the use of the aspirometer he got straight to work with the rest of the remains on the table in front of him. Drake noticed Sara clearing her throat a couple of times and moving her weight uncomfortably from one leg to the other. He gave her a how-are-you look which she returned with a brief shake telling him silently he need not worry.

Once he was finished with Longman, Crewe looked pleased with himself. Denver produced the weak tea Crewe had asked for and moments later he wheeled out another trolley. Lee Kings took the lead and completed the same detailed tests on Michael Capon while Crewe sipped his drink. After completing the aspirometer test Kings' work rate increased and soon he was busy at work on the corpse of Michael Capon. Occasionally Crewe made a suggestion in his customary clipped formal tone. Kings would acknowledge and, from what Drake could judge, follow his colleague's direction.

Drake had expected Crewe and Kings to break after the second post-mortem but they carried on, encouraging Denver to wheel in Victoria Rowlands.

'We're going to get a coffee,' Drake said.

Kings and Crewe grinned in unison.

They retreated into a small kitchen and Sara flicked on the electric kettle. After opening a couple of cupboards Drake found a jar of cheap instant coffee and tea bags.

'I don't think I'll go back inside,' Sara said, staring at the blue light at the base of the kettle, its bubbling sound gradually increasing. 'I don't think I'll sleep tonight if I have to see two more...'

Drake had been thinking the same. Usually attending a post-mortem meant watching one body being dissected. With the four bodies in the mortuary, the human decay was more advanced and the smell was unbearable. It was a ghoulish sight, worse than any horror or zombie film, because it was real. These had been human beings. Their bodies had been placed in caskets buried underground, out of sight. There was something unnatural and defiling about the exercise being undertaken in the room adjacent.

'I understand,' Drake said eventually. 'It's a pretty sickly sight. I hope we get some sort of result after all this.'

Fortified by adding sugar to the instant coffee Drake sat with Sara in Lee Kings' office. Denver put his head round the door a couple of times and grunted noncommittally when they told him they wouldn't be rejoining the pathologists. After all it was only the result of the aspirate tests that interested Drake and Sara. Positive confirmation that pointed to 'criminal intervention' in all four deaths meant they had a serial killer to catch. The immediate imperative of the normal murder inquiry when the few hours after the death were crucial didn't apply.

It was late in the afternoon and Drake's stomach grumbled a complaint when Kings and Crewe bustled into the room. Moments later the radiologist he had met previously arrived.

'We've finished, Detective Inspector,' Crewe said rather formally.

Kings interjected. 'We'll be concluding the second post-mortem on Emyr Isaac tomorrow.'

'Which means I get to spend a weekend in Llandudno,' Crewe said. 'That celebrity chef has a restaurant in Colwyn Bay that I've heard good things about.'

Kings and the radiologist looked over at Crewe who continued. 'I think I'll let Dr Penrose outline his conclusions from the CT scans.'

Penrose straightened and paused for breath. 'All the

scans suggest air embolism in the ventricles.'

Crewe nodded. 'And the spirometer tests and our microscopic examination of the lungs which revealed intra-vasal air locks all lead us to be able to formally confirm a diagnosis that the four individuals – William Longman, Michael Capon, Victoria Rowlands and John Kerr died from an air embolism.'

Silence filled the room for a few brief seconds. Drake's throat constricted, drying up as it did so.

Kings continued the explanation. 'We've also examined the medical and hospital records for all four and there's no reason to suggest the air embolism could have entered the body iatrogenically, that is to say, because of medical intervention. Therefore we must conclude a criminal intervention.'

The disclosure stunned Drake. He gathered his thoughts in the silence that followed Kings' announcement. He croaked out a response. 'How? How was it done? Injecting the patients, I mean?'

Crewe replied using the tone of an academic delivering a lecture. 'One cannot be certain. But air could be injected into the veins using a large syringe connected to a canula.'

'But there'd be evidence of a puncture wound.'

Drake's interruption earned him a brief reproachful glare. 'Elderly patients could easily have had a canula fitted for a sedative or drugs to be administered. There'd be nothing out of the ordinary with that. But it would take probably two 50 ml syringes to inject enough air to kill a patient. And before you ask, syringes of that size are not commonplace in hospitals or surgeries.'

Crewe cleared his throat. 'Using a syringe is rather clumsy although it could be simple to use and relatively quick to administer. But there would be no absolute guarantee that enough air would be injected to kill the patient. That raises the possibility that some other mechanism was employed – possibly an oxygen cylinder. It would have the advantage of being able to inject large quantities of air at a high pressure.'

'But—'

Crewe cut across Drake. 'Oxygen cylinders aren't the easiest things to carry around although they are standard kit on ambulances. Which tends to favour the explanation that syringes were used.'

Drake sensed the medics staring at him, waiting for a response. 'We'll need a full report.'

Crewe nodded.

Having his suspicions confirmed gave Drake certainty.

Certainty that a killer was responsible for five deaths, possibly six.

And certainty that he had to do everything possible to prevent any more deaths.

Chapter 25

Drake's worst fears became a painful reality when he sat at the kitchen table the following morning listening to the news broadcast referring to 'four exhumations in the Gwynedd and Anglesey area'. At least the journalist didn't suggest a link to the deaths of Emyr Isaac or David Morris. Drake could imagine Susan Howells' salty language had the reporter done so. It would have been irresponsible in the extreme, but was it only a matter of time until some hack decided to make a name for himself or herself and ignore the imperatives of a police investigation.

Drake explained to Annie where he had been the previous evening. He spared her the full description of the images that had swirled around his mind as he had driven home. She sat wide-eyed, concentrating on every word. 'I've never heard of exhumations being undertaken before.'

'I haven't been involved with such a procedure previously and I'm not going to rush to repeat the experience.' For the second time in two days Drake left a half-eaten piece of toast on his plate, his appetite evaporating. He stood and stared at the espresso machine, conscious that not seeing his daughters that Saturday created a spasm of guilt. It was his weekend for contact, after all.

His mother's pending birthday party had meant changing the arrangements. Sian had reluctantly agreed, but only after Drake had told her his sister and her children were visiting. Mentioning Mair Drake's ulterior motive of introducing her new 'man friend' to the family had elicited a typically brusque response from Sian: 'Will there be any more mysteries to emerge from your family's closet?' Her comments still rankled.

Drake shook off the rumination, dismissing it to a distant corner of his mind. He loaded the coffee filter into the espresso machine and waited until the lights told him the boiler was ready. It dribbled the hot liquid into a cup which he topped up with recently boiled water. He returned to the table.

'What time will you be back tonight?' Annie sounded matter-of-fact. Despite the permanence of their relationship it continued to surprise him that she accepted easily the demands of his job whereas Sian would have screwed up her eyes and given him a critical glare. Policing was never a nine-to-five lifestyle.

'I'm not entirely sure, but I'll message you later.'

'I'm going into the department. I need to collect some papers and it'll give me time to do some work when it's nice and quiet.'

Drake envied the flexibility she had as a lecturer. A murder inquiry was a demanding and unforgiving mistress. His mobile rang as Annie cleared the dishes. He recognised Susan's number.

'I've just rung Mam. That man answered.' Susan's voice was shrill, borderline hysterical.

'Do you mean Elfed?' Drake glanced over at Annie who gave him a quizzical turn of her face. He mouthed Susan's name.

'Who else do you think I mean? Oh, come on, Ian, don't be silly. It's still early in the morning and I wanted to speak to Mam. He told me she was in the shower. How would he know?'

'He probably heard the water running.'

'You are impossible when you're in this sort of mood. I think it's shocking. He must be staying there. I don't know how you can stand it.'

Susan was well and truly on her high horse by now. Drake wanted to put the phone down on the table and allow her to gallop off into the sunset, but he held it pinned to his ear.

'Is he living with her now?' She didn't wait for Drake to reply. 'I mean what will people think, what will the neighbours say?'

'Hopefully they'll want Mam to be happy.'

'Happy... How can you be so frivolous at a time like this? Is she sleeping with him? I mean are they having...'

'Do you mean, sex,' Drake managed to get a spicy edge to the word.

'But she's in her seventies, for goodness sake.'

'People do have sex in their seventies, you know,'

A disgusted silence permeated down the line.

'I think it's revolting. I never thought they would, you know, be in bed together. I thought they were ... friends. The way I feel now I can't face seeing her next week.'

Now Drake gave his voice a determined tone. 'She'll be very disappointed not to see you, Susan, and the boys.'

'This is all such a surprise.' Susan sounded on the verge of tears and she rang off.

Annie had all the dishes tided when Drake finished. He got up from the table and readied himself to leave. 'She's shocked that Elfed might be staying overnight with Mam. The very idea that people in their seventies could be having sex repels her.'

Annie reached out a hand and drew a finger over his face. 'She should get used to it.' Then she kissed him. 'I hope we'll still be making love in our seventies.'

Drake smiled, before threading a hand around her waist and pulling her close.

As Drake made for the main entrance at headquarters, his mobile rang; he recognised Lee Kings' number. 'Good morning, Lee.'

'Have you spoken with Superintendent Hobbs this morning?'

'No, why?'

'He was on the phone first thing asking for an update on the post-mortem of Emyr Isaac.'

'I see.' Drake tried to shake off Hobbs' invisible hand on his shoulder but failed. 'And what was the result of the Isaac post-mortem?' Drake took the steps towards the main entrance.

'Nothing to suggest an embolism. The original conclusion that a blood clot on the brain was the cause of death stands.'

A mix of emotions filled his mind, frustration uppermost – it meant he didn't have a direct link from Isaac to the other five deaths.

Drake pushed open the door and the warmth of headquarters enveloped him. Kings continued. 'Superintendent Hobbs suggested meeting Dr Crewe for dinner.'

'Really. Did he accept?'

'Apparently not. Crewe made some comments about having known Superintendent Hobbs when he was working in Cardiff. I got the distinct impression that having dinner with your superior officer will be the last thing Crewe would entertain. He's going for one of his 'brisk constitutionals' over the Great Orme this afternoon and then Conwy Mountain tomorrow morning before, as he put it, 'motoring back to Cardiff'.'

Drake smiled to himself. 'Have you sent me a copy of the report on Isaac?'

'Emailed a moment ago.'

Drake settled at his desk where he switched on his computer and waited, his mind turning to the priorities for the day.

Before turning to his inbox, he adjusted the photographs of his daughters a couple of millimetres – dealing with the columns of different coloured Post-it notes on the desk could wait until later.

He read Kings' email and downloaded the report. An embolism was definitely not the cause of Isaac's death. Could they still justify the suspicion that his death was linked to the other five? Several emails from the PR department caught his attention. Susan Howells was covering her back – that much was clear from the tone of her correspondence.

But it was Superintendent Hobbs' email that unsettled Drake.

It informed Drake that a meeting with a Professor Grant Ibbott, a psychological profiler, had been organised for that morning.

Drake glanced at his watch. He had barely any time to prepare – what the hell was Hobbs doing? He hadn't consulted him about involving a psychological profiler in the inquiry. A tingling sensation made his chest heavy.

Quickly, Drake tapped the name of Professor Ibbott into a Google search and was directed to Ibbott's page on the website of the university where he taught, which outlined his career and achievements. It mentioned cases with other police forces where he had assisted in solving tough cases. Ibbott had a world-renowned reputation in the field of clinical psychology and he'd published several papers on the psychology of serial killers.

Drake's previous experience of working with a profiler, on a case where two police officers had been killed, had been constructive and frustrating in equal measure. But in the end, Drake had valued her contribution.

Drake read the time, realising his meeting with Hobbs was imminent. He got up and left his office intent on exchanging greetings with his team and then making his way to the senior management suite.

He didn't have to bother. Superintendent Hobbs entered the Incident Room followed by a short man with a pronounced paunch.

Hobbs gave Drake a cursory nod. 'I thought it best that all of my team were included in the briefing from Professor Ibbott.'

My team. What the hell does he mean? Drake thought.

As the SIO, Hobbs could make the decisions, Drake determined, although it still angered him. He was convinced that Hobbs was testing him, seeing how far he could push him until he complained.

Hobbs stood in front of the board, Ibbott by his side.

'Good morning, everyone.' Hobbs used his most formal tone. 'This is Professor Grant Ibbott who is an academic with a specific interest in criminal psychology. He's written several papers on serial killers and, in particular, killers within the health care system.'

Drake pulled out a chair and sat down, scanning the faces of his team. Sara gave him an inquisitive look as though she couldn't quite understand what was going on.

'Potentially the persons of interest are healthcare professionals and for that reason I've invited Professor Ibbott to advise.'

Hobbs nodded at Drake. 'Inspector Drake, perhaps you could outline the barest circumstances of each death.'

Drake cleared his throat, noticing Hobbs hadn't said murder – only 'each death'. 'Emyr Isaac, an elderly gentleman was found one morning by his carer. There was evidence of a break in and from bruising on his arms we suspected he had confronted a burglar. He had suffered a crack to the head and died from a blood clot to the brain. So, we focused our inquiries accordingly. However, a second death, again a man in his late eighties became a murder inquiry when we established his cause of death was an air embolism – a bubble of air injected into the body.'

Ibbott nodded agreement – Drake's explanation sounded normal, a perfectly acceptable pattern of activity.

'Irregularities in four other recent post-mortems led to the bodies being exhumed and more detailed post-mortems, including CT scans, being completed. All indicate that the cause of death in each was an air embolism.'

'And you believe you may have a serial killer at work.' Drake was expecting rich vowels from a well-educated academic, but his accent was actually a thick Yorkshire twang.

Drake continued. 'Paramedics saw both of the first two

victims hours before they died. Both were patients of the same surgery and were being treated by the same district nurse.'

'Do you have the names of the paramedics?'

Drake shook his head. 'We've got a meeting with the ambulance service later today.'

'Good, excellent. And is the same carer involved?'

Drake nodded.

'Excellent, that's a good start. A lot of work was done by an academic called Ramsland several years ago. She identified twenty-two red flags associated with a HSK profile.'

Drake interrupted. 'HSK?'

'Healthcare serial killer. Forgive the jargon. I can send you details of the flags you should be looking for, but they involve things like a person frequently moving from one hospital to another, a history of mental instability. Of the twenty-two flags, five were considered to be most frequent when an assessment was made of known HSKs.' Ibbott shared a look around the room before continuing. 'The first was a higher incidence of death on his or her shift, a history of mental instability or depression, then making colleagues anxious, possession of drugs at home or in their locker at work and the appearance of a personality disorder.'

'We're not going to find most of those without talking to colleagues or the employer,' Drake said. 'Although one of the district nurses has a conviction for possession of cannabis.'

'Another red flag, Inspector. All I can tell you, is the basis of the academic assessments made to date.'

Sara made her first contribution. 'Is there a typical age range for HSKs?'

'Yes, thirty-one to forty. And before you ask there doesn't seem to be any gender bias. And interestingly they don't appear to target a particular gender. The most prominent victim types in terms of age group are elderly people.'

'Fits our victims,' Winder said.

Hobbs gave him a sharp glance, as though he hadn't expected Winder to say anything.

Ibbott continued undeterred. 'And that is not surprising as elderly people are more vulnerable and are least able to protect themselves.'

'Is there anything in the academic research to identify what the motives could be for HSKs?' Drake said.

Ibbott shrugged. 'Nothing definitive. Ridding themselves of demanding patients, freeing up beds and facilities and benefiting financially from the patient's death have been identified. It's also been suggested a variation of Munchausen syndrome by proxy – where parents or caregivers induce illness in their children in order to gain medical attention – may be relevant in understanding such cases. Some academics have referred to this as 'hero complex'.'

Drake noticed Winder raising startled eyebrows while Luned looked on perplexed.

Sara played with a ballpoint through her fingers before adding. 'How do HSKs evade detection?'

'In many ways the health service isn't set up to identify them quickly enough. That's why the twenty-two red flags can be most helpful. A checklist is only a relevant tool in preventative and possibly limiting interventions.'

'Do you mean we can't use it as evidence?' Drake said.

'Let me explain further.' Ibbott managed a scholarly tone. 'Even if your suspect attends, or is linked to, the scene of each death, it doesn't automatically mean you have good evidence. There's a disconnect between what I, as a scientist, can prove and what you, a police officer, and the prosecuting authorities can prove in a court of law.'

Hobbs added. 'We appreciate Professor Ibbott that the burden of proof we have to discharge is far greater than that which you can use to come to academic conclusions. What I and my team want to be able to know is how far academia will assist us in discharging that burden of proof.'

'Thankfully, superintendent, HSKs are rare. They are a complex phenomenon and establishing motives can be highly challenging. You may well be left in a situation where his or her motive isn't clear. All three of your persons of interest – the carer, the district nurse and a paramedic could be likely suspects.'

'There was a meals on wheels delivery driver who visited the home of Isaac and Morris, the second victim,' Sara said.

'Does he have a health care background?' Ibbott said.

'No.'

'Then you can probably discount him.'

Drake looked over at Rachel's image on the board alongside Boxford, the district nurse. They'd have to make a place for a possible paramedic too, in due course.

Ibbott continued. 'All I can suggest is that you use the red flags I mentioned. They should help you focus your investigation. Go about your usual procedures – gather enough evidence to build a strong case.'

Drake still stared at the board, paying little attention to Hobbs's formal thanks for Ibbott's assistance. Hobbs stood up, Drake followed suit, shaking Ibbott's hand mumbling his thanks.

'I'll see you down to reception,' Hobbs said.

Drake sat back down on his chair. Three sets of shell-shocked but eager eyes looked over at him. They had a lot to do.

Chapter 26

Sara parked outside the large detached property set in landscaped gardens in one of the villages overlooking the Menai Strait. A brief Google search told her that similar properties sold for over £1 million and with the average price on Anglesey well under £200,000 it made John Kerr's home one of the more select houses on the island.

A three-year-old Land Rover Discovery and a Mercedes C class were parked nearby. Before leaving her car, she checked the names of John Kerr's two children – Sadie Appleyard and Neil Kerr. Normally she would have accompanied Inspector Drake, but the urgency demanded by Superintendent Hobbs meant the team had split up.

An overweight woman in her early fifties wearing heavy make-up opened the front door.

'I'm Detective Sergeant Morgan,' Sara gave the woman enough time to study her warrant card. 'Mrs Sadie Appleyard?' The jowls under her flabby chin shook as she nodded.

'Come in.'

The hallway was wide and the sound of domestic activity – dishes being washed, a meal being prepared – drifted from the kitchen. Appleyard led her into a sitting room overlooking a lawn leading down to the Strait. A RIB carrying passengers strapped into seats crashed and bounced its way over the water's surface.

Neil Kerr paid as much attention to his diet as his sister. The buttons of his shirt strained and the skin on his face carried a blotchy complexion.

'This is Detective Sergeant Morgan,' Appleyard said to her brother. The accent was Scouse, but only just.

Kerr gave Sara a flaccid handshake.

They sat down on matching cream-coloured sofas.

'As you know, concerns were raised by the North Wales pathologist about your father's post-mortem.'

Appleyard and Kerr said nothing, but their eye contact

was fixed and focused.

Sara continued. 'We've had the results of the latest post-mortem. I'm afraid I have to inform you we now believe your father was murdered.'

'Jesus Christ,' Kerr exclaimed.

Appleyard gasped and put a hand to her mouth.

'What the bloody hell happened?' Kerr said.

'Somebody injected air into your father's veins. It meant he suffered a heart attack caused by an air embolism.'

'And why the hell wasn't this picked up on the original post-mortem?'

'It is very difficult to spot an air embolism if you aren't looking for it specifically.'

Sara reminded herself of the articles she had read on the Internet the evening before about serial killers in Europe injecting their victims with air bubbles. None had been caught immediately.

'Who would do such a thing?' Appleyard said.

'We need to establish the exact details of who visited your father the day before he died.'

'Of course,' Kerr said. 'Anything we can do to help.'

'Did either of you visit your father that day.'

Appleyard was the first to respond. Her voice incredulous. 'I hope you don't think we had anything to do with it?'

Sara shook her head. 'It's routine, I assure you.' She couldn't very well tell them there were four other similar deaths.

It took a few minutes for them to establish that Appleyard had visited her father late on the afternoon of the day in question on her way back to Warrington. She had been staying at her holiday home in a village on Anglesey and had left at about five pm. Her brother had been to see his father earlier that day. He had taken over running the pub ,café and restaurant his father owned several years previously and lived just a few miles from his father's house.

'The carer from Caring Wales would have arrived shortly after I left. She would have prepared an evening meal and tried to persuade him to change into pyjamas. But he could be stubborn.'

'Do you know the name of the carer?' Sara checked the details from Caring Wales as she spoke.

Appleyard shook her head. 'But Rachel would have called last thing.'

The name grabbed Sarah's attention. She knew Rachel Ackroyd was listed as one of John Kerr's carers, but she hadn't been rostered to visit John Kerr the evening he died. 'Rachel who?' Sara smothered any suspicious overtone to her question.

'Rachel Ackroyd. She's very good, goes the extra mile and we pay her privately to visit last thing at night to make certain dad is tucked up in bed.'

'And did she call to see your dad?'

Kerr nodded. 'I spoke to her. She called the paramedics because dad had fallen. We were dead busy in the pub and shorthanded that night. I couldn't spare the time to come down and she said everything was under control.'

'Do you know what happened?'

'You'll have to talk to Rachel in detail, and the paramedics I suppose. When the carer called to see him in the morning… she found him… He had died in his sleep.'

The dawning realisation on the face of Appleyard made her voice tremble. 'Surely you don't think that Rachel was responsible? She liked dad. She got on very well with him. He gave her gifts and he thought the world of her. She'd stop and listen to him, spent time with him.'

Sara sounded a note of caution. 'Until we've been able to establish all the details, I'm sure you appreciate it's important everything is kept confidential.'

Appleyard and Kerr nodded their understanding.

Winder paid insufficient attention to the notice at the end of the drive for Bodnant Residential Home telling visitors to follow the signs for the car park and he found himself having to reverse back to a junction. Eventually he parked next to a van from a cleaning company. A flat roofed extension made Bodnant look ugly, although Winder guessed the house looked elegant years ago.

At first, he didn't notice the keypad on the wall but when he tried to yank open the locked door he checked for a doorbell. He pressed the buzzer and a crackly voice emerged from the speaker asking who was calling. The door bleeped open once he'd establish his credentials and the warmth and stifling atmosphere smothered him. The tang of disinfectant laced with urine and another sickly smell tickled his nostrils. The corridors were narrow, the skirtings scratched and the walls above them scuffed. Winder retreated into a doorway when a carer came round the corner with an elderly resident in a wheelchair. As she slowed her progress she gave Winder a brief smile.

A room opened and Winder peeked inside. A carer stood by the threshold talking with a resident sitting in a chair, her voice a decibel too loud. The furnishings looked old, the decoration shabby. It was difficult to imagine a building less suited to the demands of looking after elderly patients, Winder thought. How many people finish their days in a residential home? It wasn't something Winder relished. He had only recently come to the realisation that he wasn't going to live forever but the prospect of being hauled around in a wheelchair dribbling and farting was definitely not for him.

He found the manager's office and gave the door a polite tap before pushing it open. A desk sat underneath an oblong window high on one wall. Every square inch of the walls was covered with shelving units each crammed with lever arch files and piles of paper. A woman with a long dreary face and thin hair looked up at Winder.

'Heidi Toomey, I'm the manager.' She introduced

herself in one long breath as though she carried the weight of the world on her shoulders.

Winder didn't bother with his warrant card. He pulled up a chair and sat down. 'You may be aware that the body of Victoria Rowlands was exhumed last week.'

Toomey nodded weakly.

'Certain irregularities arose following a review of her post-mortem.'

'I know, there was that piece in the news about the exhumations. Somebody took some photographs. It all looked like something out of a horror film. If you're looking for a serial killer, you won't find him here. Or her for that matter.'

'We need to get a clear picture of what happened to Victoria Rowlands the day she died.'

Toomey stood up and walked over to one of the shelving units. She tilted her head and searched the folders and lever arch files. When she couldn't find what she was looking for she moved on to the next unit. Standing up her figure was just as thin and long and gangly as she appeared sitting down.

'Got it,' Toomey exclaimed before returning to her seat. 'We don't keep a record of every minute of every single day for all the residents. That would be impossible.' She opened the file and flicked through the various sheets.

Toomey looked up at Winder. 'Not a lot to tell you really. She had her medication at lunchtime with her meal. She didn't have a big appetite and one of the girls tested her diabetes – it was within acceptable boundaries. She had a visitor after lunch – one of her former colleagues and one of her daughters came at the end of the afternoon after she'd eaten tea.'

'What was Victoria Rowlands like?'

Toomey sighed. 'Old.'

Winder expected a little more embellishment. 'Did the staff get on with her?'

Toomey seized on Winder's comment reading into it an implication he hadn't intended. 'You don't think any of the staff here would have killed her?'

'I was asking how they got on with her.'

Toomey roamed Winder's face searching for some hidden meaning. 'She was more popular than some of the cantankerous old buggers we have in here.'

'I understand she went to hospital the evening she died.'

'When the night staff couldn't control a nosebleed we called the out of hours doctors service. They advised we call an ambulance. When the paramedics attended, they arranged for her to be admitted.'

Intrigued that paramedics saw Rowlands as they had Isaac and Morris, Winder asked. 'Do you remember their names? Perhaps you may have seen them before?'

Toomey looked blank. 'Sorry. I don't know their names.'

'I'll need a full list of the carers working that evening as well as a list of your employees.'

Toomey shuffled through paperwork on her desk and found two sheets of A4 that she handed to Winder. 'I thought you might ask for that.'

It took her a few moments to photocopy the documents Winder needed. He tucked a folder with the papers under his arm and, after thanking Toomey, left. Outside he stood for a moment allowing the clean crisp autumn air to bathe his face. Then he wondered if the paramedics who called to see Rowlands were the same as those who visited Isaac and Morris.

Chapter 27

Drake arrived at the ambulance service regional headquarters at the hospital near Bangor, having taken the precaution of arranging a warrant. Drake needed the names and details of all the paramedics involved with the victims and the treatments offered to finish building the draft spreadsheet pinned to the board in the Incident Room. Drake already knew the name of the person he needed to speak to – Frank Ogden, the administration manager.

'Is Mr Ogden expecting you?' The woman on reception asked. Her accent was local but the attitude was abrupt and borderline antagonistic.

'Just call him,' Drake turned his back without bothering her with his warrant card, as she pouted.

Moments later he heard his name being called. 'Inspector Drake.'

Ogden even managed a good morning greeting – '*Bore da*' in Welsh – explaining he was learning the language. They shook hands and Drake followed him from reception down the corridor and up a flight of stairs to the first-floor landing and then on to a room with 'Manager' printed on the plaque screwed to the door.

'I spoke to one of your officers and told him we couldn't disclose any information without a warrant,' Ogden said after settling himself at his desk waving a hand at a chair for Drake to do likewise.

Drake slipped the paperwork over the desk and gave Ogden a moment to read it.

'Has this got anything to do with those exhumations?'

'We've been asked by the coroner's office to conduct a detailed inquiry into four deaths that occurred recently while the regular pathologist was on secondment. The post-mortems were undertaken by a locum and concerns have been expressed about the standard of his work. At the same time, we have two ongoing murder inquiries and we need details of the paramedics who called at the homes of Emyr

Isaac and David Morris.'

Ogden frowned.

'As part of the inquiry it has come to our attention that various paramedics attended at the homes of five of the individuals on the evenings before they died. We need the personnel files for the paramedics involved. It's routine at this stage. A Victoria Rowlands died in hospital after she was admitted, and we shall be asking the hospital about the nurses who treated her.'

'This is most unusual. I'll need to speak to my superior... My line manager...' Ogden stammered.

Drake measured his response. 'I'm sure you realise the sensitivity of this request necessitates that as few people are involved as possible.'

Ogden stared at the warrant again.

'Mr Ogden,' Drake said sharply obviously aware the manager's attention was drifting. 'As you can see from the warrant, the files and documents listed need to be produced today so that I can remove them. Now.' Drake added softly, 'I'm sure I can rely on your confidentiality.'

It took a few minutes, but eventually the printer behind Ogden purred into life spewing out reams of paper. Ogden tidied them into a neat order before stapling them together. He turned to look over at Drake. 'These are the rotas for the paramedics on duty on the dates you've given me. They would have run a standard set of tests whenever seeing someone of that age: blood pressure, a test to check blood sugar, oxygen levels. The details of all those tests and any treatment recommended would have been recorded. Details would have been sent to the GPs.'

'Do you have copies?'

'Yes, of course but...'

Grudgingly Ogden looked again at the monitor and reached over for his mouse. A few clicks later more paper had been churned out by the printer. Ogden used the stapler again before handing sheets to Drake. 'I hope you can make sense of all these.'

'And the personnel files?'

Ogden darted a glance at the filing cabinets in the corner of his office. They must contain the files, Drake guessed. Ogden reached a hand over towards the phone but drew back at the last minute picking up a ballpoint instead which he turned through his fingers. He flicked through the papers on his desk making notes Drake assumed were the names of the paramedics involved.

He stood up and walking over the laminate floor yanked open a drawer from the second cabinet that squeaked a protest. He pulled out several files and returned placing them in front of Drake.

Drake made to leave. 'You've been very helpful.'

Back in the car he examined the various sheets Ogden had given him. One name was common to all, except Victoria Rowlands, a paramedic called Luke Holgate. Drake stared at the name wondering if, by the end of the afternoon, Holgate's name was going to take centre stage. He started the engine and drove back to headquarters.

Drake sat at the nearest desk to the Incident Room board and laid out the spreadsheet he had unpinned from it and shared a glance between the officers of his team. It was Saturday afternoon. They would want to get home, have a few hours break, relax with family and friends, have a cold beer or glass of wine, eat a pizza, do the ordinary things of life. Tomorrow they could enjoy an unstructured day away from headquarters and he hoped that by Monday morning there would be fresh minds ready to deal with the next stage of the inquiry.

'Let's identify if we have any names common to all six deaths. I'll do the paramedics, Sara you do the carers and Luned and Gareth you do the GP records.' Drake announced sorting the papers in front of him. 'Let's start with Emyr Isaac,'

Sara piped up. 'Rachel Ackroyd saw him the night before he died.'

'And the paramedics who attended were Holgate and Faulkner,' Drake said.

'District nurse Boxford saw him that afternoon,' Luned added.

Drake turned to the second death – David Morris. 'David Morris was seen the evening before he died by paramedics called Owen and Holgate. So Luke Holgate is common to the first two deaths.'

'Rachel Ackroyd too, boss,' Sara said.

Luned shook her head as she read from the GP notes. 'Morris hadn't been seen by the district nurse for over three weeks.'

'Which of the district nurses attached to the surgery visited him?' Drake said.

'They both did,' Luned added.

Drake paused and looked at the spreadsheet. Rachel Ackroyd and Luke Holgate were common to both Isaac and Morris. Would the same pattern recur for the other four names?

He started with Capon. 'It was late when Capon called emergency services. He complained about chest pains and pins and needles in his arm. The paramedics arrived and checked him out.' Drake paused. 'It was Faulkner and a Geoff Davies. They checked him out and left. But the following morning he was found dead by the carer.'

Sara took her lead from Drake finishing. 'Carers had seen him that afternoon and evening but Rachel Ackroyd isn't one of them.'

Drake tipped his head at Luned.

'Boxford saw him that afternoon too, sir. A preliminary background financial search came in this morning. She has a lot of credit card debt. And a big mortgage.'

Drake annotated the spreadsheet and then he turned to John Kerr. Drake jabbed the ballpoint towards Sara. 'How did you get on with John Kerr's family?'

'Caring Wales provided regular carers. The last called at the end of the afternoon.' Sara dictated the name and Drake scribbled them in the carers column. 'But they had a special arrangement with Rachel Ackroyd.'

Mentioning her name had the effect of refocusing Winder and Luned's attention. It was a link Drake hadn't anticipated. 'What do you mean special arrangement?'

'She would visit after she finished her normal shift to check Kerr was okay and make certain he got to bed. The Kerr family thought the world of her. They were shocked by even the remotest possibility she could be involved.'

Drake added her name in capitals in the carers column.

He sat back for a moment. 'We may need to interview Rachel Ackroyd again.'

Sara continued. 'When Ackroyd arrived at the house Kerr had fallen and she was unable to get him back to bed, she was worried he might have broken something, so *she* called the paramedics. She wasn't the last to see him alive.'

'How many paramedics are there in North Wales?' Winder said. 'I thought the health service was understaffed these days.'

Drake reached for the ambulance records announcing Luke Holgate and a Penny Upton were the paramedics who had attended.

Winder announced unprompted. 'There's no record of him being seen by the district nurses on the day he died.'

Drake checked his notes and the spreadsheet – two more names and nothing so far to link one name conclusively to all the deaths.

'William Longman next,' Drake looked over at Sara.

'Caring Wales provided some of his carers that included Rachel Ackroyd but she hadn't been there for several days.'

Luned contributed. 'When I spoke to Longman's son, he mentioned that his father alleged that items had been stolen from the house. He'd dismissed it because his father was becoming confused. I've inputted the items into the system.'

Drake nodded. 'On the night he died paramedics attended earlier in the evening. He couldn't get his breath and complained of breathing difficulty.'

Drake shuffled the papers on his desk before reading that Luke Holgate and Christopher Chandler had been the paramedics who called at Longman's home. He read their names out loud as he wrote them in the relevant column.

'What's interesting, boss, is that Boxford called at Longman's home that afternoon.'

Drake scribbled down the details.

One more name – Victoria Rowlands.

'I hate nursing homes,' Winder said.

'They're residential homes,' Luned corrected him.

Winder ignored her. 'There's this odd smell of old people and death and decay and...'

'We don't treat older people with enough respect,' Luned managed her best school mistress tone.

'Tells us about your visit,' Drake said.

'She had been living in the care home for a few months. She wasn't in the best of health. I've got a list of the carers that worked on the day she died, none match those linked with the other cases. She was seen by paramedics on the night she was admitted to hospital because the care home had been unable to staunch a nosebleed.'

Drake read off the names of the two paramedics who attended – Penny Upton and Christopher Owen.

Drake looked over at Luned, who piped up. 'Neither of the district nurses had been to see Rowlands in the days before her death.'

Drake scrutinised his notes. Then he made a simple calculation. How many times could they link Holgate to the victims – four out of six. And a similar calculation proved that on the day of the deaths, Rachel Ackroyd and Boxford were linked to three of the six. Did that make Holgate the most likely culprit? Drake wasn't certain but instinct made him discount Rachel. After all, if they were dealing with an HSK then Holgate and Boxford were more likely to fit that profile.

Drake ran a hand through his hair and sighed heavily. Then it struck him that they hadn't checked the movements of Mervyn Ostler. 'First thing Monday check out the meals on wheels guy – even though Professor Ibbott discounted him.'

Winder stifled a yawn; there were bags under Sara's eyes.

'And get a full background and financial search done on Holgate.' Drake tipped his head towards Sara. 'First thing Monday we'll go to Liverpool. We need to discover more about District Nurse Boxford.'

Chapter 28

The following morning Drake fed enough coins into the parking meter and after pressing the green button the machine made a whirring sound and a preprinted ticket dropped into a slot in the front. Annie was finishing tying the laces of her boots when he returned to the car. He placed the ticket on the dashboard and pulled on a light-weight red walking jacket over a fleece before reaching for the rucksack in the boot. Gazing up at the summits towering above them he recalled his first murder case when, as a young detective inspector, he had attended the scene of what had looked like a murder–suicide. Since that tragic case he had visited Cwm Idwal many times, often with Helen and Megan. He never tired of the spectacular scenery around the ancient glacial valley. Although it was a short walk from the car park near Llyn Ogwen up into Cwm Idwal the sheer cliffs and the changing patterns of light and cloud swirling around could transport Drake away from the hubbub of everyday to the magnificent isolation of the mountains. He hoped the walk that morning would be no different. He couldn't share the details of the inquiries with Annie, couldn't divulge who they suspected, or how they hoped to proceed. Circumstantial evidence was one thing but persuading a Crown prosecution lawyer to press charges was quite different.

They took the path up towards Cwm Idwal, passing through the gate, its top fashioned to mimic the skyline ahead of them. Large, flat stones marked the footpath and by the time they were clear of the shelter of the car park Drake zipped up the jacket against the chill of the autumn breeze. To his left the jagged summit of Tryfan reached up to the sky and Drake noticed figures silhouetted against it.

After tramping along the path of flat worn slabs they reached a bridge that led across the stream that emptied from the lake at the floor of the cwm. They paused and gazed around the sides of the cwm. Small dots of colour from brightly coloured jackets moved as if in slow motion. Others were stationary, gazing upwards at the ropes dangling against the cliff face and the climbers above them. Despite it being October Drake had expected to see more walkers – it was the right weather for a hike in the mountains.

They hiked around the right-hand side of the lake towards the base of the Devil's Kitchen where the two bodies from his first case had been discovered. They found a comfortable rocky outcrop and sat eating their lunch as Drake recounted to Annie the circumstances that had brought him here as a young detective. She listened attentively, shocked when he finally revealed who the culprit had been. The faces on the Incident Room board came to his mind as he briefly thought of what faced the team in the days ahead, knowing he had to make real progress. Contemplating failure was out of the question so he shooed the images into a safe corner to await his attention in the morning.

Over to the right, climbers were scrambling up the sheer cliff face. Drake had never seen the attraction of climbing and didn't relish the prospect that his life depended on a rope and another person's complete attention. High above them clouds milled around Glyder Fawr and Glyder Fach. Behind them they heard walkers chattering as they descended from the top of the Devil's Kitchen.

It was another two hours before Drake and Annie returned to the car.

The fresh clean air of Cwm Idwal had re-energised Drake. Later, he and Annie would enjoy a rich Bolognese sauce with some fresh pasta and a bottle of wine before getting to bed early. Perfect preparation for the week ahead, Drake thought.

Chapter 29

'We'll need to remember to pay the toll, sir.'

Drake had paid little attention to the traffic signs as he sped across the new bridge over the Mersey estuary. Rather than taking Drake up the Wirral and through the Mersey tunnels the satnav had directed him along the M56 and on towards the Runcorn Bridge. The last occasion when Drake had taken the route was when he and Sian were flying from John Lennon airport in Liverpool for a weekend in Barcelona. The toll bridge had been a building project at the time – at least the old bridge had been free of charge.

Drake glanced to his left and saw the outline of the old Runcorn Bridge in the distance. It was a world away from the steep cliffs of Cwm Idwal that had surrounded Drake the previous day.

'I slept most of yesterday,' Sara said. 'Or it certainly felt like that. I went for a run in the morning but when I got back, I was exhausted. Did you relax, boss?'

'A walk in Cwm Idwal.'

'I hadn't realised how tired I'd become. I was supposed to go out in the evening, but I had to cancel. I was in bed by eight.'

Drake sympathised. The life of a detective often meant a creeping exhaustion not only from the physical demands of the job but from the mental strain. 'You don't realise until it hits you on your day off.'

Sara nodded.

She didn't have to reply, he could imagine how her thoughts could be dominated by the imperative of chasing down their killer, contemplating the consequences of not doing so. If there were more deaths might it be down to something they had missed?

After crossing the bridge, the satnav bleeped, warning Drake that the junction he needed was imminent. The screen showed they had another twenty minutes until they reached their destination. Alpha Medical had an anonymous sounding address in a business park in one of the suburbs on the southern side of Liverpool. Drake followed the directions until he reached the entrance, where he slowed to inspect the directory. Drake looked around for a place to park near the building displaying a prominent sign advertising the services of the agency. He toured around getting more and more annoyed with the absence of a parking slot.

'It's as bad as a bloody hospital,' Drake said.

'There is a slot over there,' Sara said pointing over to Drake's right.

After parking Drake and Sara walked over to the office block and flashed their warrant cards at a disinterested woman in her mid-fifties at reception. 'We'd like to see Ray Johnson.'

She jerked her head at the seating area nearby. 'Take a seat. I'll check if he'll see you.'

Sara idly flicked through an edition of Nursing Times that sat on the coffee table in front of the sofa where they sat. 'The NHS spent £3 trillion a couple of years ago on agency nurses.'

'How much?' Drake sounded surprised. Sometimes this sort of expenditure grabbed the headlines, usually in the winter months when there was a bed crisis or at elections when one political party or another wanted to argue they could manage the NHS better than their competitors.

A tall man with a thick wave of dark hair joined them, reaching out a hand. His crisp white shirt looked expensive, the tie an immaculate silk variety knotted carefully. The designer stubble and Rolex completed the executive look. 'Ray Johnson, how can I help?'

Drake expected a Scouse accent, at home on the terraces of Anfield or Goodison Park but Johnson's English accent was neutral and educated.

'We'd like to ask you about Elaine Boxford.'

Johnson frowned. 'Who?'

'She was a nurse you employed. She was placed with a

surgery in Liverpool a couple of years ago. She's now working as a district nurse with a practice on Anglesey.'

'What's this about?'

'Is there somewhere more private we can discuss this?'

Johnson led them to a room in the corner of the first floor which they reached by walking through an open plan office with staff peering at computers, others in discussions on the telephone. A few gave them disinterested glances.

Johnson waved a hand at the visitors' chairs before sitting down and clicking open his computer. Without looking at Drake he asked again, 'Why do you need to know more about Elaine Boxford?' He continued to peer at the screen until eventually he shared a glance between Drake and Sara. 'I've got her details.'

'It's part of a coroner's inquiry. One of the constables on my team spoke to the practice manager of a surgery here in Liverpool who indicated she was employed by your agency.'

The explanation satisfied Johnson. He turned back to the monitor and started reading, frowning occasionally, lines crossing his forehead, his eyes studying the details.

'She was with us for eighteen months. And she was placed in a number of surgeries around the Merseyside area but... '

Johnson squinted, his eyebrows drawing together.

'Is there anything wrong?' Drake said.

'Normally we would make an assessment once she joined our agency, but I can't find any confirmation about her previous employment although it does state she was a nurse in one of the hospitals.'

'We'll need copies of her personal details,' Drake said.

Sara added. 'Do you have any appraisals of her employment with you? Did she go on any training courses?'

Johnson's brow wrinkled again as he stared at the screen. 'This is most unusual.' He clicked his mouse and the printer behind them purred into life. 'But I know someone who can help.' He picked up the handset of his landline telephone and punched in a number.

Drake and Sara listened to the one-sided conversation as he tracked down an Angela. He relaxed as he spoke and nodded his recognition to Drake and Sara. 'I'll send the officers over to see you.' Johnson finished the call and reached over behind him scooping up the papers from the printer. 'You need to go and see Angela Ackerman at the Royal St James Hospital. She is the last person we have down as the immediate supervisor for Elaine Boxford.'

Johnson gave them a helpful, dismissive smile and pushed over the printed sheets. 'I hope you find the information you need.'

Johnson's parting shot was to provide a card with his contact details and on the back he had scribbled the address and postcode of the Royal St James Hospital. Sara punched in the details into the satnav and the disembodied voice dictated instructions.

It was another half an hour before they wound their way through the streets of Liverpool and found the sprawling hospital complex. Luckily Angela Ackerman had treated seriously the fact that two detectives had wanted to speak to her and was waiting for them in reception.

'I'm Angela Ackerman.' No expensive Rolex or power dressing. 'I'm one of the senior personnel managers. Follow me.'

Ackerman's computer and monitor were the only similarities with Johnson's office. It had a tired and worn-out feel, the paint was faded and the door into the room needed to be heaved into place before it closed.

She sat down heavily announcing as she found a notepad, 'I'd better make a formal note of your names and the nature of your inquiry.' Drake and Sara produced their warrant cards for Ackerman who took plenty of time to read them carefully jotting down the details she needed.

'The North Wales coroner is investigating a series of

deaths. We are building a complete picture of all the medical staff that looked after the patients. An Elaine Boxford is attached to the surgery and—' Drake broke off when he saw Ackerman nodding seriously.

'I am familiar with Elaine Boxford.'

Drake took a beat. 'What can you tell us about her?'

'There was a near miss incident about five years ago.'

'Near miss?' Sara said.

'Yes, Elaine Boxford and another nurse were working nightshift in a general ward with a lot of elderly and very frail patients. If it wasn't for the diligence of another member of the nursing staff, Boxford might well have administered inappropriate medication to a patient.'

Sara again. 'What do you mean inappropriate?'

Ackerman leaned over the desk, her eyes taking on the serious edge. 'It was enough to threaten the life of the patient and question Boxford's professionalism.'

'What happened?' Drake said.

'We took steps to ensure Elaine Boxford was given the opportunity to explain herself and some of the senior staff made certain she was aware of prescribing practices. However… '

Ackerman let her gaze glance up to the ceiling as though she was struggling to find the right combination of words.

'Were you worried?' Drake said.

She nodded. 'I know we are all supposed to flag up any worrying incidents, but I was told that because Elaine Boxford was one of those rare people that preferred to work nightshift, I wasn't to rock the boat too much.' Ackerman raised her hands in the air exasperated with the system. 'Very few nurses volunteer to work nights.'

'So what happened? Why did she leave to join an agency?'

'Lots of nurses do that. They get more flexibility, and more variety, I suppose.'

'What was she like to work with? I mean, did she get on with her work colleagues?'

Ackerman sighed. 'She was a bit of a loner but there was never any complaint from her colleagues. Has something happened, has someone she was responsible for died?'

'We'd like the personal history of Elaine Boxford,' Drake said.

Ackerman took a moment to ponder. She had guessed that Boxford was implicated in something far more than a routine coroner's inquiry. She shifted uncomfortably in her chair before clearing her throat. 'I don't want to sound uncooperative but I'm sure you appreciate that I shall need a formal request before I can release any documents. And I'm sure you realise my comments about Elaine Boxford are my *personal* comments and not those of the hospital.'

Drake nodded. 'I understand, of course. I wouldn't want you to do anything that was in breach of your protocols. We'll organise to have the paperwork emailed later today.' Only one more question to ask; Drake hoped he had done enough to secure Ackerman's cooperation. 'How long did Elaine Boxford work here?'

'Five years and before that I believe she worked at a hospital in Manchester.'

Drake stood up. 'You've been very helpful, Mrs Ackerman. We'll be in touch later with the appropriate paperwork.'

Drake and Sara threaded their way down to reception and then out towards the car where Drake paused. 'I'll call Gareth and get him to organise a warrant.' He dug his mobile from a jacket pocket and dialled the number.

Winder replied but before Drake could dictate instructions the officer said,. 'You'd better get back here, boss. There's someone you need to speak to.'

Chapter 30

When Drake and Sara arrived back in headquarters by early afternoon, indigestion was making his stomach grumble – so much for the healthy meal deal he'd bought at the services on the way back from Liverpool. He gave the door of the Incident Room a hefty push with his left hand and it crashed against the wall behind it. Inside a uniformed police officer stood alongside the board with Winder. He wasn't in the mood for small talk, so unless this officer had something relevant to add, he didn't want his team distracted.

Three faces turned towards him. Winder took the initiative. 'This is Constable Simon Yeo. He has some information about the items stolen from Longman's home.'

'Afternoon, sir,' Yeo said.

Drake nodded to Yeo. 'Let's hear it then.'

'I was at the car boot sale near Llangefni on Anglesey over the weekend. I recognised Mervyn Ostler behind a stall but when he saw me, he darted out of the way. I've come across him before, so I decided to take a bit more interest in the tat and junk on the table he and his wife were selling.'

Drake recalled the district inspector had referred to Mervyn Ostler as a known burglar in the Menai Bridge and south Anglesey area.

'A couple of people were haggling with his wife about some china. It didn't look like much to me, but one of them offered over a hundred quid for three pieces. And the more I looked at them the more their description matched the stolen goods.'

Drake turned to Luned. 'What items did Longman's son think had been stolen?'

'There were various pieces of china and six expensive wooden boxes he collected. There are also some watches missing.'

'Did he give you any idea of their value?'

Luned shrugged. 'He didn't seem too concerned.'

'All right for some,' Winder complained. 'Some of us

have to work for a living.'

Yeo held up his mobile. 'I took a video of the stall without Ostler and his wife noticing.'

'And did you photograph the people who bought the items?' Drake said.

Yeo nodded.

'We'll need those images downloaded.' Drake leaned against one of the desks as Winder fiddled with Yeo's mobile, allowing his gaze to drift to the image of Mervyn Ostler pinned to the board.

Boxford and Luke Holgate warranted far more attention, although Drake hadn't abandoned the possibility that Rachel Ackroyd and her husband were implicated. It couldn't be ruled out that multiple killers were involved, however, although the prospect seemed remote. Drake sensed they had already identified the culprit amongst the persons of interest. But everything was back to front. They couldn't prosecute without evidence, couldn't make an arrest without a suspect. At the moment they had fingers of suspicion being wagged at too many different people.

Once Winder was finished, Yeo retrieved his mobile and left.

Drake set about rearranging the images of Longman, Rowlands, Capon and Kerr to one side. Then he tidied the images of Ostler and Holgate and Boxford. Pinning them precisely parallel gave Drake a sense of order and neatness. He turned around and registered the uncertainty on Luned's face which combined with the apprehension on Winder's made clear they expected him to make a decision.

'Gareth and Sara, you go over to Menai Café. I want to know if they delivered meals to the homes of any of the exhumation victims. And ask if they have any connection to the residential home where Rowlands lived. Luned you're with me, we're going to talk to Mervyn Ostler.'

Coordinating the activity meant Drake and Luned had to

wait outside Ostler's home until Sara and Winder reached Menai Café.

'Has there been any mention of thefts of any property owned by Kerr or Capon?' Drake addressed Luned although he was staring at the screen of his mobile while waiting for contact from Sara and Winder.

'I'm not aware of any, sir.'

A jogger ran past the car and stood for a moment by the front gate catching his breath. Drake peered through the windscreen, wondering if this was an unexpected caller, but the man restarted and sprinted away. Soon Sara texted confirmation they were outside the café. So they left the vehicle and pushed to one side the rusty gate, its hinges loose in the post. Two large Griselinia hedges grew on the square of garden in front of the property. Drake pressed the doorbell, which chimed inside.

Ostler opened the door giving Drake and Luned a challenging glare. The photograph adorning the Incident Room board flattered Ostler. Only five years had elapsed since his prosecution for burglary, but from the wrinkles, blotchy complexion and unhealthy eyes it might have been fifteen.

'Fucking cops,' he spat out.

Drake did everything by the book, giving Ostler enough time to read even the small print on his warrant card. Luned did the same. 'Mervyn Ostler – we'd like to speak to you. Can we come in?'

'Do I have a choice?'

'It won't take long.'

Ostler kicked the door open wide and jerked a head for Drake and Luned to step inside. They followed him into the living room at the front of the property. Drake and Luned sat down on a sofa and Ostler slumped into a chair opposite.

'What's this about?' Ostler said.

'We're investigating the circumstances that led to the death of William Longman.' Drake said keeping direct eye contact with Ostler expecting the slightest indication of evasion, a lie coming, a bluff being called.

'I don't know who you're talking about.'

Straight off denial – good start, Drake thought.

'He was a wealthy gentleman who lived in Beaumaris. He died recently.'

Ostler's face settled into a granite like stare.

'His next of kin is a son who reported missing some personal items belonging to his father.' Drake's mobile bleeped and he nodded at Luned for her to continue.

'There were several items of china and crockery as well as wooden boxes the family couldn't trace after Mr Longman's death.'

Drake half listened whilst he read the message from Sara. It confirmed Mervyn Ostler regularly delivered meals both to Longman and Kerr.

Luned continued. 'We were provided with photographs of the stolen items.'

'You said they couldn't be traced, love.'

'It's Detective Constable, Mr Ostler.' The venom in Luned's voice impressed Drake. It made him realise she was cut out to be a detective after all. 'We understand that you've been selling some of those items at a car boot sale. Can you explain that?'

'Am I under arrest or something?'

Drake cut across. 'Answer the question.'

'Fuck off, *Detective Constable.*'

Drake scanned the room wondering what a lawful search would produce. 'Mervyn Ostler, I'm arresting you on suspicion of theft of items belonging to William Longman. You don't have to say anything… '

Once Mervyn Ostler had been deposited in a cell Luned and Drake headed off to the canteen for a coffee. They were joined by Sara and Winder who launched into an update.

'He was a regular, boss,' Winder said cracking open the

cellophane wrapper of a chocolate biscuit. Sara blew over the surface of a brown-coloured drink in a plastic cup. 'Ostler went to both properties at least twice a week. So he knew Longman and Kerr.'

Luned sounded a cautionary note. 'But the Kerr family didn't mention that anything was missing.'

Drake read the time on his watch, trying to work out how long the search team needed to complete their work at Mervyn Ostler's property.

'We wait until the search has been completed.' Drake sipped on the tasteless liquid. An interview meant he would be late home so he texted Annie telling her when she could expect him. Whatever the outcome of the interview with Ostler later that day, Drake determined it wouldn't interfere with his mother's planned party the forthcoming weekend.

His mobile rang and he recognised Susan Howells' number. Making excuses he left the team and found an empty room to speak to the public relations officer.

'The press is going ballistic, Ian.'

'What's happening?'

'There are journalists from London throwing money around, trying every angle to create a story about the 'serial killer prowling North Wales'.

'Nothing's been published yet though has it?'

'No, but it's only a matter of time. Do you have any thing I can use? Have you made any progress?'

'It still far too early—'

'Jesus, Ian. I thought you'd arrested somebody.'

'News travels fast. And it's far too early for me to authorise you to make an announcement. You'll have to wait, Susan.'

'Did you *have* to do all those exhumations on the same day? People have been talking about zombies and ritualistic killings. There's even a blog discussing Welsh Druids getting in on the act with human sacrifices.'

'When we've made progress, you will be the first to

know.'

Howells gave a disgusted grunt and ended the call.

An hour later Drake had finished a conversation with the search team supervisor who had finished at Mervyn Ostler's property. He had described the garage and the house as an 'Aladdin's cave' with a well organised storage system of plastic boxes full of china and glass and others with children's toys and several containing DVDs of Hollywood films. All the items would be cross referenced against reports of stolen property and Drake relished the prospect of interrogating Ostler.

Winder and Luned returned to headquarters tasked with searching the databases of items reported stolen while Drake and Sara remained at the area custody suite preparing for the interview.

Ostler's regular solicitor was finishing a case in a magistrate's court that afternoon so it meant a delay before they could talk to him.

'What would be his motive?' Sara's question pressed the pause button on their discussion. Gathering evidence usually led to a person of interest and then the suspect who would have a motive. But they were dealing with the possibility that one individual had killed six people. Serial killers were a breed apart, motives could be garbled, thought processes scrambled.

Sara continued. 'It strikes me that Mervyn Ostler is a petty criminal.'

'Burglary isn't petty crime,' Drake scolded her.

'What I meant is that his profile doesn't suggest he's capable of killing six people. And neither does Rachel Ackroyd's, come to that.'

A nagging sense that she was right returned to Drake's thoughts. 'We've still got to interview him about the items stolen from Longman's home.'

Mervyn Ostler had a contented, smug look on his face as

Drake and Sara settled into the hard-backed plastic chairs on the opposite side of the table to where he sat alongside his solicitor. Nigel Garland wasn't a lawyer Drake had come across previously. He had narrow, shifty eyes which made Drake instantly distrust him. The stink of stale cigarette smoke hung over his clothes and although Drake guessed he was early fifties the wispy grey hair clinging to his scalp made him look ten years older.

'My client wants to make a statement,' Garland announced before Drake had cracked open the wrapping of the tapes he'd use to record the conversation.

'All in good time, Mr Garland.'

Once the tape-recording machine had let out a long shrill whine indicating it was ready Drake glanced over at Ostler and Garland. He invited everyone around the table to identify themselves and then turned to Ostler. 'Do you know why you're here?'

Garland replied. 'My client wishes to make a statement.'

'I'll ask the questions,' Drake said sensing his annoyance rising.

Ostler and his solicitor ignored Drake. Garland handed his client a sheet of paper and Ostler cleared his throat before reading the details. He had known William Longman as he had regularly delivered a lunchtime meal to him from Menai Café. Longman had often engaged him in conversation, and they had established a rapport. Ostler had frequently returned to visit Longman, explaining that the old man was lonely and needed company and always enjoyed their conversations. He would have done nothing to harm William and explained that he had gifted him various items recovered from his property which he had been selling at car boot sales.

Ostler must have realised that Simon Yeo had clocked him that previous weekend. He had his explanation ready.

Ostler had never met Longman's son who visited infrequently and who he thought had little interest in his father's well-being.

Another clever comment, Drake thought.

Once Ostler had finished Drake began questioning him.

'Let's go back to the beginning. When did you begin delivering meals to William Longman?'

'I have nothing further to add to the statement that I have already made.'

Drake's second and subsequent questions were met with the same reply. Without Longman's direct evidence that his property had been stolen, Ostler wouldn't face prosecution for theft. Very few suspects refused to answer questions in Drake's experience. A person's instinct was to reply, engage with questions. Things were different with Ostler.

Drake tried one last throw of the dice. 'We executed a lawful search of your property and the contents of the garage have been removed pending further inquiries.'

'I daresay suspicion has fallen on my client because of his previous record,' Garland said, 'but the fact that his hobby is buying and selling and visiting car boot sales hardly gives you the right to suspect he has stolen Mr Longman's items.'

Drake didn't reply. He stared at Garland and then at Ostler. He regularly visited the properties of four people who had died in suspicious circumstances and for now Drake wasn't going to dismiss the possibility that Ostler was the killer.

Nothing further could be achieved, so Drake formally requested the custody sergeant to consider releasing Mervyn Ostler on bail. Once they'd been through all his possessions, had all his clothes examined for any possible shred of forensic evidence to link him to the burglary at Emyr Isaac's property, only then could he be dismissed from the inquiry.

It was after ten o'clock that evening when Drake watched Ostler and his lawyer leave the area custody centre. His eyes burned and the small of his back ached. It was time to go home.

Chapter 31

Tiredness still lingered in Drake's bones when he woke the following morning. It felt as though he hadn't moved in bed all night. Dozing through the sound of Annie showering and then moving around the bedroom, dressing, making small talk he slowly surfaced. In the shower he let the water drench his head and face. Mervyn Ostler's smirk returned to his mind, as did the self-serving comments from his solicitor about the motive for involving Ostler. His previous record would always create suspicion. Once a criminal, always a criminal, surely he understood that.

Later he would get a mind map drafted, see how all the pieces fitted together. He had to make sense of everything. Showered and dried and back in the bedroom he chose a dark grey suit, a striped blue shirt and a navy tie. His black brogues were scuffed in one corner and he made a mental note to polish them at the weekend.

He joined Annie in the kitchen and listened as she shared with him the latest developments in her parents' house-hunting. 'Mam wants me to visit one of the properties and get a detailed measurement of the kitchen and utility room. She's thinking of knocking both together and she needs the correct measurements.'

Drake hadn't visited the property but after seeing the online particulars he'd made complimentary comments about the size of the rooms and the interior decor.

Annie continued. 'The estate agent is meeting me at the property later.'

'Have they finally decided on that particular house?' Drake said.

'It looks like it.'

Drake made for the front door, finding an overcoat before kissing Annie and promising not to be late. A raised eyebrow told him she didn't believe him for one moment. The overcoat was folded neatly onto the back seat and Drake drove towards the A55 where he joined the dual carriageway snaking its way along the North Wales coast.

His mind turned again to Mervyn Ostler and the reality that his explanation about William Longman's possessions seemed plausible, too plausible. And as far as they knew Ostler had no connection with the health care system. But the preliminary searches Gareth Winder and Luned Thomas would be doing that morning would tell them definitively. Mervyn Ostler was the only one they could connect to the homes of four of the victims. He regularly delivered meals which gave him access to the properties.

Access to the property.

The words kept playing around in his mind like a broken record.

The killer needed access to the property. Their focus had been on establishing that the culprit had a legitimate reason to visit the house – Elaine Boxford as a district nurse, Rachel Ackroyd as a carer and Luke Holgate as the paramedic.

Access to the property.

Then it struck him they had missed something, and he slammed a fist against the steering wheel.

He saw the sign for Llanfairfechan and indicated left, pulling up onto a verge.

Rachel Ackroyd accessed the properties by using the key in the key safe. The code was known to the carers. Punching in the code was straightforward. Other carers must have known it too – it wasn't likely to be a state secret. It would not be known to Boxford and Holgate, unless…

Another scenario, a darker version played in his thoughts. What if Elaine Boxford and Luke Holgate did know the code? He scrambled to find his mobile and called headquarters. Sara had arrived early.

'I need to check something. I need some dates.'

Once he gave Sara the details he sped over the bridge back onto the A55, heading back the way he'd just come. He floored the accelerator, flashing at cars in the outside lane.

He reached Maes yr Haf quickly, and parked by the gate to Isaac's drive. He read the email on his mobile with the details he needed.

Leaving the car, he paced up to the front door of Isaac's home. He opened the flap on the key safe and looked at the keycode pad inside. Then he checked Isaac's date of birth from the information Sara emailed. After inputting the numbers into the key safe he turned the switch on the top and the front panel opened, revealing the aperture where the key would have been stored.

It took an hour to check the homes of David Morris, Capon, Kerr and Longman.

The codes for the key safes of all were their dates of birth.

Information easily available to Boxford and Luke Holgate. It changed everything. All the persons of interest could have accessed the property at any time. Priorities swirled around his mind and he raced back to headquarters, ignoring the speed limits.

Drake took the stairs to the Incident Room two at a time. Brushing aside the door which crashed against the wall behind it he made for the board.

He turned to face the team. 'Things have changed. All five of the victims who lived at home had key safes where the codes were their dates of birth. We've been making the assumption the killer was with *each* victim for a *legitimate* purpose. Remember what Professor Ibbott said – even if we could connect the killer to the date and time when we thought the victim had been killed it might not be sufficient. Well you can forget all that.'

Drake paused focusing on the possible scenarios. 'If Isaac struggled with Holgate and fell against the fire surround, he might have decided to return later that evening to stage the burglary.'

Steely faces looked over at him.

'Or Boxford could have decided to pay Isaac a visit.

She would have known the code. But things don't go according to plan and he fights back. He's strong but not strong enough – after all he is eighty-nine.'

'Makes sense, boss,' Winder said. 'Sounds plausible to me.'

'But what about Victoria Rowlands?' Sara said.

'I know, I know,' Drake sounded exasperated. 'Let's focus on solving five deaths. Maybe we've overlooked something about Rowlands' death. We may need to get the medics to look at her PM again. And ask for details of whether the paramedics or district nurses ever called to see Capon.'

'One other thing, sir,' Sara added. 'I've checked the records from Caring Wales about the employment record of Rachel Ackroyd and she was on holiday when Rowlands and Longman were killed.'

'Do we know where she was on vacation?'

Sara shook her head. Another detail to be established.

'What do you want us to do, boss,' Winder said.

'Let's start with CCTV footage. I want to know exactly where there are cameras in the immediate vicinity around the homes of all five. Get the registration numbers of all the vehicles registered to Rachel Ackroyd, Mervyn Ostler, Elaine Boxford and Luke Holgate. Let's get to work. There's a piece of evidence out there. Let's find it.'

Back in his office Drake sank into his chair, blew out a mouthful of air before turning on his computer. He turned to his emails and read a message from Superintendent Hobbs announcing Professor Ibbott would be arriving for a further meeting that afternoon. It was the last thing he wanted. So he turned his attention to building a detailed picture of what they knew about Boxford and Holgate.

He still had a mind map to get organised. But a whole room full of cobwebs cluttering up his thoughts had been brushed to one side like taking a breath of fresh air at the top of Cwm Idwal. He had to hope this was the right direction.

Superintendent Hobbs had made copies of the HR assessments from Detective Inspector Drake's personnel file which he read occasionally to remind himself his decision to assume the role of senior investigating officer was entirely justified. After all, he couldn't allow an officer whose judgement had been challenged previously by a difficult case to be in charge of this inquiry.

Emyr Isaac's death had initially appeared to be a burglary gone wrong. There were plenty of similar examples. A case several years previously when an elderly farmer disturbed a burglar, killing him with a shotgun, had made headline news. The tabloid press had gone into meltdown about a householder's right of self-defence. Hobbs wasn't going to run the risk of allowing the inquiry to be handled by a detective inspector who didn't command his full confidence. His predecessor's reassurance that Drake was an excellent detective had struck Hobbs at the time as a little too gushing. Was there something to hide? Something he wasn't aware about in Drake's past or, indeed, in Superintendent Wyndham Price's past?

Hobbs' promotion to superintendent had been long overdue and he had little doubt his ability fully justified his new status. In three years' time, a chief superintendent's position in Western Division would be vacant and Hobbs saw that as a small step towards an assistant chief constable role. Another career move might entail applying for a chief superintendent's position outside Wales. It might bolster and improve his curriculum vitae when it came to the application for an ACC appointment in Cardiff.

And making certain the murders of Emyr Isaac and David Morris were solved quickly had more than justified bringing in Professor Grant Ibbott. He recalled the moment his pulse spiked when he had learned the pathologists believed a serial killer was responsible for six deaths.

More than anything he salivated at the prospect of being

the superintendent who solved the case of the North Wales healthcare serial killer. Papers would be written, academic articles analysing the way the case had been conducted would secure his legacy. But he had to make sure Detective Inspector Drake and the team were making progress and progress in the right direction. Professor Ibbott was expected later that afternoon so Hobbs took time to read all the latest memoranda prepared by Drake and his team. Hobbs' insistence on being kept in the loop with formal reports had avoided unnecessary team meetings and briefings. He never felt comfortable with listening to officers referring to 'I've got a feeling, boss'. Building a case around evidence was the important thing.

When Hannah announced that Ibbott had arrived Hobbs wasted little time before inviting him into his office. Hobbs turned up his nose when he noticed that the academic hadn't shaved for at least three days and that part of his shirt tails were hanging out of his trousers. Such a dishevelled appearance might be okay for a politician wanting to ingratiate himself with the voting public but this was the Wales Police Service.

Ibbott reached out a hand. 'Superintendent Hobbs, good afternoon.'

'Good to see you again Professor Ibbott.'

Hobbs did his best to try small talk with this expert, but his wife's recommendation that he needed to lighten up and be a little bit more relaxed and normal with people never seemed to work. It made him feel uncomfortable. So he ushered Ibbott through to the Incident Room.

Hobbs opened the door and nodded an acknowledgement to the three officers seated around the desks, computers humming, monitors flickering. Hobbs and Ibbott sat near the board as Inspector Drake joined them.

'We need to do a formal team briefing,' Hobbs said. 'Professor Ibbott is keen to learn about progress.' Hobbs nodded towards Drake. 'Detective Inspector Drake perhaps you could start.'

'We arrested a Mervyn Ostler yesterday on suspicion of theft of items belonging to William Longman, one of the victims,' Drake jerked his head towards the board. 'His explanation was that Longman had given him the items.'

Winder piped up. 'And we did a full background check and can't find any possible link to Ostler working in the health service.'

Ibbott now. 'And what about his family?'

Winder shook his head. 'No connection to the NHS.'

Ibbott turned his head and ran his gaze across the faces of the four persons of interest on the board. 'In that case it looks as though you can exclude Mervyn Ostler.'

'We've made some progress with Elaine Boxford's background,' Drake said. 'Sara and I interviewed a manager in the hospital where she worked for five years. There were concerns about her competence – there was a 'near miss' incident involving the administration of some medication.'

Ibbott scribbled notes. 'Any problems with her interacting with other members of staff? Any suggestion of mental health issues?'

'Our preliminary assessment of her personnel records doesn't suggest that, but we did find that she preferred to work nights.'

Ibbott reacted positively. 'Good, excellent. That's a positive sign. I suggest you dig deeper into her background.'

'And the latest on Ackroyd?' Hobbs said.

'She was on holiday at the time of two of the deaths but we need to establish if she was out of the area,' Drake said turning his attention to Luke Holgate without waiting for Hobbs or Ibbott to ask. 'And we've established that Holgate has moved around a number of different hospitals.'

'Good, good – another red flag indicator.'

Ibbott made it sound so matter-of-fact, as though they were discussing the performance of a premier league football team.

He continued, 'Have you more details about his employment history, after all, he hasn't been in North Wales very long.'

Drake paused. 'Sara and myself are going to Shropshire tomorrow.'

'Good, good.' Ibbott's use of the same words grated with Drake. 'So we are narrowing the persons of interest to Elaine Boxford and Luke Holgate – progress!'

Chapter 32

The Shropshire County hospital was set in substantial grounds outside Shrewsbury. An accident on the main road south of Wrexham had caused a lengthy delay to Drake's journey and driving around the car park trying to spot an empty slot increased his frustration. Fortunately, a car drew out of the first row of the second car park and Drake parked.

Several conversations at the end of yesterday afternoon had given him the name of the person to contact and he tramped through the corridors of the hospital, Sara alongside him, following the signage for the administration department.

An overweight woman with enormous spectacles perched on her nose examined his warrant card and then Sara's with a mixture of surprise and interest. Then she stared at Drake and Sara's faces as though she had to double-check the warrant cards belong to them.

'Just a moment.' Drake clocked the intonation as a watered-down version of a Stoke-on-Trent accent, but it could have been Shropshire – middle England for certain.

A couple of minutes passed until a tall man with round horn-rimmed glasses appeared in reception. He wore a short-sleeved shirt despite the season and a striped tie. His baldness was complemented by a thick red beard. 'I'm John Cavendish. I understand you've asked to speak to me.'

'Is there somewhere we can discuss things in private?' Drake said.

Cavendish gave him a worried look, as though he were uncertain whether to agree or not. 'Follow me.'

Instead of Cavendish's office, the HR manager led them into a conference room and waved a hand over a well-polished table towards the chairs. He pulled one out and gazed over at Drake and Sara.

'What's this about?'

'I understand a Luke Holgate was a paramedic here until nine months ago.'

Cavendish nodded his head. Drake hadn't expected confirmation quite so quickly.

'I remember. I dealt with Luke Holgate.'

'What can you tell me about him?'

Cavendish sat back in his chair. 'I was certainly glad to see him leave this hospital.'

'What were the issues with Holgate?'

'Why do you want to know?'

'It's part of a coroner's inquiry. We'll need full details about his employment here.'

Cavendish paused, scanning Drake's face. Would he probe any further? Satisfied, he stood up. 'The records may well be in storage so it may take some time.'

The manager left Drake and Sara. He reappeared a few minutes later announcing they'd have to wait, and offering them coffee. He repeated Drake and Sara's order to make certain he didn't forget. An administrative assistant arrived with a coffee for Drake and a milky tea for Sara. No china cups and saucers just mugs with the names of pharmaceutical companies printed on them – it was the NHS, after all.

Half an hour passed before Cavendish returned. He sat down at the table and opened the folder in front of him.

'Luke Holgate was far from a model employee. He'd been disciplined on several occasions for inappropriate comments to other members of staff, bullying and poor timekeeping. He tried to excuse his behaviour because of underlying mental health issues – depression and so forth.'

'How long did he work here?' Drake said.

Cavendish flicked through the papers. 'He'd been here for fifteen months.'

Now Sara checked her documents. 'Are you certain? The employment records we have state he'd been here for four years.'

'No, definitely not. Only fifteen months.'

Sara scribbled on a note she passed Drake – *mental*

health, one of Ibbott's red flags.

'How did you deal with his mental health issues?' Drake said.

'That was one of the problems, Inspector. We could never get to the root of what the problem was. Personally, I think he suffered from a borderline personality disorder. He was completely unsuited to be a paramedic and I had advised my superiors to begin the process of leading to his dismissal when he gave notice.'

'Were you asked for a reference?' Drake said.

'I don't believe we were.'

'Isn't that a bit unusual?'

Cavendish paused. 'I certainly wouldn't employ anybody without one. Perhaps the hospital that now employs Luke Holgate took a different view.'

Sara fumbling through her papers distracted Drake who looked over at her. She pulled out a sheet of A4 and pushed it over the table towards Cavendish. 'These are the references on Holgate's current personnel file.'

Cavendish took a moment to read the documents. He grimaced as he finished the first and grunted as he read the second. 'The first is a forgery. It purports to come from someone in our HR department here. I've been here for ten years and all requests for references have to come through me. The second is from a hospital in Newcastle upon Tyne. I have no record of Luke Holgate ever having been employed there. When he applied to work here, he told us he'd been working at a hospital in Dover.'

'How many hospitals has Holgate actually worked at?' Drake said.

Cavendish spent a few seconds searching for Holgate's CV and Sara took the opportunity of scribbling another note to Drake – *another red marker – moving jobs frequently.*

Cavendish continued, 'Apparently he had been in five hospitals.' Cavendish pushed over the document towards Drake. Sara reached over and set it alongside Holgate's CV.

It was easy enough to establish that of the five hospitals on Cavendish's CV, only one matched the CV Holgate had provided to the Bangor hospital.

'It certainly looks like he's been employed in several different hospitals,' Drake said.

'His employment history is chequered to say the least.' Cavendish agreed.

'Did you have any other issues with Luke Holgate?'

'Such as?'

'Did you notice any apparent increase in death rates during shifts that Luke Holgate worked?

The silence that gripped the room snuffed out Cavendish's ability to speak. Drake watched as the colour slowly drained from his face. 'Are you suggesting...?'

'We are investigating a number of unexplained deaths where suspicion has fallen on Luke Holgate and his work as a paramedic. There are certain features of Holgate's employment with your hospital indicating a propensity for behaviour which is consistent with the profile of a healthcare serial killer.'

Cavendish gasped, clasped a hand to his mouth.

They left a serious-faced Cavendish who promised utter confidentiality, mumbling he would discreetly establish if a high death rate had occurred during shifts worked by Luke Holgate.

Would that help them? Drake wasn't certain of the answer. Perhaps only Andy Thorsen, the senior Crown prosecutor, and Superintendent Hobbs could decide. As they approached the revolving doors at the exit Drake's mobile rang. He recognised Winder's number. 'Boss, we might have a lead from CCTV footage.'

Drake peered over Gareth Winder's shoulder at the monitor on his desk. Sara stood alongside him next to Luned. Drake preferred to stand, complaining that after three hours driving the small of his back ached.

Winder explained, 'We've inputted the registration numbers of Boxford and Holgate's vehicles into the automatic number plate recognition system. The ANPR hasn't produced any hits yet. But we've traced CCTV footage from all known locations in and around the addresses for the five victims.'

Luned announced, 'We haven't requisitioned any footage for the day Victoria Rowlands died.'

It made sense. Rowlands died after being admitted to hospital. She hadn't been treated by Elaine Boxford or Luke Holgate and Drake was beginning to conclude there had to be some other explanation for her death.

Winder continued. 'We've got CCTV footage of Elaine Boxford leaving Beaumaris on the coast road a little before midnight on the evening William Longman died. I know there are other roads out of Beaumaris but they all involve a much longer journey.'

'Any sightings of Holgate for that evening?' Drake asked.

'None, boss,' Winder replied.

'I looked at the CCTV footage for the day of John Kerr's death,' Luned said. 'And we have Holgate in the forecourt of a supermarket filling station in Menai Bridge at a little after ten pm and Elaine Boxford crossing the Britannia Bridge at eleven-thirty pm.'

'And anything from the date that Capon and David Morris were killed?' Sara said.

Winder nodded. 'Holgate was seen crossing the original Menai Bridge at eleven twenty-seven but we haven't found any footage for Elaine Boxford that day. But we do have her car recorded in another garage forecourt at eleven pm the night David Morris was killed. And we haven't got any footage for Holgate on the night David Morris was killed – at least not yet.'

Drake made a quick mental calculation. It meant they could trace Holgate's movements for the evenings of two of the five deaths and Boxford for three of the five deaths. Did it mean that they had to concentrate their attention on Boxford?

Drake stared at the map, pleased that Winder and Luned had already annotated it with different coloured pins and a legend explaining where they knew Holgate and Boxford had been spotted and recorded on CCTV. At the top of the map was a red dot indicating the location of Emyr Isaac's home on the outskirts of Menai Bridge. It was surrounded by fields and Drake recalled the comments by one of Isaac's neighbours about lights in the field at night. The killer wouldn't have been lamping, of course, but he wondered if there had been trespassers on the fields the night Isaac was killed. 'Do we have any statements from the landowners or farmers next to Isaac's property?'

The only sound behind him was Winder and Luned clicking on their mice and Sara flicking through some paperwork on her desk.

'One of the officers who did the house-to-house inquiries called at Bryn y Neuadd and left a card. The land agent was supposed to call but we haven't heard anything.'

Drake nodded at Winder and Luned. 'Get onto that tomorrow after you've finalised the employment history for Boxford and Holgate.'

Drake returned to his room intent on writing yet another formal report for Hobbs. He settled down to the task, finding himself using the jargon and platitudes he thought Hobbs would appreciate. He emailed the completed report and stared at the monitor. Hobbs would read it, probably even send a copy to Ibbott. Drake wasn't sure what he made of Hobbs. Was he clever or just accomplished at climbing the greasy pole? Hobbs hadn't endeared himself to Drake or his team yet and he couldn't help but feel that a little humanity, the occasional flash of humour, a word of praise and encouragement, wouldn't go amiss.

He reached over to adjust the photograph of Annie and

his daughters. Then he'd tidy the columns of Post-it notes and leave for the day. But the final rituals were interrupted by the telephone.

'Inspector Drake. It's Dr Cadwalader from the Afon Menai Medical Centre. I thought you should know that we've suspended District Nurse Boxford.'

Chapter 33

The receptionist at the Afon Menai Medial Centre strangled the words 'please take a seat' as Drake discreetly flashed his warrant card over the counter. He and Sara were the first people to arrive that morning and from the whispered exchanges among the reception staff it was clear they were aware of what had happened to Elaine Boxford.

Drake and Sara had barely sat for a few seconds before the door opened and Dr Cadwalader appeared jerking his head for them to join him. Silently he paced down the corridor before holding open the door to his room and closing it firmly after Drake and Sara.

Cadwalader wore a powder blue short-sleeved shirt and a pair of expensive-looking teal chinos. He cleared his throat noisily. 'The health board recently introduced a protocol compelling us to undertake more stringent checks on our doctor's bags and drugs cabinet. But we were also required to undertake a workplace test to identify possible misuse of controlled drugs.'

Cadwalader paused sharing a glance with Drake and Sara indicating the serious part was yet to come.

'The test we undertook of the staff lockers produced a positive result for District Nurse Elaine Boxford.'

Drake sensed a tingling surge of euphoria in his chest. It was another red flag. He heard Sara ask, 'Is that why she's been suspended?'

Cadwalader nodded briskly. 'We had no other choice. Our standard protocols insisted she be suspended without delay and the health board informed.'

'Did she say anything?' Drake said.

'She denied any knowledge or use of controlled substances.'

Drake stood up abruptly, his mind alive to the urgency. They needed to talk to Boxford, quickly. And the suspicion created by this positive test gave them the perfect reason. 'Do you have any idea where she might be?'

'At home, I assume. She threatened to get her solicitors and union representative involved.'

'Thank you, Dr Cadwalader.'

Drake broke out into a jog as he left the surgery and made for his vehicle. Sitting in his car he turned to Sara. 'We've got enough to justify Boxford's arrest.'

He could see the encouragement on Sara's face. 'And that means we can search her property.'

'And while she's suspended, she's no longer a threat to patients.'

'But she'll be expecting us, she might already have disposed of any evidence in the house.'

Drake started the engine. 'No time to lose.'

Drake floored the accelerator and after a journey of ten minutes parked in a small hammerhead of tarmac and glanced at the house. The semi-detached property was on two floors set on a slightly elevated position. A patch of moss-filled lawn at the front clung to life. A garage at the rear had been extended and the garden banked steeply behind the house. At the top he spotted a summer house and a shed.

Something made Drake hesitate. Perhaps it was because he wasn't the senior investigating officer or perhaps it was Superintendent Hobbs' piggy eyes squinting at him. But what if the tests carried out at the surgery were unreliable? Would an arrest be justified? He decided to call his superior officer. If he alone made the decision to arrest Elaine Boxford then Hobbs would be the first to complain if things became awkward.

Drake decided to give himself deniability. Hobbs was the SIO, he could take the glory and the flak. He had hoped Superintendent Hobbs would have sought his assistance, asked his opinion, valued his judgement but his superior officer's lack of interaction made Drake wary. Was Hobbs a risk taker or a by-the-book officer?

Drake called headquarters and Hannah put him through

immediately.

Hobbs listened as Drake outlined the facts. Then Drake paused and waited for Hobbs to respond. 'So we've got enough prima facie evidence to justify an arrest for possession of controlled drugs,' Hobbs said as though repetition cemented a justification for the chosen course of action.

Drake said nothing.

'Make the arrest and I'll organise a search team.'

Drake's relief that they could interview Elaine Boxford was tempered by a wariness he couldn't explain.

'And you need to be back here this afternoon for a meeting with Professor Ibbott.'

'What!... I mean—'

'I did email you, Inspector.'

Hobbs finished the call. Drake turned to Sara. 'That bloody academic is back again this afternoon.'

He reached over to the door handle. 'Let's go.'

Drake sat in a vacant inspector's office in the area custody suite listening to Winder and Luned detailing Elaine Boxford's employment history. It'd been a convoluted process but eventually they had established that her CV was false. Transferring her allegiance from one agency to another and working in several different hospitals meant she had been able to cover her tracks. Of the five red flags highlighted by Professor Ibbott – moving from one job to another – this was something Boxford had done regularly. Even if they could establish that issues existed about her conduct in each hospital where she worked, it didn't give Drake evidence. The prospect of Boxford escaping justice dragged at his thoughts like a heavy weight.

Evidence, they had to get evidence.

He could imagine any half decent barrister taking apart a case against Boxford built on insinuation and the five red flags.

And he had to hope the search of Boxford's property would throw up a crucial piece of evidence, a glass fragment from Isaac's property clinging to an item of clothing or the kit described by the pathologists used for injecting a lethal amount of air into the patient's veins.

Winder and Luned left, allowing Drake and Sara to focus on preparing their interview plan. If Boxford's solicitor complained when they moved on from questions about possession of drugs, Drake would plough on. Would he have to arrest Boxford for murder midway through the interview to justify carrying on?

He was going to be in charge no matter what Boxford's solicitor might say.

The interview room was hot and stuffy, and Elaine Boxford looked uncomfortable sitting next to her solicitor. Drake had expected her to look nervous and avoid eye contact. Instead she looked directly into his eyes and followed him as he sat down at the table, plonking a folder in front of him. A few inches separated them. Drake could see the ageing skin and the developing double chin. She shook her head briefly before sharing a feigned expression of disbelief with her solicitor. Tom Williams was a regular in the interview rooms of Northern Division.

Once pleasantries had been exchanged Drake switched on the tape recorder and turned to Elaine Boxford. 'You've been arrested in relation to an offence of possession of controlled substances. A search of your locker at the Afon Menai Medical Centre resulted in you being suspended. Do you have anything to say?'

'I don't know what this is about,' Boxford said. 'I mean I've never done drugs. I've always been a nurse. And I'd never dream of using any banned substances.'

'You do admit the locker at the surgery where the test was undertaken is used by you.'

'Yes, of course.'

'And you were present when the test was carried out in

accordance with the proper protocols.'

Another nod of the head.

'You have to say something for the purposes of the tape. Miss Boxford,' Drake said.

'Yes. I was there.'

Williams interjected before Drake could continue. 'Can you explain why my client has been arrested when this matter should clearly go through the health board's standard protocols first?'

Drake used a kindly smile. 'Our involvement is part of the health board standard protocol.'

'But surely not an interview under caution by a detective inspector and a detective sergeant.'

Drake continued to look at Boxford. 'Have you ever used drugs?'

Williams again. 'She's already replied to that.'

Drake ignored him. 'I'll ask you again, Elaine, have you ever used drugs?' Drake ran a finger down the edge of the buff file on the desk in front of him. A denial would be stupid, he had the police national computer printout to prove her previous conviction.

'No, of course not.' Boxford looked over at Drake nonplussed, as though what he was asking was utterly incredulous.

He opened the folder and read the details of the date of Elaine Boxford's conviction at the Preston Magistrates Court eighteen years before for possessing cannabis.

'Why did you lie to me?' Drake said.

'That was nothing to do with me. I wasn't involved. I was with some friends and we were at a party.'

'You pleaded guilty.'

'I wasn't in possession.'

Williams said nothing but scribbled energetically in his legal notepad.

'You do know that it is an offence to possess a controlled substance and that you should have disclosed your conviction as part of your employment application.'

Williams pitched in, his voice a shade too loud. 'I think you'll find, Inspector, that the conviction is spent under the Rehabilitation of Offenders Act and that my client does not need to disclose it.'

Drake was ready for this line of attack. 'Applications for a nursing role require full disclosure.'

He turned to Boxford again. 'You failed to disclose this conviction when you applied for a role as a nurse with the Alpha Medical recruitment agency. Is that correct?'

Boxford replied. 'I never had any drugs. It was all a big mistake. I've never smoked cannabis. I wouldn't dream of taking cocaine or anything like that.'

'Why didn't you mention your conviction when you applied for employment with the agency?'

'I don't know. I don't know.' Boxford raised her voice.

Drake removed Boxford's curriculum vitae and pushed it across the table towards her. 'Is this a copy of the employment history you submitted when you joined the Alpha Medical recruitment agency.'

Boxford stared at the pages, her eyes scanning the contents but her mind not taking anything in. 'I think so.'

'You were employed at St James's Hospital in Liverpool for four years.'

Boxford nodded. Drake continued.

'But the details of your employment before you joined the hospital aren't accurate. Why did you lie on that application form?'

Williams dropped his notepad on the desk. 'Where exactly is this interview going?'

Drake ignored him.

'You lied on your application to the Afon Menai Medical Centre because you told them you had been employed by the surgery in Liverpool for four years. That wasn't correct. It was four months. Why did you lie?'

'It was four years. I loved it there. This is all a mistake.

I loved the patients there. I wanted to live near the sea so I moved to Anglesey.'

Perplexed, Boxford looked over at her solicitor and then at Sara as though she were inviting them all to assist against Drake, the overbearing bully. 'This can't be happening; all of this is a lie. I know what the truth is. I love my patients. I was working in a practice in Liverpool before moving here. And I've never used cannabis.'

Drake paused for a moment. How would Tom Williams react to his next line of questioning?

'Do you recall a patient at the practice called Mr David Morris?'

Williams straightened in his chair.

'Yes, he was a nice gentleman.'

'We are treating his death as suspicious and I need to establish your movements on the evening he died.'

Williams wasted no time in raising his objection, his voice now almost a shout. 'What the hell do you think you're playing at? This hasn't got anything to do with a possible offence of possession of controlled substances.'

'I'll ask the questions, Mr Williams.' Drake injected a defiant edge to his voice. He turned to Boxford. 'Your car was seen in a garage forecourt in Menai Bridge at eleven-thirty pm on the night he died.' Drake repeated the day and date. 'Can you explain why you were there?'

Williams retorted. 'You don't have to answer that.'

'I was filling up with petrol. You said it was Wednesday. I'd probably been to choir practice.'

Williams was angry now. 'Don't make any further comment, Elaine.'

Drake checked the day and date of the next time Boxford's vehicle had been recorded on CCTV – crossing the Britannia Bridge at eleven pm the evening John Kerr died. Now he knew what her reply might be.

'And Mr John Kerr was also a patient of your practice.'

'I don't believe this.' Williams again.

Drake continued, without acknowledging Williams, sharing with Boxford the date Kerr died before asking. 'You were seen crossing the Britannia Bridge at eleven pm that evening. Can you account for your movements?'

Another bewildered look. 'Like I said, if it was Wednesday it would have been choir again.'

Drake had one further roll of the dice. 'Do you remember William Longman another patient of the surgery?'

'Yes.'

'On the evening he died you were seen travelling from Beaumaris at midnight. Can you account for your movements?'

'I can't... ' Boxford's voice faltered.

Williams got to his feet. 'We've had quite enough of this charade. This interview is terminated.'

Boxford left with Williams once processing her release on bail pending further inquiries had been completed. Drake watched Williams talking animatedly to Boxford as they walked to the car park. What was he telling her?

Relieved that for now she was no danger to any of the surgery's patients, a more thorough questioning of District Nurse Boxford would have to wait for the search result of her property. There was something off about her behaviour – denying her criminal conviction and her lies about her employment made him wary. But was she a killer?

He glanced at his watch and cursed silently when he realised he might be late for the meeting with Ibbott.

Chapter 34

Professor Ibbott looked as though he had slept in his clothes all night. There were dark bags under his eyes that made Drake think he had travelled overnight on a train, getting little sleep. Greedily he attacked the plate of pastries and biscuits Winder had organised.

'Will Superintendent Hobbs be joining us?' Ibbott asked through a mouthful of raspberry doughnut, a dollop of the jam sticking to his fingers. Then he reached over for his coffee on the table in front of him and slurped noisily.

The prospect of asking Ibbott to give expert evidence about the profile of healthcare serial killers faded as Drake contemplated what a jury would make of him, what a judge would make of him. Being persuasive, authoritative, required a certain presence, Drake thought, looking over at the shambolic appearance of Grant Ibbott. If it came to a court hearing, Drake decided, the professor would need advice on his attire and haircut.

'He should be here any moment,' Drake said.

Drake could read the expression of disbelief on Sara's face. It was more difficult to figure out what was on Winder's mind, but Drake guessed he would share his colleagues' suspicion that Ibbott wasn't a valuable contribution to their team.

Ibbott finished eating and gazed at his sugar tipped fingers. Surely, he wasn't going to lick them? Thankfully he found a tissue and wiped his hands. But it wasn't enough to remove all the particles so he excused himself to go to the bathroom.

Superintendent Hobbs arrived, barging into the Incident Room, a thin mist of cologne drifted in alongside him. Drake was about to explain Ibbott's absence when the academic returned.

He shook hands with Hobbs and sat down.

'Let's get on, shall we?' Hobbs said.

Drake nodded for Winder to play the footage of his

interview with Boxford. Silently the team watched the large monitor on the nearby table.

'Can you replay it?' Ibbott asked.

Occasionally Professor Ibbott jotted something in his notepad during the second viewing, before turning to look up at the board. 'So we have eliminated Rachel Ackroyd and unless Ostler has a link to the health service then he's not your culprit.'

Hobbs piped up. 'That leaves Elaine Boxford and Luke Holgate. What did you make of Boxford?'

'Interesting, very interesting. She clearly has a borderline personality problem – she can't accept the reality of the situation, wasn't concentrating on what Inspector Drake was asking her and seemed to be in a state of complete denial.'

Drake pitched in. 'Boxford has worked in lots of different hospitals. And she has been reprimanded for inappropriate use of medication.'

'That's typical of HSKs.'

'We've been focusing our attention on building a picture of Elaine Boxford and Luke Holgate based on your advice, Professor Ibbott. Where do you think we should go from here?'

'Well, we know that Elaine Boxford is now suspended which means she is technically no longer a danger. I certainly think you should be advising all the elderly patients of the Afon Menai Medical Centre who have key safes to change the codes.'

'That's already been done,' Luned announced.

Typical of her, thinking ahead and not banging her own drum. Hobbs gave her a nod of approval.

'Do you have details of Luke Holgate's employment history?' Ibbott continued.

Sara replied. 'The details on his personnel file at Bangor hospital have inconsistencies.'

Putting it mildly, Drake thought.

'Over the past fifteen years he has worked in seven different hospitals and each time he moved on he created a false employment history for his new employer.'

'It doesn't surprise me.' Ibbott said. 'The NHS systems can be atrocious at picking up inconsistencies like this.'

'He faked some of the references used to support his job applications.' Ibbott sounded animated now. 'And I suppose they talk up his skills and expertise?'

Sara nodded her confirmation.

Drake cut in, gesticulating a finger towards Winder. 'Detective Constable Winder interviewed Rachel Ackroyd because she was with John Kerr when the paramedics arrived.'

Drake jerked his head at Winder, knowing his discussion with Rachel Ackroyd that afternoon needed to be shared with the team.

Winder got the message. 'Rachael Ackroyd confirmed that Luke Holgate was one of the paramedics who attended John Kerr. He kept boasting that he was brilliant at his job and she says he came on to her whilst he was there treating the patient.'

Ibbott nodded appreciatively. 'Doesn't surprise me. And promiscuity is a red flag, as is an inflated opinion of his own abilities.'

Winder continued. 'And we've been able to establish that both Holgate and Boxford called at Capon's house in the week before he died.'

'How does that help you?' Ibbott said.

Drake replied, 'We believe the killer memorised or recorded the code for Capon's key safe. It would have been easy then to return and access the property at a time suitable to them. And Boxford and Holgate would have access to their victims' dates of birth which were used as the codes.'

Ibbott nodded. 'I understand. So likewise for Mr Isaac.'

'That's correct.' Drake paused before continuing. 'We've spoken to a manager of the Shropshire County hospital who tells us there were repeated complaints about Luke Holgate. They were delighted to see him move on.'

'Tell me about the burglary again,' Ibbott narrowed his eyes at Drake.

'Luke Holgate and another paramedic called to see Emyr Isaac. He was elderly but still reasonably strong. They treated him and left the house. He was found in a pool of blood the following morning by his carer. There was evidence of a break in. The post-mortem indicated Isaac died from a blood clot to the brain. But there was bruising on his arms which we believe was caused when he struggled with the intruder. And he cracked his head on the metal frame of a gas fire in his bedroom.'

Ibbott stared at Drake, frowning. 'And your theory is that Isaac fought with Holgate when he was there. Thereby making it necessary to return and fake a burglary to avoid suspicion falling on him as one of the last people to see Isaac.'

The academic had neatly summarised Drake's working hypothesis. But it was no more than that. They had no specific evidence to link Holgate to the scene, no DNA and no eyewitness seeing him approaching the house late at night. More importantly he had a legitimate explanation for any fingerprints or DNA that might have been found in the house, having been there earlier.

Nobody knew quite how to react.

Ibbott sounded worried now. 'Troubling.'

More silence as the Professor deliberated. 'Has Luke Holgate been suspended?'

Hobbs shared a glance around the officers. Drake watched him composing his reply.

'Holgate prefers working night shifts and—'

'That's another red flag,' Ibbott said, 'as are odd comments and talk about death which can make colleagues anxious or suspicious.'

Ibbott's comments took Drake back to that first

morning when he had arrived at Isaac's home. An ambulance was parked outside, as well as a first response vehicle. He looked over at the image of Luke Holgate on the board and realised they had met that morning. Then Drake recalled the comment he'd ignored at the time.

Another one of our old fogeys kicking the bucket, then.

Drake repeated the words out loud.

Four sets of eyes looked over at him, inviting him to explain himself. 'I met Holgate on the morning we were called to Isaac's home. That's what he said to me.'

Ibbott was the first to break the silence. 'It looks like he's your man.' Professor Ibbott continued deliberating his words carefully. 'I think you should be concentrating on Luke Holgate.'

'It's a shame we can't catch him in the act,' Winder said.

Luned's comment caught everyone's attention. 'Maybe we can.'

Chapter 35

'It's a crazy idea,' Sara said.

After Luned had shared her suggestion that she pose as a paramedic and be allocated to work with Luke Holgate, she recounted in detail her paramedic training before joining the Wales Police Force. The lack of direct evidence linking Holgate to the crimes and Professor Ibbott's reservations about the evidential value of proving Holgate's attendance at the homes of the victims made Luned's proposition superficially attractive. Drake's face was etched with incredulity, Winder looked perplexed.

Catching the killer was a priority and perhaps they all had to think outside the box. Develop a different mindset to solving problems. Hobbs had heard the clichés a dozen times already in different management meetings. He imaged the press conference after the successful prosecution of Holgate. It would attract journalists from far and wide. His name would always be associated with an audacious and clever plan to catch a serial killer.

'You would need to witness Holgate attempting to murder somebody,' Drake said.

Luned had obviously thought the proposal through. 'Rachel Ackroyd referred to Holgate being alone with John Kerr, which would have given him the opportunity he needed.'

'After all, Inspector,' Hobbs added, 'all we need is first-hand eyewitness evidence that Holgate attempts to inject a patient with air to create an embolism.'

Drake looked over at the superintendent, his eyes betraying his amazement that Hobbs was even contemplating the proposal. 'What about the risk to Detective Constable Thomas?'

'Holgate takes advantage of elderly vulnerable people, who cannot resist or fight back,' Luned had got an authoritative tone into her voice.

Superintendent Hobbs responded. 'That's a very good

point.'

'We could always follow Luned and Holgate,' Winder said.

Sara vigorously shook her head. 'It's too risky. And how would we get Luned up to speed with all the protocols and procedures and equipment. It's not going to work.'

Luned piped up. 'We can probably organise a refresher course somewhere.'

Drake was about to say something when Hobbs stood up and made his way over to the board. 'I don't think we should dismiss Constable Thomas' suggestion out of hand.' Hobbs paused, staring, without saying a word, at the image of Luke Holgate and then at the images of the six victims. 'I'll get authority for a covert operation. Top priority will be to provide a refresher course for Detective Constable Thomas. We'll tie off the other loose ends as we go and… ' Hobbs turned to Drake. 'You need to speak to the ambulance service.'

Then Hobbs gazed over at the team. 'We've got to catch this madman.'

Hobbs's enthusiasm to embrace Luned's proposal surprised Sara. She tried to persuade herself that she wasn't shocked by his decision. Deferring to the orders of a senior officer was something that came naturally to her. But she persuaded herself to go along with the course of action despite her reservations.

The car emerged from the tunnel at Penmaenmawr and Drake turned to Sara. 'You're still not happy with this idea?' He switched off Al Lewis singing 'The Truth In Growing Old'. The lyrics of the song seemed oddly relevant to their inquiry.

'I think it's a big risk. If we use evidence improperly obtained there could be a miscarriage of justice. I've been reading up on some of the healthcare serial killers who've had their convictions overturned on appeal.'

'What do you suggest we do?'

Sara stared out of the window at the storm clouds billowing over Anglesey and Ynys Seiriol on their way to the mainland, replicating what was happening in the inquiry. Without evidence, arresting and charging Holgate might be unwise. They had no fingerprint or DNA trace and knowing his background and his personality didn't give them enough. Sara fell into an uneasy silence. If the covert operation was sanctioned it would mean lots of preparation. And the cooperation of Frank Ogden; his reaction to it would be crucial to its success.

Drake indicated off the A55 and followed the signs for Bangor hospital and found a slot for his Mondeo at the far end of the car park. Ogden was in reception waiting for them. He practised his Welsh in a preliminary exchange with Drake and smiled at Sara before leading them through into his office.

He had a cheerful air. How long it would last once he knew what Drake wanted to discuss?

'How can I help?' Ogden pulled his chair nearer the desk.

'What I'm about to disclose is highly confidential. All the details have been authorised at the highest level of the Wales Police Service.'

Serious voice and unblinking eye contact did the trick. Ogden did a double take, sharing a frightened glance with Sara.

'We are now treating Luke Holgate, one of the paramedics, as our principal person of interest into four of the deaths we're investigating.'

Ogden's fear turned to terror as he tried to compute the implication of what Drake said. He ran a finger along his lips and then pulled at his nose. 'Are you suggesting that Luke Holgate, the paramedic, is a killer.'

Drake nodded slowly.

Realisation suddenly struck Ogden. 'Jesus Christ.'

Sara took the opportunity to repeat the seriousness of their assessment of the situation. 'I'm sure you appreciate that sharing this detail with you is unprecedented.'

Ogden nodded briskly. 'Of course, of course.' His eyes darted from Drake to Sara. 'I mean it's so hard to believe.'

'We need to discuss something with you,' Drake said.

Ogden wasn't paying any attention, he was already staring at the monitor on his desk clicking furiously with his mouse. 'We'll suspend him at once, of course, get him off duty.' He paused and read the screen. 'Thank Christ for that. He finished a nightshift this morning and isn't rostered to be back until Tuesday morning. That gives us time over the weekend to get a complaint created. But he's an awkward customer so he will probably involve his union.'

Drake wasted no time and the more he outlined the proposal the more Ogden's mouth fell open and his cheeks took on the flabby flaccid complexion. Finally, he asked meekly. 'Is the police officer qualified as a paramedic?'

'She did some preliminary training before joining the Wales Police Service and we've arranged for her to receive a crash course over this weekend on paramedic medicine and procedure. By Tuesday morning we will have created a fake background history for her.'

Ogden sat back in his chair rubbing the palms of his hand into his eye sockets. 'I don't believe this. Holgate has kept suggesting he wants to get involved with training because he's such a brilliant paramedic and that no hospital could do without his expertise. I could mention to Holgate that a new paramedic has joined us and that he needs to assume a supervisory role which could lead to more responsibility in the future.'

'That sounds like an excellent idea,' Drake said.

'How am I going to explain the urgent changes to the staffing rotas?'

Drake made to get up. 'I'm sure you'll think of something. Make it sound plausible. Suggest you overlooked an email with notification that a new trainee paramedic was joining the staff here.'

The look of terror had disappeared from Ogden's eyes, replaced by recognition he had no choice. Drake and Sara left soon after and returned to the car.

Sara turned Drake. 'Do you think he'll keep the secret?'

Drake nodded. 'I'll keep in touch with him over the weekend. In the meantime, we've got work to do.'

Chapter 36

Drake spent the following day reviewing everything they knew.

Luke Holgate's background.

Boxford's employment history.

Both had woven a complex web of deceit and it had taken hours of work to establish a detailed curriculum vitae for both. An early morning meeting with Superintendent Hobbs left Drake feeling depressed. The superior officer had been interested in outcomes only and the negative result from a wipe test of Holgate's locker had only underlined how risky the operation really was. Time reviewing the background of Boxford had proved fruitless too – the choir existed and her explanation of travelling home seemed credible. But the practice had finished an hour before the cameras recorded her car. And there was still no explanation of her presence near Longman's home in Beaumaris. It troubled Drake that Hobbs had embarked on a bold strategy with far too much risk.

Driving from headquarters to collect his daughters, the reply made by the hospital administrator when he asked about death rates on Luke Holgate's shift resurfaced in his mind. 'Do you have any idea how long that will take us? And we could discover a whole pile of shit that someone could throw at us.'

Drake had replied sympathetically. Sara and Winder had reported similar comments from the hospitals they had contacted.

Helen and Megan had interrogated him about who was likely to be at the family gathering the following day. Drake repeated the details he had given them previously, explaining the family tree and skirting around Elfed Matthews and the exact nature of his relationship with his mother.

The following morning at breakfast Annie whispered that he needed to pay attention and switch off for the weekend. He gave her a weak smile, shrugged his shoulders and pretended to agree. Helen and Megan emerged mid-morning and after lunch they drove over to his mother's home. It was a short drive to Caernarfon and then on through the narrow lanes towards the smallholding where he had been brought up.

He slowed at the top of the lane down to the farmhouse. Three cars were already parked on the gravelled area outside. He spotted his mother's Hyundai and he guessed that the Mercedes SUV belonged to his sister. It meant Elfed Matthews owned the Ford Fiesta.

In the distance Caernarfon Castle dominated the surrounding scenery. Behind it Anglesey and its flat landscape stretched out into the Irish Sea. The weather hadn't improved, despite the encouraging forecast. Over Caernarfon Bay he could see the pillars of rain from the clouds shedding their loads.

As he parked a text reached his mobile. Annie gave him a sharp look and he replied with a I-have-to-take this response. Helen and Megan ignored him and sprinted over to see their *nain* standing on the threshold of her back door. He watched as Annie kissed his mother on the cheek and then turned his attention to Luned's message that the first day's training had been a success.

Luned volunteering to undertake this covert policing had surprised Drake. He had assumed she was not a risk taker. Was he being unduly fussy thinking what she had suggested was a high-risk strategy? He fretted about texting Superintendent Hobbs to establish if formal approval had been given for the covert operation. But the tone of Hobbs' last conversation had made abundantly clear that if there was anything to report he would be kept informed. Hobbs was the SIO in any event and Drake had raised enough objections so that any fallout would be down to Hobbs. And Hobbs would bathe in the glory of any success.

Drake left the car and went over into his mother's home.

Susan was in the kitchen with his mother. They exchanged a perfunctory kiss on the cheek and Susan gave him a good look up and down. 'You've put on weight, Ian.' Then she shared a smile with her mother.

Drake joined Elfed in the living room. It was odd seeing a man the same age and generation as his father occupying the space where his father should be. Drake's first impulse was to chastise Elfed for using his father's favourite chair, but he told himself how absurd it would be. His father wasn't with them any longer and his sister's comments about her mother's new friendship had quickly been buried in the realities of family life. Annie was chatting to Elfed. He stood up and he reached out a hand to Drake. He smiled and Drake smiled back.

'Good to see you, Ian,' Elfed said.

'Where are the children?' Drake said, thinking he should say hello to his nephews.

Annie tipped her head towards the door into the rest of the house. 'They're playing games.'

Drake found Helen and Megan sitting in the front room, which had been rarely used by his parents when he was growing up, a place kept for Sunday best. But it had a lived-in feel now which he put down to Elfed and the new large screen TV which gave his nephews and Helen and Megan an opportunity of playing the latest Xbox games. The boys gave him the briefest of glances. He didn't try small talk; it would be futile he knew.

Walking back to the parlour a text reaching his mobile made him pause. The message from Superintendent Hobbs was succinct – *Preliminary approval obtained. Meet tomorrow 9 am.*

He had reservations; he had made that clear enough. He hoped everything would go according to plan. Spotting him still grasping his mobile Annie gave him a sharp glare. He switched off the handset and dropped it into a pocket.

Huw Jackson, Drake's half-brother, arrived soon

afterwards with Sioned, his daughter. Drake preferred that things didn't change. It was inevitably a part of the obsessions that could dominate his mind but since his father's death he had learned about the existence of Huw and his family. And now that Annie and Elfed were part of the family things had changed again.

And a new superintendent at work challenged Drake. He couldn't make out Hobbs and that unsettled him even more.

By the end of the evening everyone had shared a generous meal prepared by his mother. Susan had been charming, allowing her reservations about Elfed to disappear or certainly to hide them effectively. Mair Drake had had the opportunity of enjoying time with her grandchildren, telling them that simply having their presence around the house was enough to lift the spirits. It felt good to be sharing time with his family and, while his reservations still persisted, their company had strengthened his resolve to face the week ahead.

Chapter 37

Superintendent Hobbs arrived at Northern Division headquarters in good time for the briefing with Detective Inspector Drake and the rest of the team. He had dismissed all the negative and possibly adverse consequences of Luned's suggested course of action to a distant corner of his mind around which he had built a secure barricade. Persuading himself the risks were minimal, the briefing memorandum he had prepared for the chief superintendent in Cardiff focused on the possible outcomes, emphasising the importance of catching the serial killer. They could link Holgate to at least four of the deaths. He had been to the properties of each of the deceased a few hours before they had died. And using the dates of birth of Isaac and Capon would have enabled him to access the key safes for the keys to their homes.

It was simply a matter of Luned keeping a watchful eye on Holgate, observing his movements and identifying whether he acted in any way suspiciously or carried a piece of unusual equipment. Hobbs had dismissed Drake's comments that Luned had to be careful. All she had to do was ensure she didn't give Holgate the chance to be alone with any patient.

Apprehending Holgate was crucial. He had to be stopped. And Hobbs had already prepared the draft of a statement he would read out to the press conference after his apprehension and subsequent conviction. It would complement the officers under his command, mentioning their dedication and professionalism. All of which he anticipated would reflect positively on his own record. It had never occurred to him that his first major inquiry would involve such a high-profile serial killer. Although the press attention the case had garnered after the exhumation had been an unwelcome distraction, the only disappointment had been how little opportunity there had been to gain more press coverage.

Initially reluctant to accept the relocation to North Wales his promotion to superintendent had entailed, Hobbs now saw it as an opportunity. A chance to shine. Few officers ever got the chance to lead such an inquiry and Hobbs had extinguished any notion he might take a second opinion, or ask for advice from one of his superior officers. He was the senior investigating officer and his relative lack of experience in leading a murder inquiry wasn't something that troubled him.

The senior management suite was quiet and, finding his papers, he settled into reading the summaries he had prepared for himself. Admitting to Drake that he had worked on little else recently would indicate a weakness. Demonstrating he had a complete command of all the detail was something different.

At nine am sharp he entered the Incident Room. Inspector Drake and Sara Morgan were casually dressed and exchanging the normal pleasantries. Hobbs gave them a professional smile. Both officers shared their customary greetings and as Hobbs sat down at a spare table Gareth Winder arrived. Hobbs frowned slightly when he noticed his unshaven appearance. He made a mental note to remind the detective constable that even at weekends he was still a police officer and part of a major crime team.

'The detective chief superintendent in Cardiff has authorised the covert operation,' Hobbs announced.

Drake nodded solemnly and Hobbs directed what the activity would be for the rest of the day. No chance of any of the team sloping off early. In any event, he expected Luned Thomas to call at headquarters after completing her training course. It would give them all the opportunity of speaking to her before her shift started the following morning.

Hobbs suspected he saw a shadow of annoyance cross Gareth Winder's face, but Ian Drake and Sara Morgan looked over at him impassively. This is a murder inquiry, for goodness sake, Hobbs thought. Having time off on a Sunday could wait.

Sara sat down in one of the visitors' chairs in Drake's room and gave him a worried frown.

'Does the superintendent think we haven't been thorough enough?'

Drake reached over and adjusted the photographs of his daughters on his desk. He needed to feel calmed. Hearing Sara's question was taking him back to his days as a sergeant when the junior officers would gossip and discuss and dissect comments made by senior officers, revelling in the absurdity of decisions made. He felt conflicted, he had to get Sara and Gareth and Luned working effectively yet he wasn't the SIO.

'You and Gareth and Luned have done everything possible.'

Sara gave him a weak smile acknowledging the praise.

Drake continued. 'We've got the rest of the day, so let's look under all those stones.'

Sara rolled her eyes, stood up and left.

Drake sympathised. Hobbs knew nothing about managing a team, nothing about getting the best from the officers under his command. Drake turned his attention to reviewing everything about the case, again. He wasn't going to let Hobbs distract him from doing the best job he could. And perhaps having the team working that Sunday gave them an opportunity to draw breath, check and recheck statements, review reports and prepare for the week ahead.

Starting with the forensic reports Drake read, then re-read the details from Mike Foulds and his team and the conclusions about the break in at Emyr Isaac's property. It looked like a classic burglary, but the absence of any trace compounded Drake's frustration. Somewhere in Isaac's home there would be evidence pointing to the culprit, they just hadn't found it. Drake played around with the scenario in his mind that Holgate's plan to murder Isaac had gone wrong, Isaac had fought back, Holgate had grappled with him and Isaac had fallen and cracked his head against the fire surround. It would have all happened in an instant as Holgate's partner was packing up their ambulance. It meant Holgate had a mess to clear up. And knowing he could safely return in the small hours to stage a burglary gave him the chance to cover his tracks.

Completing a forensic examination of David Morris's home had been a complete waste of time. It had been window dressing of the worst sort, pandering to the pressure Morris's daughter had applied.

Winder was ploughing through the balance of the CCTV footage while Sara reviewed the house-to-house inquiries. Drake focused on the detailed background to both Holgate and Boxford. Elaine Boxford's financial problems had been caused when her partner of twelve years had met a Czech girl on a stag night in Berlin and stayed in the German capital, leaving her with a mortgage and credit card bills to pay. Her peripatetic employment record mirrored that of Holgate's but Holgate's former colleagues' comments on his remarks about the longevity of his patients troubled Drake. They hadn't been picked up then and were they troublesome now? Drake's initial meeting with Holgate on the morning Isaac's body had been found when he referred to another 'old fogey' dying replayed in his thoughts. He had dismissed it then as a bit crass, but now its significance dominated his mind.

Boxford's involvement in drugs and a clear inability to understand the consequences of a conviction and its nondisclosure as part of her employment record suggested a borderline personality disorder according to Professor Ibbott. Drake wasn't so sure – wasn't it no more than Boxford taking a chance?

Drake joined Winder and Sara for lunch in the canteen. He ate a chicken sandwich, the plastic white bread sticking to the roof of his mouth. He finished a soft drink, a chocolate bar and only Winder managed small talk, regaling them with Liverpool football team's recent success in extending their lead to eleven points at the top of the Premier League.

They traipsed their way back to the Incident Room and Drake drifted over towards the board, gazing up at the map pinned to it. Mulling over the possibility that Holgate had tramped the fields behind Isaac's home Drake asked, 'Have any of the adjacent farms to Isaac's home been spoken to about the lamping activity on their fields?' He didn't address the question to anyone in particular but he turned to face both officers and Sara replied.

'I don't think so, boss.'

Drake tipped his head to Winder. 'Something for you to do first thing tomorrow morning.'

It was late in the afternoon when Luned arrived back at headquarters and she settled into friendly chatter with Sara and Winder as Drake finished the paperwork on his desk.

Hobbs' enthusiasm for a risky operation filled Drake with doubt. Prosecuting Luke Holgate with what they knew so far could prove problematic, so he could see how Hobbs had persuaded himself that gathering direct evidence would be crucial. Drake replayed in his mind part of the conversation Hobbs had had with Ibbott about the frequency of murders by HSKs. Ibbott had sounded energised when he said that generally the pace of deaths would accelerate once an HSK had started. The last thing Drake wanted was for Luned to be exposed for longer than was necessary. They had no idea if Holgate would strike again.

Drake determined to insist her participation be short lived. Then they would put all the papers to the senior Crown prosecutor for a decision. The health board would be encouraged to suspend Holgate, remove him from frontline paramedic work. At least they would prevent more deaths, but it might mean Holgate avoiding prosecution. It went against everything he valued as a police officer – bringing a criminal to justice, locking up the bad guys.

Drake left his office and moments later Superintendent Hobbs breezed in.

'Detective Constable Thomas,' Hobbs said casually, finding a chair by an empty desk. 'How was your training?'

'It all went very well, sir.'

'Excellent, excellent. We're all good to go then. Initially you'll undertake no more than six shifts. Afterwards we shall review and take advice from Andy Thorsen the Crown prosecutor about the value of any evidence gathered.'

At least some common sense to involve the lawyers, Drake thought.

'The operational support department has put together a curriculum vitae for paramedic Luned Thomas.' Hobbs looked up and over towards her. 'It's important you commit to memory the details so that you sound consistent when you meet your new colleagues tomorrow. Apparently, you've been working in Sydney for the past twelve months.'

Chapter 38

Luned left her home the following morning a little before seven after checking she had the digital camera pen which she needed for patient report forms, a normal ballpoint, and some money. She anticipated being given an access card to the ambulance station and she already had her identity card neatly clipped to her ironed paramedic uniform. Her twelve-hour shift was due to start at eight and she didn't want to be late.

She had spent the previous evening walking around her flat committing to memory the fake background created for her, and checking out the neighbourhood in Sydney where she had supposedly lived. It all made her feel like some sort of secret agent. Her initial doubts about her suggestion had quickly been dismissed by Superintendent Hobbs' alacrity to adopt the plan. She was there to observe, after all, to gather evidence about his behaviour.

She arrived as an ambulance hurried out of the car park. She spotted Frank Ogden from the distracted look on his face as he kept peering out of the window into the early morning gloom. Once she was inside, he reached out a hand. 'Luned Thomas, I'm Frank Ogden the Clinical Team Leader.' His voice was a fraction too loud and Luned hoped he'd tone it down and act normal.

She followed him through into the kitchen where she was introduced to various paramedics and technicians. Apologising that she was poor with names met with understanding nods. Somebody offered to make her a drink and she opted for tea with sugar, deciding she needed the energy. After being allocated a locker she left her car keys and trainers, donning a pair of regulation steel-toe-capped boots. Then she returned to the kitchen and spotted Luke Holgate.

He was talking in a loud voice with one of the paramedics. Luned tried to focus on what he was saying – he was making some comment about a patient the previous day. She heard 'sad old fucker – time for him to go' and made a mental note to record all these comments when she had an opportunity. Ogden joined her feigning nonchalance. 'Let me introduce you to Luke Holgate.'

'Morning,' Luned said giving him a brief nod to which he gave her the briefest of encouraging grimaces.

'All right.'

Holgate's roving eyes inspected Luned. They were set slightly too far apart under heavy eyebrows that almost shadowed them. A little under six foot and, although a good few pounds overweight, Luned thought he carried himself well.

'Boss tells me you've been working in Australia,' Holgate said.

Luned couldn't make out the accent. Working all over the United Kingdom his accent had been moulded and changed over the years.

'I'm from North Wales originally,' Luned said dragging the conversation away from the details of Australia.

'You'll have to tell me all about Sydney. I'd love to go there. I see all the adverts for jobs there. They give paramedics a lot more responsibility. That would suit me.'

Luned sipped on her drink and winced – two sugars at least.

'Let's get the van checked,' Holgate said.

Luned made a mental note of the procedures he followed as he checked the ambulance's tyres and blue lights and made sure it was clean, tidy and fully stocked. Then Holgate checked into the computer dispatch system announcing they were ready to receive a call.

It was eight thirty-one am.

They didn't have long to wait. At eight fifty-one the first call came in.

'It's a male in his late fifties fallen at home. We don't know how long he's been in that position,' Holgate said.

Luned jogged out to the ambulance with Holgate who jumped into the driver's side and powered out of the garage. The earlier grey, overcast conditions had now turned to a persistent rain drenching the road and the pavements. The wipers swept back and forth as Holgate accelerated towards the main road. The job location appeared automatically on the screen and within fifteen minutes they arrived outside the property. Holgate directed Luned to remove an immediate response bag and defibrillator monitor from the rear of the ambulance and they took one each up the drive to the house.

A woman in her late thirties opened the door to them and explained that her father had fallen yesterday and that he was in his bedroom.

'We were told your father had fallen at home.'

The woman gave them a sheepish look before taking them upstairs to a bedroom. Holgate stood over the man lying in bed. 'Can you tell me what happened Mr Parry?'

'I fell over yesterday on my way home from the pub. I thought I'd leave it until the morning before calling my daughter and the ambulance.'

'From the pub you say?'

'Yes, my ankle is really painful.'

Holgate kneeled and examined Mr Parry's ankle. Luned expected Holgate to suggest she take blood pressure and other basic observations.

But he stood up and proceeded to give Parry and his daughter a lecture about choosing the correct service. In his professional judgement, while acknowledging that Mr Parry was in pain, he did not require an emergency ambulance. Parry's daughter looked offended. Her father looked on dumbfounded. 'I would suggest you talk to your GP or go to the minor injuries unit.'

Luned followed Holgate downstairs, Parry muttering after them, 'Call yourselves the caring profession.' They loaded their equipment back into the ambulance.

Holgate sat in the driver's seat updating his status and

then turned to Luned. 'That was a waste of time. Some people have no idea. We are valuable professionals so don't expect me to be sympathetic to a man who fell over on his way back from the pub. He should have known better.'

The radio crackled with instructions for them to proceed to a jump cover point – the local jargon for a convenient place for them to park and wait.

'Good,' Holgate said. 'There's a McDonald's at those services. We might get time for a coffee.'

Within five minutes the voice over the radio had instructed them to move to another jump cover point and before they reached that one they were diverted to a third. It was over two hours until they finally parked and waited. Holgate nodded at the services and gave his preference for a sugared cappuccino to Luned who found the right change and went in search of the machine. She had managed only two sips of her drink when the alarm beckoned. A woman was critically ill a few minutes away. Luned's pulse increased as Holgate threw the plastic carton containing his coffee onto the tarmac next to the ambulance and switched on the blue lights and then the siren.

Luned read the information on the screen that warned them the patient was having trouble breathing and that she had recently been diagnosed with asthma. Holgate floored the accelerator, peering out through the windscreen as he weaved through the traffic.

Holgate hauled the ambulance onto the pavement outside the property. Luned followed him to the rear, where he removed the equipment they needed including a defibrillator, response bag and oxygen cylinder in a bag. Luned could imagine this was exactly the circumstances Holgate thrived on. She expected he'd make an excuse to be alone with the patient. She needed to be careful.

A woman stood at the threshold and pointed into the kitchen. It looked as though a bomb had exploded inside. The gas cooker had been moved, the table was in pieces on the floor, as were the chairs. Strewn all over the floor were empty tins of soft drinks, a pack of cereal and an empty wine bottle and various plates and crockery.

In the middle of the chaos lay the body of an elderly woman.

Holgate stepped over to her, Luned joined him. It was obvious from her colour and chest movement in response to their voices that she was very unwell. Briskly, Holgate dictated instructions for Luned to go back to the ambulance and bring a trolley. 'We'll get her to A&E without delay,' Holgate announced.

For a moment Luned stood rooted to the spot. She didn't want to leave Holgate with an elderly struggling patient, but the other woman was present and Luned made a judgement that his request was reasonable and if she refused he might get suspicious. She dashed out to the ambulance, frantically removing the trolley and galloped back inside. It didn't look as though Holgate had moved and he was assisting the woman's breathing with a nebuliser. The other woman hadn't moved either.

A few minutes later Luned was sitting in the rear of the ambulance monitoring the patient, who was responding well to medication. It was another twenty minutes before the ambulance arrived at the hospital where they wheeled her into the resus department. The woman grasped Luned's hand as she stood alongside the trolley. Holgate excused himself, explaining he had to give the reception staff all the patient details. Holgate returned and soon they left.

Luned secretly heaved a sigh of relief that nothing untoward had happened while she was out in the ambulance. Nothing so far had suggested Holgate was a serial killer. But Luned hadn't met any before and she had no real idea of what to expect.

After a break of thirty minutes for lunch, which Holgate complained bitterly was unpaid, he took another series of calls that took them to various jump cover points. Luned made excuses that she wanted to stretch her legs while Holgate finished a coffee sitting in the ambulance. She knew he didn't understand Welsh so even if he had overheard her conversation with Inspector Drake, he wouldn't have understood a word. She managed to keep the conversation straightforward – everything was going okay, some of the incidents are a bit hairy, no odd behaviour from Holgate so far.

'I need to go, sir,' Luned said. 'He might get suspicious.'

'Take care.' Was all Drake said.

The long drive up from the lodge to Bryn y Neuadd – it would have been called a gentleman's residence years ago – gave plenty of time for Winder to admire the property. The external walls had been painted a dusty pink and the woodwork of the windows gleamed a glossy white. Projecting eaves of modern slate created a veranda, which was supported by slender cast-iron columns around the two sides Winder could see. He glimpsed a range of outbuildings to the rear and two Land Rover Discoveries, no more than two years old, parked in front of garages with arched wooden doors. Winder pulled up onto the gravelled area outside and then left the car.

Winder looked over the carefully manicured lawn leading down to a pond and beyond it a paddock. A search that morning had told him that Bryn y Neuadd estate owned hundreds of acres and that the land agent lived at the house. He walked under the veranda and over to the main door painted a glistening black. No electronic doorbell here; he reached for a pull on a brushed brass plate. It made no noise when he yanked it, but he could imagine a copper bell somewhere in the servant's quarters announcing his arrival.

As he waited, he thought about Luned, wondering how she was getting on and pondering if visiting this house really was a good use of his time.

He didn't have to wait long. A man in a tweed suit and a Tattersall shirt opened the door.

Winder presented his warrant card. 'My name is Detective Constable Winder. We're investigating the death of Emyr Isaac who lived at Maes yr Haf in Menai Bridge. Are you Robert Brown, land agent for the Bryn y Neuadd estate?'

'Yes, that's me.'

'We believe there's been a lot of lamping activity on the land surrounding Maes yr Haf. If you've had trespassers on your land, then it might have come to your attention.'

Brown relaxed, realising the purpose of Winder's visit. 'Of course, I understand. Do come through.' His manners and courtesy complemented the landed gentry accent perfectly. He spoke over his shoulder as he led him through the hallway. 'As it happens Reverend Canon Frank Davenport, the owner of the estate, is here at the moment. I'm sure he'd be interested to know we were helping the local constabulary with their inquiry.'

A red Aga had been built into a substantial stone fireplace in the kitchen. An expensive-looking American-style fridge–freezer stood against one wall and copper-bottomed pots and pans hung from a square butcher's hook over the island in the middle of the floor.

'This is Reverend Canon Frank Davenport,' Brown said.

A man in his sixties wearing a dog collar, a black tunic and black trousers stood up from the kitchen table and stretched out a hand as he did so. 'How do you do.' His accent was indistinguishable from Brown's.

'I'm Detective Constable Winder.'

'Do sit down,' Davenport fluttered a hand towards some chairs.

'As I've just informed Mr Brown, I'm investigating the death of Emyr Isaac who lived at Maes yr Haf.'

'Terribly sad,' Davenport said. 'Does he have any

family?'

'I had heard it was a burglary that had gone wrong,' Brown said.

'No, he doesn't have family,' Winder ignored Brown's question.

'I don't know how we can help,' Brown said.

'An eyewitness has told us about lamping activity over the fields surrounding Maes yr Haf. Are you aware of anybody trespassing on your land?'

Brown gave Davenport a glance that suggested he was looking for approval. None was forthcoming and Davenport appeared as interested as Winder to hear the response.

'We did have some trouble a few months back. My gamekeeper caught a local chap and his two sons out on our fields lamping late one night.'

'And what happened?'

'They were trespassing, of course, but as you know there's nothing we can do about that so they were given a warning.'

'Did you notice any lamping activity on the night Emyr Isaac died?' He reminded both men of the date.

Davenport replied first. 'I wasn't here, I'm afraid.'

Brown frowned. 'Now that you ask… ' He reached for his mobile. 'What was the date again?'

Winder repeated the details and Brown scrolled through his mobile before announcing. 'Probably nothing, but that night I almost collided with a motorcyclist on the lane near the house. Damn fool was speeding. I did get a chance to snap his number plate though.'

Winder's pulse drummed in his neck. Brown pushed over the mobile at Winder. The image was dark and the number plate a little blurred but clear enough to run it through the DVLA system. Who are you, Winder thought? They would know soon enough.

'Can you email me a copy?'

'Of course.'

Winder passed Brown a card with his email address. Winder wasted no further time and rushed out to his car fumbling for his mobile as soon as he left. He dictated the number plate details to Sara. He slammed the door closed, started the engine and floored the accelerator.

Chapter 39

'Are you sure?' Drake said realising he sounded stupid. The DVLA could be slow in producing records but rarely wrong.

'Yes, boss. A motorcycle registered to Boxford was spotted near Isaac's home the night he was killed.'

'What the hell was that doing there?'

Winder didn't reply. Only way to find out: they would have to question Boxford again. But that afternoon Drake was in Caernarfon police station on Hobbs' insistence, attending a meeting with other detectives from the western area of Northern Division reviewing recent statistical anomalies in burglaries and reports of racially inspired hate crime.

'We'll need to speak to her again. In the meantime, get the ANPR interrogated for details of the motorcycle and check out the CCTV.'

'Yes, boss.'

The other attendees at the meeting were filing back for the second session and Drake had to finish the conversation. 'And, Gareth, see if her mobile can be traced for the night of Isaac's death.'

Drake returned to the conference suite but all he could think of was that Luned would have to spend another few hours with Luke Holgate in the cab of an ambulance. During their earlier brief conversation, she had sounded calm, which was no more than he would have expected. Since she had joined his team her thoroughness and professionalism had impressed him.

The exuberance of youth, Drake thought as he fiddled with the ballpoint, trying to concentrate on the comments made by a detective inspector. As soon as this meeting finished, he could arrange to see Luned, get her debriefed, get up to date. It was only going to be for a few days. Then they would reassess.

A message reached his mobile.

'Detective Inspector Drake,' Drake heard his name and

looked up and over towards the front of the room. 'What you think about these statistics?'

Something hard stuck in his throat as he read the text. *Dad's had an attack. I've called the ambulance.*

Drake stood up. 'Sorry, something's come up.' He said, as he dashed out of the room.

Luned returned to the ambulance. Holgate gave her a smarmy smile. 'Boyfriend?'

'My mother. You know what parents are like.'

'Have you got a boyfriend then?'

Fortunately, Luned didn't need to reply as the alarm rang with a call. An elderly man in his early seventies with a history of heart problems was having an angina attack. It was only a few minutes from the dispatch point and Holgate negotiated through the afternoon traffic, lights flashing and siren clearing away the commuter traffic.

The directions took them into the village of Y Felinheli and Holgate indicated right, down into the marina. The road was narrow. Cars mounted the pavement giving the ambulance room to pass easily. Luned looked out for the number of the property and pointed towards the front door when she spotted the right house. An elderly 3 Series BMW stood on the drive.

At the front door a woman told them that her father, Roland Jenkins, was upstairs. Luned cast her glance towards the staircase. It was a tall thin house and the woman explained that the sitting room was on the top floor. Holgate asked all the usual questions as they took the stairs. Her father had become poorly quite suddenly that afternoon. He had been for a walk around the village, nothing too strenuous, but he had found difficulty getting his breath when he returned and his colour had deteriorated.

The staircase led into a kitchen that occupied the rear portion of the top floor. Beyond it was a sitting area where Roland Jenkins sat on the chair, a woman about the same age, presumably his wife, Luned concluded, sat next to him holding his hand. The door to a terrace allowed a fresh breeze from the Menai Strait to fill the room.

Holgate wasted no time assessing Mr Jenkins, 'My name is Luke, Mr Jenkins, and this is Luned. She's new, I've taken her under my wing today. I'm just going to start by putting some monitoring on you.' Holgate proceeded to attach ECG leads before taking Roland's blood pressure and measuring his oxygen saturations. He then placed him on oxygen before listening to his chest. 'Have you had an attack like this before?'

Mrs Jenkins replied, her voice shaking. 'There was an attack about a year ago. He went to the Heath Hospital, in Cardiff. He had to be kept in overnight.'

'Well, Mrs Jenkins, I think we'll do the same thing again. Better to be safe than sorry. We'll arrange to transport your husband to Bangor hospital.'

The front door slamming and footsteps bounding up the stairs grabbed their attention. Luned could barely believe her eyes when she saw Inspector Drake walking into the room. 'I came soon as I could. How are you Roland?' He purposefully didn't look at Luned. Then Luned realised this was Annie Jenkins, his partner, her parents.

'You got here quickly, Ian,' Annie said.

Drake shook off the question.

Holgate turned to Roland. 'We'll help you downstairs.'

Jenkins nodded his head weakly.

'Good, let's get going.'

It took them a few minutes to negotiate the staircase with Holgate going first, helping Jenkins take the steps carefully. Luned was right behind him. On the drive they helped him into the rear of the ambulance. Drake turned to Holgate. 'We'll accompany Mr Jenkins.'

'There's only space for one of you.' He turned to Annie. 'Perhaps you'd like to join your father with Luned in the back of the ambulance?'

'We'll follow behind,' Drake said.

Luned kept monitoring Roland Jenkins' blood pressure. It was a short journey and Luned reassured Annie after the door had been closed that her father would be all right.

The vehicle negotiated the various roundabouts leading up to the hospital and eventually Luned could sense Holgate reversing into the entrance for accident and emergency. He stopped the engine and the rear door opened. Seconds later Roland Jenkins was on the ambulance trolley and Holgate pushed him through the entrance doors. Then Inspector Drake appeared. Luned could see him scanning Holgate and she noticed him surveying the scene. He moved to a position in front of Holgate looking directly at Roland Jenkins. Holgate wouldn't dream of trying anything in the hospital, Luned concluded.

Holgate turned to Drake. 'Can you stay with your father-in-law for a few minutes while we go and check-in.'

Drake nodded. Luned followed Holgate inside where he handed over to the resus nurse. Returning to reception Holgate explained to Drake and a recovering Roland Jenkins what the procedure would be. Then he nodded to Luned and they returned to the ambulance. She let out a long slow breath before climbing back into the cab. Her pulse was off the scale and she gave a silent prayer that the shift would be over soon.

Once the ambulance had left the grounds of the hospital Drake pinned his mobile to his ear. 'I'm in the A&E department of Bangor hospital. I need to speak to you – don't leave your office.'

He didn't wait for a reply. He ended the call and dropped the handset back into his jacket pocket. Annie had gone to sit with her mother at the reception full of patients waiting their turn.

Drake's adrenaline had spiked when Annie had messaged him about her father's illness. And now his attention was highly focused and it gave him the opportunity of realising there was one thing they might have overlooked. One thing that might implicate Luke Holgate in one of the deaths they could not link to him.

He looked up at the CCTV cameras.

How many of them covered the A&E department, Drake wondered?

'Are you all right?' Annie said. 'Only you look very agitated. You seemed quite cross with the paramedics.'

He wished he could tell her, but that had to wait. 'Look there's something I have to do. Can you stay with your father?'

'Of course, Ian. You're frightening me. What's wrong?'

'Just make sure your dad's okay.' Drake trotted out of A&E and then sprinted towards the ambulance administrative centre. Ogden was standing in reception, a troubled frown creasing his forehead. He bustled Drake into the same conference room they had sat him previously.

'Who oversees CCTV footage recorded in the hospital?'

'I don't know, someone in security.'

'I need a name. And I need it now.'

Ogden gave him a frightened glance. 'Okay, I'll see what I can do but it's late.'

'I don't care how late it is I want to see the footage tonight.'

Drake left Ogden scanning his computer looking for the right contact number and dialled Winder who only took a few seconds to find the date and time when Victoria Rowlands had been admitted to Bangor hospital.

'There's a Jack Williams still working in the security department but he's going off shift in five minutes.' Ogden said.

'Tell him to wait.'

Drake insisted that a reluctant Ogden accompany him to Jack Williams's office. The man in his early twenties, loosened tie, casual jacket was obviously leaving for the day, an empty sandwich box propped on the top of a shoulder bag by his desk.

'What's this about?'

'I need to see the footage from A&E for a specific date.' Drake dictated the details.

Williams glanced at the time on his watch. 'Can't this wait until tomorrow?'

Drake stared at the monitor. 'Now will do just fine. How many cameras are there in A&E in any event?'

It took a moment for Williams to confirm there were six. Drake turned to Ogden. 'I'll keep you informed.' Ogden gave him a tentative look as though he wasn't certain that he was being dismissed.

'Of course, keep me posted.'

Once Ogden had left Drake pulled up a chair and sat alongside Jack Williams listening to an explanation of where the cameras were located. 'Start with the entrance.'

Watching Holgate arriving at A&E had made Drake realise he could have seen Victoria Rowlands when she arrived at the hospital. He could have made an instantaneous decision to dispatch her, pump her veins full of air. Williams clicked on the mouse and found the footage from the entrance. He began the footage an hour before the time Drake had given him and Drake watched the time elapse quickly as the speeded-up images flashed on the screen. Drake didn't recognise any of the paramedics pushing patients into the hospital and when they reached the time Winder had given Drake there was no sign of Victoria Rowlands.

Drake toyed with the idea of calling Winder to double-check the timings of Rowlands arriving at the hospital. But then the image of an elderly woman on a trolley being wheeled into the corridor filled the screen. There were two paramedics with her – no sign of Luke Holgate. They pushed the trolley through beyond the scope of the first camera and Drake almost yelled. 'Stop it there. I want images from the next camera, now please.'

It took Williams a couple of moments to find the right camera and he ran the footage for a few minutes before Victoria Rowlands arrived. She was pushed into a bay waiting for treatment.

Then Luke Holgate appeared.

He walked confidently into the footage, stopping to chat with the nurses, exchanging a joke, chewing the fat. Somebody must have mentioned the recent arrival of Victoria Rowlands because he glanced over towards her. Momentarily he disappeared from view returning wearing his high vis jacket. Instead of heading out he moved over towards Victoria Rowlands' bed.

Drake couldn't see what he was doing but he knew instinctively what the paramedic was up to.

Now I've got you, you bastard.

Chapter 40

Drake hammered a fist on Elaine Boxford's front door. Her next door neighbours gave him a cursory glance as they left for work. The door opened a few millimetres and a bleary-eyed Boxford stared at Drake.

'I need to ask you some questions.'

'What about? I've got nothing to say to you.' She made to close the door, but Drake put his hand against it.

'It's important, Elaine.'

She eased the door open slightly.

Drake took it as an opportunity and barged in. Boxford retreated into the kitchen tightening her dressing gown as she did so.

She flicked on the electric kettle. Her hair was dishevelled, her eyes barely functioning. 'Shouldn't I have a solicitor present?'

Normal protocols should have demanded that he insist Boxford get dressed and accompany him to the police station where they could conduct a further interview under caution. But he urgently needed an explanation about the presence of her motorcycle near Bryn y Neuadd, so protocols could go to hell. Eliminating her from their inquiries was the priority. He had to be able to tell Superintendent Hobbs and Andy Thorsen when the time came what her explanation was. He wasn't going to face the risk of Hobbs criticising him for failing to follow up this one lead.

'Are you the owner of a motorcycle?' Drake said reading out the registration number from his mobile.

'Yes, it's in the garage.'

'We have an eyewitness who confirms the motorcycle was seen on the evening of Emyr Isaac's death in a lane by the fields behind his house.'

Boxford frowned and continued frowning as though she were thinking. 'I haven't been on the motorcycle for months. It must have been Pete.'

'And who is Pete?'

The sound of footsteps on the floorboards upstairs took Drake's attention and he suspected the movement was probably the answer to his question. The noise of the kettle filled the room and it switched itself off as the staircase creaked before a man in his early fifties entered the kitchen.

Boxford tipped her head towards him. 'You can ask him yourself.'

Luned woke early, her mind full of the images from the previous day. Luke Holgate made her skin crawl but was that enough to make him their killer? She pulled on a pair of old jeans, found battered trainers in a kitchen cupboard before shrugging on a warm jacket. She marched down into the town, staring straight ahead, tramping the streets, breathing deeply. She wanted to face the day refreshed, determined.

After half an hour she returned to the apartment and after showering slurped on an instant coffee. She didn't feel hungry. The paramedic uniform had been neatly ironed the night before and as she took it off the hanger doubts surfaced in her mind that they would ever get the evidence they needed to convict Luke Holgate.

She drove to work, her resolve stiffening.

Holgate was a serial killer. He had to be stopped.

And she was making a small contribution towards that outcome.

Entering the ambulance station, the paramedics exchanged warm natural greetings, and it reassured her they had accepted her without question. Holgate came in from the garage announcing he had checked their vehicle. She gave him a cursory good morning. His gaze lingered a moment too long before he replied. 'You all right?'

Luned didn't need to reply.

Holgate organised tea and pushed the mug over the table in the mess where they sat waiting for their first call. He kept up a stream of banter with the two other paramedics sitting with them boasting about his expertise and how it was wasted as a paramedic.

'Maybe you should think about retraining.' A paramedic in his fifties suggested to Holgate.

Another joined in. 'They're looking for brain surgeons.'

They chuckled. Holgate ignored them as though he were impervious to the criticism implied by their comments. Exaggerating his own importance seemed second nature. Luned said nothing, but the two paramedics looked over at her one raising an eyebrow, another rolling his eyes.

Soon enough the first call came over the system – an elderly woman had fallen in the early hours of the morning. Discovered by her daughter, who was unable to help her up, she had called for an ambulance. Luned caught her breath – this was exactly the sort of circumstances Luke Holgate had taken advantage of before. She had to be wary.

The journey took fifteen minutes for them to reach the house in Llanfairfechan. The road was narrow, so Holgate had to squeeze the ambulance onto the pavement barely allowing space for Luned to open her door.

A woman in her mid-forties stood at the front door. She looked alarmed and explained she lived locally and had found her mother on the floor when she called. Holgate encouraged Luned to assist with the initial assessment. Although the patient was cold, she did not appear injured but the responses she had given to Holgate and Luned's questions suggest she was suffering from short-term memory loss. They helped her to her feet and Holgate inquired about the care arrangements to look after her mother.

'She's very stubborn. She insists on being able to do everything herself. I call in a couple of times a day but I'm working and sometimes it can be difficult. The social services can't offer her any help because she isn't bad enough.'

It shouldn't have surprised Luned from what she had learned about the adult social care system. People who could afford regular care were lucky, others, who couldn't, were more at risk.

They watched the elderly lady as she hobbled through into the kitchen at the rear of the property. Luned noticed an altered gait – she was dragging her right foot. 'She's been doing that for a while,' her daughter said, as though her mother were not in the room.

After an examination Holgate announced he suspected some tenderness to one of the bones in her foot and that it would be best for her to have an x-ray and further assessment. It pleased Luned the circumstances didn't give Holgate an opportunity to be on his own with the patient. The daughter sticking to her mother like glue made that unlikely.

Luned accompanied the woman in the ambulance to the hospital. Once triaged Luned waited until her daughter arrived, making certain Holgate couldn't be alone with her. After her brief conversation with Inspector Drake the previous evening when he had told her about his suspicions regarding the death of Victoria Rowlands, Luned was determined to be on maximum alert whenever they took a patient into hospital.

Luned took the opportunity of tidying the rear of the ambulance. Once satisfied there were no large unusual syringes secreted anywhere she realised she would have to examine the contents of Holgate's bag – the one that he usually kept fastened to his belt loop.

Once they had finished in the hospital, they were directed to a jump cover point. It was one of Holgate's favourite spots where he could buy a coffee and a cake. He parked in sight of the service area.

A call took them to a supermarket where a man had collapsed. The normal observations and ECG persuaded Holgate the man was healthy enough to accompany his wife home. Luned tried to glance inside Holgate's bag as he treated the man but the more she worked with him the more she noticed his reluctance to open it. Was this where he was trying to hide a large syringe?'

Their mandatory thirty-minute lunch break gave Luned an excuse to walk around tapping out a message to Drake telling him that nothing suspicious had happened and that she hadn't been able to see the contents of Holgate's bag.

By late morning Drake was stalking around the Incident Room demanding to know if Winder had made progress. The CCTV footage Jack Williams had emailed to Drake included additional footage Drake hadn't viewed the night before. They needed a detailed picture of Holgate's movement in the hospital the evening Rowlands was admitted.

He tried to reassure his superior officer he was working as quickly as he could.

'When will Luned be having lunch?' Drake said standing by the board.

Sara sitting alongside Winder read the time on her watch. 'Yesterday it was another hour or so before they stopped for a break.'

'And they aren't paid,' Winder added still staring at the screen.

A few minutes later Winder called over to Drake. 'I've finished boss.'

Drake emerged from his office and dragged a chair to look over Winder's shoulder as he adjusted the monitor. 'I've been able to track the movements of Luke Holgate on the night Victoria Rowlands was admitted.'

Sara cut in. 'He was working with another paramedic called Faulkner. They had arrived eleven minutes before the ambulance delivered Victoria Rowlands.'

Winder continued. 'Rowlands was placed into a waiting area for a preliminary assessment.' Winder played the footage Drake had seen the previous evening and he watched as Rowlands was wheeled into A&E and then into a bay where she was seen by triage nurses. 'We're lucky, boss, that the CCTV camera which covers that bay gives us great footage.'

Winder clicked into the footage showing the figure of Luke Holgate arriving with a patient minutes before Rowlands. He moved around the A&E reception area: it thronged with nurses and doctors and the occasional civilian. The footage moved from one camera to another. Being inconspicuous was easy in his paramedic uniform. It was easy enough for him to walk over to Victoria Rowlands lying on a trolley. There was nobody with her – perhaps Holgate had asked whether there were any relatives accompanying her in one of the conversations he had with the reception staff.

'What's he holding?' Sara said.

'It's a bag. I haven't seen any of the other paramedics use anything similar,' Winder said.

'It matches the description Luned has given us about his 'bag of tricks' he keeps on his belt loop.'

'Does it look big enough to carry a large syringe?' Sara said.

'Let's hope Luned can get a look inside his bag.'

Nobody paid any attention to Luke Holgate as he stood alongside Victoria Rowlands' trolley, his back to the camera. He was doing something, that was clear enough. And it only took him a few seconds, more than enough. Holgate straightened and fiddling with something they couldn't see, he moved away and exchanged small talk with more staff before waving at a colleague.

'That's his partner,' Winder said.

They stood watching the images silently for another few minutes. The footage didn't prove Holgate had injected Rowlands. 'It's circumstantial evidence, surely,' Winder said.

Drake stood up and blew out a lungful of breath before restarting his stalking manoeuvre around the Incident Room. 'It's no good on its own. If we can prove the others were killed by Holgate injecting them this evidence might have more weight. Jesus, we have to stop this guy.'

'We've had some preliminary feedback from the hospitals that employed Holgate,' Sara said.

Drake gave her a pained expression.

'The Shropshire County hospital and the Northern Infirmary in Newcastle have confirmed concerns about suspicious spikes in their death rates.'

'What the hell are these people doing?' Drake exclaimed.

It appalled Winder how the managers and doctors had turned a blind eye to Holgate's behaviour, ignoring possible evidence he had killed before. It was difficult to believe.

Drake continued. 'Tell them to put together a detailed analysis. It must be difficult for doctors to comprehend the possibility a paramedic might be a serial killer but if there is a pattern to previous spikes in death rates then… it beggars belief… that they did nothing about it.'

A text reaching Drake's mobile interrupted him. 'It's Luned,' he said falling over his words.

He read the message and turned to the team. 'No change. And he's still protecting his bag as though his life depends on it.'

Luned finished her banana and dropped the peel into a bag with her empty sandwich box when a call came directing them to a road traffic collision. Holgate kept up a running commentary about his expertise in assessing trauma patients of this sort and that his time in various inner-city roles had given him enormous experience. Luned had expected a degree of inquisitiveness about her previous jobs but apart from his initial comments the day before about working in Sydney, Holgate was happy to keep talking about himself. That afternoon, travelling to the collision involving two cars was no different. Luckily the accident wasn't serious, and nobody required hospital treatment although Holgate advised all that if they felt aches and pains the following morning, they should seek medical attention.

He acted normally.

He gave proper, sensible advice.

He didn't fool Luned. And he kept the bag on his belt loop carefully zipped up.

They had time for a coffee from a petrol station before the next call.

A man had collapsed unconscious with no warning and a neighbour had reported the incident. The report said he was at home, no next of kin. Luned could see it might be the perfect opportunity for Luke Holgate. When they arrived, she breathed a silent sigh of relief as she saw a police community support officer standing on the threshold. The PCSO smiled and waved a hand at them to enter. She explained that a neighbour had seen the patient collapsing and that he had banged his head.

Holgate made a provisional assessment and when he announced to the PCSO that he wouldn't be needed any longer apprehension gripped Luned's chest. Holgate managed to take the man into the downstairs bedroom where he measured the patient's blood pressure which he reported as abnormally low. Holgate touched the bag on his belt loop and turned to Luned. 'It might be advisable for us to take the man to hospital. Can you go and get the portable chair?' He avoided looking Luned in the eye.

It was the sort of circumstance she wanted to avoid. How quickly could she get to the ambulance and return with the equipment he requested? At the sound of a voice from the front door Luned relaxed. 'Hello, can we come in?'

Footsteps approached along the hallway and a face appeared in the doorway. A woman smiled broadly. 'Are you a neighbour?' Luned said to her hoping she didn't sound too relieved to see her.

The woman nodded and Luned continued. 'I've got to get a piece of kit, perhaps you'd like to keep your friend company?' Luned hurried to the ambulance worried her ruse might alert Holgate. There were straps and clips to undo. She fumbled, her fingers uncoordinated – she was taking minutes to complete a simple task. Returning inside she heard the neighbour's voice keeping up a loud conversation with the patient.

When Holgate and Luned drew away from the property the neighbour was still standing on the drive looking intently at the ambulance. At the hospital Luned made certain she accompanied Holgate as he checked into reception, spoke to the triage nurse and then she hung around near the bay were the man was waiting to be treated.

They left soon afterwards, returning to the ambulance station at the end of their shift. Once the ambulance had been locked and the end of shift tasks completed Luned made for her car.

She sat in her vehicle, her body shaking, fighting back the nausea.

Had she prevented another death?

She drove home worrying she wouldn't get more than a few hours' sleep.

Chapter 41

Frank Ogden was waiting for Luned the following morning in the ambulance station. He kept running his hand over his lips and cheeks and Luned wanted to tell him to stop. 'Good morning, Luned.' The courtesy was forced, and it sounded rather odd but none of the other paramedics paid him any attention. Or so it seemed. 'I thought you could tell me how you've been getting on.'

Luned followed him out of the mess room and into the empty garage. Ogden whispered. 'What's happening?'

Luned hissed back. 'You know I can't discuss things.'

Ogden looked around checking who else might be present. 'I hope this whole damn thing will be worth it.'

Holgate emerged from the mess. He gave Ogden and Luned a frown. Ogden announced in a voice a shade too high. 'Well I'm glad you're settling in satisfactorily. I'll undertake a formal review and appraisal next week.'

He gave Holgate a cursory nod and left.

Holgate turned to Luned. 'You're very honoured. Ogden doesn't usually grace us with his presence.'

Ogden's attendance had created suspicion, so she needed to gain Holgate's trust. 'I don't like him. He's a strange one, isn't he?'

Holgate nodded his approval of Luned's criticism. He tipped his head towards the ambulance. 'Are we ready to go?'

The first two hours involved moving from one jump cover point to another waiting for a call, listening to Holgate's small talk and exchanging gossip about other paramedics. The first substantive call of the morning was to a child who had collapsed at school. After an assessment Holgate decided to take him to hospital and Luned breathed a sigh of relief that one of the teaching assistants accompanied the child. The assistant didn't move from the child's side once as they reached the hospital telling Luned the boy's mother would be arriving very shortly.

After an hour at a jump cover point drinking coffee a call came about a woman with an ear infection and complaints of dizziness. 'Another bloody whinger,' Holgate remonstrated as he accelerated out of the services. 'Don't they know we have better things to do with our time?' After seeing the woman, he spoke to her GP who arranged for an appointment later that afternoon.

The woman was left in her home. Both the patients that morning had been young: not the profile of the elderly vulnerable people Holgate allegedly targeted.

Luned couldn't avoid sitting with Holgate as they ate lunch in a café at the services. Only then did he start asking her about Sydney.

Did she enjoy the sunshine? Where had she lived?

Had she ever been swimming in Bondi Beach?

Had she walked over Sydney Harbour Bridge?

Luned convinced herself she had answered his questions with effective, plausible responses. But he had shown undue interest in her Australian adventure. She couldn't tell whether he believed her, but she certainly hoped so.

At two pm an emergency transfer request reached the ambulance. It meant travelling eighteen miles to the hospital in Holyhead on the other side of Anglesey under emergency driving conditions to pick up a patient from one of the wards and transfer them to a specialist unit. It would mean a round-trip of at least ninety minutes, Luned calculated, even allowing for high-speed driving.

Holgate flicked on the blue lights, got the sirens blaring and left the hospital. Holgate bragged that he had been top of the class when he had undertaken the specialist emergency driving course. And the speed at which he was throwing the ambulance around suggested he was enjoying himself. Once on the A55 he floored the accelerator and Luned grasped the seatbelt tightly hoping he wouldn't notice her discomfort as he hurtled along in the outside lane flashing at the occasional dawdling motorist.

Reaching the hospital in Holyhead meant negotiating various small roundabouts that crisscrossed the retail park on the outskirts of the town. At least Holgate had the common sense to slow down and all of the traffic slowed or stopped allowing him to proceed. After loading the patient quickly they were soon heading back towards Bodelwyddan.

When they arrived at the hospital Luned jumped out of the ambulance as soon as she could, letting out a lungful of air. Holgate took charge of the patient transfer and when he returned simply remarked. 'What have they got in store for us now?'

The final call of the afternoon was to an elderly lady who lived on her own, which immediately put Luned on edge. Rachub was a small village clinging to the foothills of the mountains of Snowdonia. The ambulance powered up towards the bungalow where Jean Jones lived. A BMW X1 sat in the drive, which Sara assumed belonged to the GP who had requested the ambulance.

The front door was ajar and a man wearing casual trousers and a thick navy fleece stood in the hallway reading his mobile telephone. 'Dr Ralston?' Holgate said.

Ralston nodded. 'She's in the bedroom.'

Luned followed Holgate and the doctor into a room at the rear of the property. Ralston sat on the bed where Jean Jones was propped up on pillows against the headboard. The doctor explained to Mrs Jones in Welsh that the paramedics would take her to the hospital. She nodded with relief thanking the doctor profusely.

Ralston stood up and spoke to Holgate. 'She lives on her own and she hasn't got any family. She's become severely dehydrated and I think she may have sepsis. She needs IV fluids, and antibiotics when she gets to hospital. I've already told A&E to expect you.'

'Thanks, doc,' Holgate said.

Ralston picked up his bag and left. Holgate fussed over

Mrs Jones, sitting on the edge of her bed and then turned to Luned. 'You had better get the portable chair from the ambulance. I'll get everything ready for Mrs Jones.'

He made it sound so reasonable. But Luned stood rigid, unable to move, staring at him. He had already looked away, conversing with Mrs Jones who didn't look well. It would only take her seconds now that she knew how to disconnect the portable chair.

'I won't be long,' Luned said.

She left the front door wide open and trotted down to the ambulance, yanking open the rear door and getting inside unclipping and disconnecting the portable chair from its storage position and almost falling over herself in her panic to get back inside. She got back to the front door and found that it was closed.

He's locked me out. Luned's mind darkened.
I might have been able to stop him.
This whole thing is a mad idea.
I should have known better; Superintendent Hobbs *should have known better.*

She reached out a hand to knock on the door.

It opened and Luned noticed the latch was up.

She breathed a sigh of relief, realising Holgate might not have noticed when he pushed the door closed. She walked straight through into the bedroom pushing the portable chair in front of her.

She caught a startled Holgate with his precious belt loop bag open on the bed a syringe laid on top with another smaller alongside it.

'What are you doing?' Luned said.

Holgate looked up and gave her a polished anthracite stare. 'I was about to give Mrs Jones some analgesia.' He snapped his bag shut. 'But it's probably not necessary.'

Holgate kept up a running commentary for Jean Jones' benefit as they manoeuvred her into the ambulance, complementing her extensively on how well she was doing.

It was a short journey to Bangor hospital where they transferred her to A&E. Luned kept a close eye on Holgate.

As it was twenty minutes after the end of their normal shift Holgate announced they could return to the station and finish for the day. They left A&E, Luned carrying the portable chair they'd used to put back on the ambulance. She opened the rear door and clambered aboard.

She heard small talk from the entrance and then the click of the door as it closed behind Holgate.

Kneeling she reattached the chair safely in place for the next shift.

She didn't have the opportunity to straighten up. A hand grasped her head, covering her mouth stifling her scream and then something hard and metallic struck the back of her head. For a second the pain was unbearable.

After that: darkness.

Chapter 42

Drake's anxiety grew when an hour had passed since Luned had finished her shift and she still hadn't made contact. The agreed protocol was for her to call or message him at lunchtime and at the end of the day. He had barely touched his evening meal and he'd glanced at his watch frequently.

'What's wrong?' Annie asked. 'You seem distracted.'

Drake glanced at the mobile sitting on the kitchen table by his side. 'I need to make some calls.'

Downstairs in the spare bedroom he called Winder. 'I haven't heard from her, boss. She hasn't checked in?'

'I'll call Sara,' Drake said.

He finished the call and dialled his sergeant. 'It's not like her,' Sara's voice reflected the concern bubbling up in Drake's mind. Luned was reliable, punctual. He couldn't escape the conclusion that something was wrong.

'I'm going around to her flat.'

'Contact me once you know something, sir.'

Drake finished the call pondering how to explain things to Annie. He had to tell her. So he dropped the mobile back into his pocket and joined her in the kitchen. She looked on open-mouthed as he explained that the paramedic she had met was in fact one of his team. 'I don't believe it. I mean… that you suspect a paramedic of killing people.'

'I need to go and find Luned.' Drake stood up.

'Yes, of course. I hope she's all right.'

In the hallway Drake dragged on a jacket and caught his reflection in the mirror. He looked tired, the bags under his eyes sagged, nothing that a decent night's sleep wouldn't solve, he reassured himself.

He drove to Luned's address and parked a short distance away from the property. The old Edwardian terrace had been converted into flats several years ago and Drake rang the bell of the ground floor apartment. The delay in anyone answering only heightened the apprehension pumping through his veins. A woman opened the door. 'Can

I help?'

'I'm looking for Luned Thomas.'

'She lives in the bottom flat. I haven't seen her tonight.'

'Are you sure?'

'Yes. If I see her can I tell her you called?'

Drake was already on the pavement when he replied. 'No need, thank you.'

Once out of sight of the house he jogged briskly back to his car.

Then he made two telephone calls, telling Winder and Sara to join him at the Caernarfon police station. And asking Winder if he knew the registration number of Luned's car. He fired the engine into life and toured around the immediate vicinity checking for her vehicle. He crawled along the various side streets until he was satisfied there was no sign of it. Then he drove on to the police station.

He cleared a desk in a sergeant's room and instigated the appropriate protocol to pinpoint Luned's mobile. When he was asked to confirm the matter was urgent he raised his voice. 'Just get it bloody well done.'

Next, he requisitioned every piece of footage from the automatic number plate recognition system covering the Bangor and Caernarfon areas that evening. He had to hope that somewhere her vehicle had been recorded. It was after nine-thirty pm when Winder and Sara arrived, both casually dressed. Deep creases wrinkling Sara's forehead. Winder's face etched with worry.

Drake leaned on the desk, staring at both officers. His throat constricted so he kept his voice flat hoping to smother any suggestion he was frightened. 'She completed her shift with Holgate over two hours ago. She was supposed to call me within an hour of finishing, but she didn't do so. I've been to her flat and she hasn't been seen. I toured around the side streets and I couldn't find her car.'

'And her mobile?' Sara said.

'No response. It's not even ringing out. Do either of you

know her friends – anyone she could have gone to stay with?'

Sara made the obvious comment. 'But she would have made contact as agreed.'

Drake looked at Sara, who was still pondering then she added. 'Perhaps we should ask her parents?'

The same thought troubled Drake. Contacting them might alarm them unduly but they had to be told and sooner rather than later.

Drake had to decide. He looked over at Winder. 'I've requisitioned a triangulation report on Luned's mobile. Do the same for Luke Holgate.'

'We won't get the results until the morning.'

'I don't care, Gareth, get it bloody well done. I've already requisitioned ANPR for Luned's car for this evening. Do the same for his vehicle and then get over to his house.'

Drake stood up. 'I'm going to see her parents.'

The drive from Caernarfon to Nefyn took Drake five minutes less than the forty minutes the satnav had predicted. The evening gloom meant he couldn't enjoy the spectacular scenery as he skirted the coastline passing the three peaks of Yr Eifl before turning right for Nefyn. The road was narrow, the traffic was light but even so he couldn't travel at speed.

He found the property without any difficulty and Mr Thomas answered the door. He was a short man with a stubbly moustache and spikes of silver hair dotted all over his skull. Once the introductions had been made, he showed Drake into the kitchen where he sat at the table with his wife. Mrs Thomas was younger than her husband and her demeanour and questions told Drake she was a good deal smarter. Drake explained in clear and unemotional terms that Luned's whereabouts were unaccounted for and that if she spoke to them, they needed to contact him immediately. He didn't dwell on the details of the covert operation, explaining simply that their daughter had been on police business.

'Should we be worried?' Mrs Thomas said.

'I'm sure everything will be fine. Does she have friends she could have gone to stay with at short notice?'

Luned's parents shook their heads in unison.

Mrs Thomas adding. 'She's very quiet, and very private. She really does enjoy her work, Inspector.'

'Although she never talks about it,' Mr Thomas added grudgingly.

His wife implicitly scolded him with her reply. 'She speaks very highly of you, Inspector Drake.'

Mrs Thomas' comments sent a jagged edge of guilt through his mind as he drove from Nefyn. If anything happened to Luned he had been partly to blame – and he'd never forgive himself. He should have objected more vociferously to Hobbs. It was almost midnight when Drake arrived at the police station where Winder was slumped over the computer monitor. 'It could take hours, boss.'

Drake fell into a chair. His mobile rang and he read Sara's number. 'There's nobody at Holgate's property. I called next door on the pretence of making house-to-house inquiries about a local burglary. He hasn't been seen since yesterday.'

Frustration and despair filled his mind and he paced the room until he stopped by the window where he thrust his fingers through the Venetian blinds. The lights of Caernarfon lit up the evening sky. Where was Luned at that precise moment and was she being badly treated? Hobbs would have some explaining to do if things went badly but he couldn't dismiss his own culpability. Should he have objected more? Fear had turned his stomach rigid.

He knew one thing.

He, Sara and Winder weren't going to get much sleep that night.

Chapter 43

Drake couldn't remember the journey to headquarters when he arrived a little before seven the following morning. Guilt mixed with anger and a sense his judgement had been at fault in allowing Luned to participate in such a risky enterprise knotted a thick piece of bile in his stomach. It was urgent they find her.

He bounded up the stairs to the Incident Room and detoured into a bathroom. Drake sensed the need for order tugging at his thoughts, demanding he follow all the right rituals to set his mind at ease.

He had to get clean. His face and hands were grubby. After finishing he looked at himself in the mirror, water dripping off his chin, dotting his white shirt. They had to make progress: find Luned, trace Holgate and then lock him up. Things were never that easy and he knew the first thing he'd need to do was get the columns of Post-it notes on his desk in proper order. He wouldn't be able to think properly until his mind was settled.

He fumbled for the electric switch in the Incident Room and the lights flickered on, illuminating the board and the desks his team would soon occupy. If only it were that easy to make sense of this case.

Comforted when he realised that his office had been cleaned overnight, he booted up his computer, found a duster from a desk drawer and ran it over the keyboard, focusing particularly on the section above the F keys. Then he adjusted the photographs of his daughters and Annie from their holiday in Disneyland Paris before turning his attention to the columns of Post-it notes. He would need to start a new one with the priorities for the day, so he reminded himself of the contents of the previous notes hoping for some inspiration.

His focus was broken when Winder and Sara arrived.

He paced out into the Incident Room exchanging greetings.

Winder was already staring at his monitor. 'We should have the results of the trace on Luned's phone soon.'

'And Holgate's?' Drake said.

Winder continued to peer at the screen. After a few seconds he announced. 'Both the mobile telephones are switched off. I'll arrange to make sure we can monitor in real-time if they're turned on.'

'I want every scrap of ANPR coverage for a fifteen-mile radius from where she was abducted scrutinised.'

Abducted. One of his officers had been kidnapped.

It made him feel sick.

'Then circulate details of Luned and Holgate's vehicle to every traffic cop, every police officer, every community support officer. Somebody, somewhere has seen them.'

Hobbs made a grand entrance before Drake could continue. He was in full uniform and he tugged off his cap before sitting down and gazing over at Drake. There was an edge of menace to his voice. 'Bring me up to date, Inspector.' Drake had spoken with his superior officer twice the previous evening, giving him a summary.

Hobbs nodded his agreement as Drake outlined the action he had authorised that morning. 'I thought Detective Constable Thomas had specific instructions that if she had grounds to suspect Holgate, she was to contact you immediately.'

'We don't know what—'

'I do hope Detective Constable Thomas didn't flaunt the established protocols. I think I made it perfectly clear we didn't want to take any risks whatsoever.'

Drake narrowed his eyes. Now he could see what Hobbs was really made of. He was more concerned about protecting his own reputation, planning his reaction when culpability was to be apportioned. He was going to walk away blameless and he was taking the first steps like some canny politician to point the finger at anyone apart from himself.

'My priority now is to do everything we can to trace Luned and apprehend Holgate.'

Hobbs gave a regal nod of approval. Then he stood up. 'I want hourly updates.' Drake tightened his jaw, wanting to conceal his seething from the rest of his team. He mumbled as he continued. 'I'll organise a search warrant for Holgate's property.'

Sara piped up. 'I'll requisition the latest details of Holgate's financial records. There might be something that will give us a clue as to where he might be.'

Drake nodded but his mind was thinking about what Hobbs was plotting.

Winder said, 'We should find out where Luned and Holgate had been on their last call yesterday afternoon.'

'I agree, get it done. I'm going to call Ogden,' Drake announced. 'Surely one of Holgate's work colleagues must know something about him.'

Luned's abduction changed everything. They needed to find her and if that compromised any future prosecution of Holgate then so be it. The integrity of gathering evidence against Holgate could go to hell. Luned's life was more important. He requisitioned a search warrant and then he called Frank Ogden.

Ogden sounded nonplussed. 'I'm not certain, I never knew much about Luke Holgate.'

Drake stared at the clock on the computer screen. 'I'll be with you in an hour. I want to talk to every single paramedic who has worked with Holgate.'

There was a gasp and a mumble down the telephone which Drake ignored.

He trotted out to the car knowing the formalities for the search warrant could be emailed to him. Complaints from the operational support department that they didn't have anyone available to break the lock at Holgate's property were brushed aside by Drake. 'Have them meet me there in half an hour.'

'Half an hour?' Came the strangled reply. 'And have you got a warrant?'

Drake wasn't going to stand by protocol, the absence of search warrant wasn't going to stop him getting into Holgate's property.

It was thirty-five minutes later when Drake parked his Mondeo on a patch of ground fifty yards or so down from Luke Holgate's home. He'd give operational support another ten minutes before he'd ring and complain.

Holgate's end-of-terrace was in a rural setting in a hamlet on the western side of Anglesey. Behind the three properties were garages and beyond them were a collection of detached houses, a small cottage and then a bungalow that lined the road as it ascended towards the brow of the hill and the junction.

The scientific support vehicle pulled up behind Drake and he got out of the car nodding to both of its occupants to follow him around to the rear. As he did so his phone alerted him to a message, and he smiled as he saw the formal paperwork with the search warrant.

A small paved area led to the back door. The green and black bin and a trolley with recycling bins stood nearby. Drake knocked on the door – no reply. No drawn curtains, no lights and no sign of life. Then he hammered on one of the glass sections – again no reply. He gazed through a window into the kitchen extension. The place looked lived-in, a mug and bowl on the draining board. He jerked his head at the door and an officer broke the lock. Soon he was standing inside Luke Holgate's kitchen.

What was he expecting? To see Luned tied to a chair in one of the rooms?

Even Holgate wouldn't be that stupid.

The downstairs rooms were furnished simply – a dining table and chairs in one and a sofa with a television and a coffee table covered with car magazines in another.

Upstairs were two bedrooms but only one with furniture

– a double bed and a simple wardrobe. Few clothes hung inside. Did Holgate actually live at the property? Drake retraced his steps down to the kitchen and then outside. Two uniformed officers had arrived. 'We're trying to trace the occupant of this property. I want you to make detailed inquiries with all the neighbours. Somebody must have talked to him or seen his car or somebody arriving.'

Both nodded and Drake made for his car.

Holgate had a bolthole and they needed to find it.

Drake reached the main road where he turned south towards the bridge over the Menai Strait and then on to Bangor hospital. He pulled the vehicle onto the grass verge near the entrance of the ambulance service office and stuffed the police 'On Police Business/Heddlu Swyddogol' sign onto the dashboard.

He ran over to the entrance. One of the reception staff waved him through to Ogden's office. The manager stood as he entered, motioning for Drake to sit down. He moved the monitor and Drake saw the flickering images of CCTV footage.

'I found this footage of Holgate and Thomas arriving at the hospital last night.' Ogden said. 'They had brought an elderly woman into A&E. Apparently, she lived alone and the GP had requested she be taken for tests. I double checked with the doctor and he left Holgate and Luned in the house with the patient.'

Drake's stomach lurched.

Holgate's ideal circumstances.

What if Luned caught him in the act? Then the significance of what Ogden had said sank in. 'Is the patient all right?'

Ogden nodded. 'She was sitting up eating her breakfast this morning.'

'Thank Christ for that.'

Drake's focus turned to the CCTV footage. He watched as Luned manhandled the portable chair back into the rear of the ambulance followed moments later by Holgate who closed the door behind him. It was only a few seconds but it felt like minutes until Holgate re-emerged, reclosing the door behind him and walking round to the driver's side. Then the ambulance moved away.

'It wouldn't be normal for Luned Thomas to remain in the rear of the ambulance,' Ogden added sombrely.

A message from Winder reached Drake's mobile before he could reply. *Luned's car has been found.*

Chapter 44

Luned woke and the searing pain that had cracked through her head the night before was no better. It was almost unbearable. She tried to move, but her hands were tethered to the bedstead, as were her ankles. Frantically she shook them hoping to free herself, but she was held in place tightly. The tape that covered her mouth felt chalky and she moved her tongue against the tacky surface. She would kill for some water and she wanted to go to the toilet and her stomach grumbled from hunger.

It was difficult to tell how long she had been unconscious.

She had to think clearly and logically and ignore the pain in her head.

Sunlight pierced through the cracks in wooden slats screwed to the windows outside. She guessed it was mid-morning, maybe even lunchtime.

She had been out for over twelve hours.

Then she heard voices and her heart pounded against her rib cage. Was Holgate returning? Was this the end? What could she do to save herself?

There was more than one voice. How many? She strained to hear. She forced herself to focus and concentrate – four, yes, at least four, perhaps five, men. Some distance away by the sound of their muffled voices. Then the sound of metal against metal and more chatter. If only she could get their attention, if only she could find a way to scream.

She tugged and yanked her ankles and then her arms but she only succeeded in tightening the knots and grazing her skin until she felt the stinging pain and blood flowing on her skin. She paused for a moment deciding that somehow she would have to escape.

The voices didn't stay around for too long and gradually they faded, as her hopes did of being able to summon help. Then she looked around the room. Apart from a chair in one corner and a bucket and a bottle of water alongside it the only other furniture was the bed on which she lay securely bound. Old-fashioned quarry tiles dirty with age covered the floor There were two doors – one by the boarded-up windows and the second near the chair.

She focused on listening to her surroundings.

No sign of traffic, no more conversation but she caught a rhythmical swishing sound. Was it her imagination? Was the lack of water and food having an impact on her mind?

She wanted to believe she could overcome Holgate. But he was taller and stronger than her. She had no doubts now he had been responsible for the six deaths. No doubt at all. Her thoughts turned to her parents. They'd be terrified. She was terrified. She could rely on Drake and Sara and Winder doing everything possible to trace her, but she was in the middle of nowhere. How would they know where to begin looking?

It was late afternoon when she heard the sound of a key in the lock.

She stiffened as Holgate entered. He walked over to the bed removed the tape and she winced in pain. From a plastic carrier bag he produced a bottle of water which he held to her lips. Eagerly she drank the contents although most of it fell over her shirt.

'Why are you doing this?'

Holgate ignored her. Wordlessly he cracked open a supermarket sandwich and fed her. Luned almost choked on the dry bread and chicken filling. When she choked he paused, gave her more water. Then he let her finish the meal. He stepped over to the chair and picked up the bucket and he returned to the side of the bed. Holgate untied the rope binding Luned's legs and her right arm. Then he retreated and sat on the chair.

Luned swung her legs off the bed and looked at the bucket. She knew exactly why it was there and her bladder was bursting. 'Can I have some privacy?'

Holgate said nothing, did nothing, just stared at her.

Luned had no choice. She removed her trousers and underclothes and squatted over the bucket. She turned her back at Holgate – he wasn't going to get the satisfaction of watching her face. When she was finished, she sat back on the edge of the bed. He gestured with his finger for her to lie down. She did as she was told and then he re-tied her ankles to the bottom part of the bedstead.

He reattached the duct tape after her right wrist had been rebound securely to the bedstead.

Then he left her alone again.

Chapter 45

Sand swept into Drake's face as he strode over to Luned's car. It was parked in a layby on a road leading to Aberffraw, a village on the southern coast of Anglesey. Over to his right hillocks of sand dunes dotted the landscape. A uniformed officer from the marked police car at the other end of the layby joined him. Drake snapped on the pair of latex gloves and reached a hand over to the driver's side door and looked inside. No sign of a struggle, no blood. Why was it in this isolated layby on the south of Anglesey?

Drake took a step back. 'Get the CSIs to remove the vehicle. I want it treated as a crime scene.'

The officer nodded.

Drake scrambled to the top of the wall, scanning the surrounding countryside before realising Holgate wouldn't be anywhere nearby. He'd be miles away. The layby had simply been a convenient spot to dump the car.

A message reached his mobile from Superintendent Hobbs requesting a meeting, so Drake jumped back onto the tarmac surface and sprinted back to his car.

At headquarters Drake ignored the yellow disabled driver paint markings on the parking slot and rushed upstairs to the Incident Room.

'I need to update the superintendent,' Drake said between deep breaths.

'I'm working my way through Holgate's finances but I haven't been able to spot anything so far. He withdrew a hundred pounds from a cash machine the evening Luned went missing.'

'Where was that?'

'One of the supermarkets in Bangor.'

'Any CCTV?'

'I've requested all available footage.'

'Good, then we can build a detailed picture before…' Drake stifled what he was really thinking. None of them wanted to contemplate the worse-case scenario.

Drake turned to Winder. 'Any joy with Holgate or Luned's mobiles?'

He shook his head. 'Still switched off.'

'But one piece of good news is that the ANPR system has picked up Holgate's car crossing the Britannia Bridge the evening Luned disappeared.' Winder sounded pleased with himself.

This sliver of information energised Drake.

He looked at Sara. 'Anything from traffic?'

Sara shook her head. It was the same when he asked about reports from community support officers and whether there had been reports about unusual activity, people acting suspiciously. He blew out a mouthful of breath in desperation.

'After I've spoken to Superintendent Hobbs we'll go over to Bangor hospital and interview the paramedics who worked with Holgate.'

'What do we tell them?' Sara said.

Drake was on his feet when he replied. 'We'll think of something.'

Superintendent Hobbs kept Drake standing while he interrogated him about the detail of everything being done to locate Luned. His face disclosed little emotion which Drake found difficult to fathom considering a fellow officer was missing. If he wanted to lay the blame on somebody other than himself then surely it could wait until after she had been discovered. Hobbs gave him a penetrating, razor-like glare with his small dark eyes.

'We may need to make a formal announcement that Detective Constable Luned Thomas is missing and ask for the public's help. Perhaps a press conference might be helpful.'

Shouting his defiance at Hobbs wouldn't help and neither would a press conference, Drake concluded. He managed through gritted teeth. 'Perhaps that could wait. It's not a priority.'

Hobbs nodded his acquiescence and Drake left before he could change his mind.

A convoy of three cars hurried along the A55 towards Bangor, Drake taking the lead in his Mondeo, checking occasionally in his rear-view mirror that Sara and Winder were behind him. At the hospital they parked close to each other and paced over to the ambulance administration centre where Ogden was waiting for them.

'I've got two paramedics here, but others are working, and more are on rest days.'

'Give the details of those not here to Detective Constable Winder – addresses and mobiles. We have to speak to them today. Urgently.'

Drake looked over Ogden's shoulder. 'Where are they?'

He led them through into a conference room.

Drake wasted no time. 'We need to ask you about Luke Holgate.'

'What's this about?' The older of the two replied.

'This is part of a routine inquiry.' Drake used a tone that made quite clear there would be no further explanation.

The younger of the two paramedics left with Sara.

After twenty minutes Drake had exhausted every possible avenue of interrogating the paramedic about Holgate's personal life. He knew little about him and described him as 'odd', and a 'bit eccentric'.

Sara finished the same time as Drake and they sat together comparing notes.

'It only confirms what we know already. Holgate is a sad individual; he's got no friends and likes talking about his medical expertise.'

Drake nodded. 'Let's hope Gareth has more success.'

Drake retraced his steps to his vehicle. His mobile rang and it wasn't a number he recognised. 'This is Sergeant Frost of the BTP.' Drake recognised the shorthand for the British Transport Police, who had responsibility for policing the railways. 'We found a vehicle belonging to Luke Holgate, that I think you're looking for.'

Chapter 46

The city of Bangor nestled between two hills and the railway station was located at a narrow point, the platforms almost spanning the space available between tunnels at either end. Drake arrived at the car park to the south side of the railway station and noticed Sergeant Frost sitting in his marked police vehicle. Drake joined Frost, who led him to the far end of the car park where he pointed to Luke Holgate's vehicle. Instinctively Drake surveyed the surroundings. Two weak lights lit up the car park and a train emerged from the tunnel on the eastern side. It pulled up to a platform and dozens of passengers disembarked, most making their way to their vehicles parked nearby.

Within a few minutes the car park had emptied.

Luke Holgate's vehicle hadn't moved and Drake turned to Frost. 'Are there any CCTV cameras in the station?'

'Not in the car park but there's a camera covering the platforms.'

Drake looked over into the town. Had Holgate simply parked the vehicle and gone over the footbridge crossing the railway and taken a bus somewhere? 'We'll need to see all the footage for the past two days.'

'I'll see what I can do.'

Drake gave him a sharp look. 'How long will it take?'

Frost shrugged unhelpfully. 'Let's go over to the office.' He nodded towards the building at the end of the opposite platform.

Drake's frustration at the volume of red tape needed to requisition the relevant footage made him raise his voice to the woman at the other end of the telephone. She was in a call centre in Crewe and she was about to finish her shift for the evening. 'There's no point shouting at me, dear. I'll do what I can to get the footage you need to Sergeant Frost by first thing tomorrow morning.' Drake didn't say anything but accepted angrily the inevitability he couldn't do anything further.

He left the BTP officer as the Holyhead to London train hauled its way from the tunnel into the platform. Passengers prepared to embark, and Drake hurried over the bridge back to his car. He called Winder for an update – two paramedics he had spoken to had little constructive to add to the picture of Holgate as a loner, an oddball, but they knew that already. None socialised regularly with Luke Holgate. None of them knew anything about his private life. All of them had expressed revulsion at comments Holgate had made on his social media pages.

Drake looked over at Luke Holgate's car. How did you get away with this for so long? Indulging eccentric and strange people was one thing but how had so many people turned a blind eye to Holgate over the years?

Drake drove home. Annie made a meal that he picked at. She asked about progress – he told her as much as he could.

A nightmare dragged him from unconsciousness a little after five am. He was walking towards an ambulance near a deserted farmhouse and the police officers and paramedics passing him all shook their heads mournfully. Then a hearse drew up and Lee Kings the pathologist shouted over at him. He couldn't hear what was being said. But he knew things were bad.

Splashing water over his face in the bathroom he tried to shake off the possibility that Luned had been killed. But he knew that unless they found her very soon the probability was becoming more and more likely. Without disturbing Annie, he showered and left the house. He detoured around the car park at Bangor railway station and saw that Holgate's vehicle was still there.

He drove through the quiet, deserted streets of Bangor heading for headquarters.

When Sara and Winder arrived, Drake sat with them around the desks in the Incident Room quietly determining priorities for the morning. From the bags under their eyes and their drawn complexions Drake guessed that neither Winder nor Sara had slept much.

'That final paramedic I spoke to couldn't add anything.' Winder said. 'He was still in bed when I arrived at his place and he was really pissed off. He only worked with Holgate on a couple of shifts. He told Ogden he didn't want to be rostered with him again, thought the guy was strange.'

Sara nodded. 'All the paramedics confirm the same.'

Drake let out an exasperated grunt. 'How the hell could they let a man like Holgate continue as a paramedic?'

By mid-morning Drake had ploughed through several hours of CCTV footage from the cameras at Bangor railway station. Their precise positioning made it difficult to be confident that every single passenger had been recorded. Sara watched the footage for the eastbound platform whereas Drake had chosen the trains departing westwards for Holyhead.

Winder had been uncharacteristically quiet and through the open door of his office Drake had heard him chasing traffic officers and contacting the various police stations checking on any sign of Luke Holgate being spotted. There was mention of a motorcycle at one point but Drake kept his focus on the footage playing on the monitor on his desk.

When he saw a figure resembling Luke Holgate walking underneath the camera towards the two-carriage train and entering the first door Drake guessed that the paramedic had been skulking out of sight. The short length of the train and the way that it had stopped at the platform forced him to act as he did. Drake bellowed at the other two officers. 'Get in here.'

Sara and Winder bustled into his office and stood staring at the monitor.

'That's him all right, boss,' Winder said.

'What time is that train?' Sara said.

Drake already had the information. It left at 2.43 pm. It was one of the trains that calls at all the stations on

Anglesey.

'I'll get details of the staff working on the train. They might remember if he got off before Holyhead.'

Sara now. 'There might be CCTV footage from the terminus station at Holyhead.'

Drake nodded.

Sara hadn't slept well and after tossing and turning she found herself staring at the ceiling worrying about Luned. She got up and went running, hoping it would help clear her mind, prepare her for the day ahead.

Inspector Drake looked pale and, after his briefing, Sara checked again if Luned's mobile had been switched on. The disappointment cut into her like a scalpel. Updating the latest financial reports on Holgate she discovered he had used his debit card at a garage. Her adrenaline spiked and she grabbed the telephone and then googled the number.

A lazy voice answered. 'Yes.'

'I need to speak to the owner.'

'Just a sec.'

The second lasted for minutes or so it seemed until she heard a voice. 'I'm the manager.'

Sara got to her feet as she explained what she needed.

'I'm not sure I can send you the CCTV footage.'

'If you don't send me what I need in the next half an hour I'll personally come and arrest you for obstructing justice.'

'Okay, okay. I'll do what I can.'

Sara couldn't concentrate on anything else and she distracted herself in the kitchen making tea. It was thirty-five minutes later when an email appeared in her inbox and she opened the attached CCTV footage. Her heart pounded as she watched Holgate, clad in biker gear walking up to the counter. It took her another few minutes to locate the footage from outside but then she saw Holgate heading back to a motorcycle.

She yelled for Winder and Drake. 'I've found him,'
Both men joined her and stared at the images.
'Where was this?' Drake said.
'Pentraeth, on Anglesey.'
'What the hell is he doing there?'

Chapter 47

After a few hours of fitful sleep, Luned had woken in the middle of the night convinced someone was in the room, that *he* had returned. But she was alone, and she dozed until a stabbing pain jolted her awake. She prayed it wasn't cramp announcing its arrival in her left leg so she tried to flex it until she winced in pain. It only made the discomfort worse.

Scratching from the far corner took her attention as she squinted through the darkness, willing her eyes to discover the source. The occasional flash of meagre moonlight through the cracks in the boards over the windows didn't help. Outside the sound of an animal sniffing the ground, rubbing the soil reminded her she had nocturnal neighbours.

She gave the binds holding her legs in place a useless jerk. If she kicked hard enough could she wrench the rope off the bedstead? She would probably break her ankle in the process. If she wriggled any more they'd be blood around her wrists. An opportunity would arise to overpower Holgate, she persuaded herself. How would she do it? Could she grab the bucket and throw its contents at him? Not if she was still tied to the bed.

Despite the scant mouthfuls of water, she wanted to urinate again. If she peed on the bedding perhaps that might give her more of a chance. But she couldn't bring herself to contemplate it. She fell into a thin, restless sleep, her mind tortured about how Holgate had behaved, cursing herself for having allowed him to get the better of her.

She woke later but had no sense of time. She could have slept for two hours or four. She blinked against the narrow shards of sunlight that forced their way through the cracks in the boards on the windows that had become her only measurement of time. How strong was the sun? Were the windows facing west or east?

She despaired. It was so difficult to fathom out where the sun set.

Holgate had taken her watch, so it was impossible to

measure time.

She would have to lie and wait. She felt dirty, her face sweaty and oily and her clothes filthy.

Then she heard muffled conversations. The voices neared, grew louder and excitement at the possibility of attracting attention grew. The intensity of the chatter slowed, and she tried to shout through the tape. Her muffled cry was useless. She gave the bedstead another heave. If only she could get her hands free, tear off the tape and raise the alarm.

The sound of a strimmer, maybe even more than one, broke the silence. The engine raced as its line tore through grass and weed as the revs peaked and it struggled against resistance.

Her muffled screaming made her jaw ache but she discovered that the movement had loosened the tape. A glimmer of hope flickered in her mind. First she used her tongue and pushed it against the tape. It tasted disgusting but she continued pressing at the gap between her lips hoping to dislodge enough of the tape so she could scream out loud. Then she wiggled her jaw relentlessly backwards and forwards. There was little movement in the tape and when she contemplated that none of the men outside would hear her above the strimmer's noise her exertions seemed pointless.

But they were her only hope. Minute after minute passed and she felt her jaw would break and that she might be sick from the taste of the adhesive in her mouth. Luckily Holgate had used the same tape as when he had first locked her in the room.

It must be an isolated spot she told herself. He wouldn't risk the incarceration where a chance encounter might discover her.

The strimmers stopped. Conversations reignited. She pressed harder with her tongue and jaw sensing she was making infinitesimal progress. She dropped her chin and the bottom corners of the tape sagged.

Success. At least in part.

Please don't restart the strimming, Luned pleaded to herself. But it was no good. First one and then a second strimmer roared into life and worst of all they moved away, the sound diminishing.

Soon there would be silence again.

Soon Holgate would return.

Soon it meant her one opportunity was passing.

She thought of her mother and that she would always tell her to do her best. Luned got back to wiggling her jaw and pushing her tongue but the gap between her lips was narrow and her jaw ached. But she was making progress and soon enough her mouth widened – the tape was loosening but at the same time the sound of the strimmers had vanished into the distance. She hoped her chances of discovery weren't disappearing as well.

Seconds later her bottom lip loosened from underneath the tape.

Then she screamed.

It amazed her she had any saliva in her mouth to enable her to shout so loudly. But the strimmer's noise made it hopeless.

But she continued her yelling – bellowing at the top of her voice – help!

When the strimmer's abruptly stopped, she paused for a second and heard the voices. They were men talking and laughing and joking in Welsh. Workmen nearby?

She prayed they were near enough to hear her and that she was screeching loud enough. Then she had one voice louder than the others. She couldn't quite catch what he said. Then she heard distinctly. *Mae 'na rhywun yn yr hen le.*

Relief crashed over her like a chunk of melting glacier smashing into the sea. The voice knew that there was somebody in the 'old place' and it had to be her. So she carried on shouting for help. Seconds later the little light that streamed through the cracks was obliterated by silhouettes, one at first, then two and then three.

She cried for help. *Helpwch fi. Plîs.*

She heard a voice announcing they had to find a way in. Moments later she heard a rattling beyond the two doors into her room but nothing else and her despair returned. A voice kept up a running conversation with her asking if she was all right. She explained that she had been kidnapped and was tied to a bed. It sounded melodramatic, absurd even.

Wood splintering and the chatter of men heaving metal against timber filled the air.

Tynna'r blydi peth.

Luned realised that if they were close to removing the slats she was almost free. She wanted to cry.

Daylight flooded into her makeshift cell once the largest section had been removed. A voice told her to turn her head away as he gave the glass a gentle tap. The shards fell on the floor and hands reached in to pull outside the large fragments of glass. It felt like minutes, but it was probably no more than a few seconds by the time two burly men in high visibility jackets were inside untying Luned. She hung on to them as they helped her through the shattered window.

She stood on an old concrete railway platform in the middle of the countryside, she couldn't see another house for miles, the tracks from the old railway snaked away into the distance, the permanent way nearby shrouded with cuttings of bramble and gorse and thick grass. In a field nearby the blades of wind turbines turned relentlessly and Luned recognised the swishing noise. The movement took her gaze and her head spun. Then she collapsed in a heap.

Chapter 48

Drake's telephone rang as he finished speaking with the guard on the train Holgate had boarded. The man had no recollection of the passengers who alighted at the various request stops on Anglesey. Anger and frustration made Drake snatch at the handset on his desk.

'Drake.'

'I have an urgent call for you.' The sound of the woman on reception sounded deadpan.

'Is that Inspector Drake?'

'How can I help?'

'We've got Luned Thomas here.'

The shock made Drake stand up, then he bellowed Sara's name before asking the caller.

'Who are you.'

'My name is William Parry,' Drake recognised the Anglesey accent. 'We were clearing an old section of the railway line between Llangefni and Amlwch when we heard someone shouting.' Sara reached the threshold of his office, Winder behind her. Drake gesticulated energetically for them to enter. 'How is she?'

'She's okay, I suppose.'

'Give me your mobile number and postcode. We'll be there as quick as we can.'

He leaned down scribbling the details on a Post-it note before he turned to Sara and Winder.

'Luned's been found.'

'Thank God for that,' Sara said.

'Let's go.' Drake scrambled for his jacket and they jogged out of the Incident Room down the staircase to reception and then out to the car park. En route Drake called the duty inspector for Anglesey demanding he send a vehicle urgently to the address he'd been given.

Sara, sitting in the passenger seat, looked over at Drake, her voice heavy with concern. 'Did he say if she had been harmed?'

Drake shook his head. 'He said she's okay.'

After taking the exit slip for Llangefni he drove through the town and then northwards. The roads narrowed, the hedgerows thickened and the settlements thinned to the occasional group of cottages or farmhouse nestled around a yard and outbuildings.

The road crossed a narrow bridge and Drake caught a glimpse of the outline of an overgrown railway track snaking northward into the distance. After fifty yards, give or take, an officer stood at a junction. Drake slowed and followed the instructions towards a dilapidated property. It looked like an old station building. A van had been parked nearby and Drake drew up alongside. He could see Luned in the rear covered in a blanket the lapels of a high visibility jacket peeping out underneath it.

He left the car, and with Sara they made their way over.

A man in his late sixties sat in the passenger seat, and he jumped out when he saw Drake and Sara approaching. Drake got into the rear of the vehicle followed by Sara who gave Luned an enormous hug pulling her close to her body. Luned looked awful, pale and shrunken, her hair matted, her eyes exhausted.

'There's a gang of us who work with the Anglesey Central Railway. We're trying to reopen the disused railway line. We worked up from a crossing to the old station. Then we heard the screaming.'

Sara produced from a bag the sandwiches and drinks they had purchased from a convenience store on the journey. Luned ate hungrily.

'How do you feel?' Drake said.

She gave an exhausted exclamation. 'It was Holgate.'

Drake nodded. 'We need to get you to hospital.'

'I'll be all right.'

Drake turned to Parry. 'Show me where you found her.'

Drake looked over at Sara, giving her a look that told her to stay with Luned.

Parry led Drake to the building. 'It was one of the stops on the line that closed in 1965 at the time of the Beeching cuts.'

It was a squat building of red brick and tall chimney stacks. The windows on the side they'd approached had been bricked up. It had the feel of a typical substantial Victorian building. Drake could imagine staff employed when it first opened: a station manager, a porter even. The platform was a narrow, small concrete construction, its surface thick with weeds and grass. Cherry trees had invaded one end, spreading down onto the tracks that were totally overgrown and obliterated by the vegetation. Parry walked up the platform towards the end nodding for Drake to follow him. He stopped and looked over at the smashed window and broken timber. 'She was inside.'

Drake stared in. It looked cold and miserable.

The germ of an idea formed in his mind. He faced Parry. 'How many of you are there?'

Parry dipped his head northward along the track bed. 'Five of us. We worked up along the track from the gate over there.'

'Has anybody else been around this morning?'

Parry shook his head. 'This is quite an isolated spot.'

Holgate had made that assumption and he must have planned to return. But seeing the van and the cars would spook him. 'I want you to listen very carefully. I want you and the others to gather your kit and leave. We'll look after Constable Thomas from here.'

'What happened? I mean why was she abducted?'

Drake kept his voice low. 'I'd really appreciate if you said nothing at all to anybody.'

Parry looked shocked. 'Of course, I understand.'

Drake retraced his steps along the platform and his attention was taken by another door and the window next to it. The lock on the door looked new and he jerked the handle but it was locked. Then he cupped his hands and peered through the glass but the inside surface was filthy. Even so Drake made out the outline of furniture and clothes draped on a chair. He returned to the makeshift car park where he organised for the marked police car to take Luned to the local hospital for a check-up.

Once they had left, Drake turned to Sara and Winder. 'It looks like he was using a room in the old station building. Now we wait for him.'

Before leaving, Parry and the other volunteers patched up the boards over the broken window. Holgate would approach the old station building on his motorcycle, so Drake opened a map of the surrounding area on his mobile. What would they do without Google maps?

Finding a place to park their vehicles without drawing attention was difficult. Drake walked back over the railway bridge and the road turned sharply to his left. Nearby was a typical Welsh cottage, its slate roof sagging. A gate nearby led to a small garage at the rear. It would have to do.

Returning to the entrance for the station building Drake met Sara and Winder returning from the T-junction a few metres beyond the entrance. Winder piped up. 'We're parked in a field gate but it's only giving us a fairly limited view. We need more officers.'

That would take time, involve more activity and Holgate could arrive at any moment to check on his captive. Luned was safe, their main priority secure. 'We'll do what we can. I don't want to scare him off.'

A few minutes later Drake had spoken with an elderly couple living in the cottage down from the bridge who looked at him in wide-eyed amazement. He reversed the Mondeo into the gravel strewn drive, it was narrower and shorter than he had first assessed. The nose of his car almost jutted onto the tarmac and he hoped it wouldn't draw Holgate's attention.

Then he waited.

He called Hobbs: the relief evident in his voice. 'I'll call her parents.' Drake called Ogden notifying him too that Luned had been found. 'Thank Christ for that.'

'Have you had any contact from Luke Holgate?'

'None.'

'If you do, call me immediately. And don't mention anything about Constable Thomas.'

Drake called or texted Winder and Sara every few minutes, but as the light faded by the end of the afternoon Drake fretted that Holgate had been spooked, that he wasn't going to return. How long would they wait?

He didn't need to answer that question as a motorcyclist flashed past him.

There had been little activity on the road until then. Drake notified Winder and Sara and pulled the Mondeo out of the drive and up the road towards the crest of the bridge over the railway. The motorcyclist was stationary at the junction staring down at the railway building.

Drake heard the blood thumping in his veins and drove his vehicle up to the brow of the bridge, pausing for a moment. Beyond the motorcyclist Winder had stopped at the T-junction.

Holgate was trapped. He glanced to his right, then to his left.

Then he fiddled with the handlebar controls and in a fraction of a second his motorcycle hurtled its way down towards the railway building. Where was he going? There was no way out.

Drake paused. Sara rang. 'Where's he gone, boss?'

Holgate hurtled down the platform passing the station building. 'Christ, he's going down the railway line.'

Then Drake recalled the comments by William Parry about a field gate crossing the line so he powered the car down off the bridge towards Winder and Sara flashing his headlights, gesticulating with his arm for them to head northwards down the road.

They reached a junction and Drake noticed a

dilapidated gate in front of the crossing. The fence alongside it was flat and ahead of them Drake heard a motorcycle accelerating away into the twilight of the late afternoon. Winder and Sara were in front of him as both vehicles sprinted ahead.

He fiddled with the hands-free on his mobile calling area control yelling instructions for every available road traffic unit and officers to make their way to the north-east corner of Anglesey.

They would trap him soon enough.

He had nowhere to go.

The last thing Drake wanted to do was criss-cross the narrow country lanes of Anglesey. A motorcyclist could do it so much easier than two vehicles. They pulled up at a T-junction and Winder and Sara ahead of Drake paused before taking a left. He followed them and as the road headed towards Parys Mountain, Drake saw in the distance the motorcycle speeding away. Copper mining over centuries had disfigured the place, scarring the land a dark rusty colour. Holgate pressed on. Where on earth was he going?

At the top of Parys Mountain, Winder and Sara's stationary brake lights shone. Ahead of them Drake saw Holgate's discarded motorcycle.

He parked and leapt out of the car, jogging to join Winder and Sara.

'Where the hell has he gone?' Drake said.

They set off running along different paths. It took Drake down into the old workings. The place looked like something from a dystopian television drama. He half expected Mad Max to appear driving some enormous tractor but there were just pools of red water and industrial decay. And no signal. He couldn't contact Winder or Sara.

He ran on and found the entrance to an old working, a metal frame covered in chicken wire discarded to one side. He darted inside switching on the torch function on his mobile. This wasn't a place to be running in black brogues and a suit so he slowed. To his right he caught sight of the figure darting into another tunnel. And then the sound of urgent footsteps. Drake retraced the steps, his heart clawing at his rib cage as he found the entrance.

Seconds later the same figure ran past him back up the track. Drake set off in pursuit. He wasn't going to let Holgate escape this easily. The paramedic glanced over his shoulder and put on a spurt that gained him a few valuable yards. At the top of an incline Holgate peeked at Drake, smirking as he did so.

It didn't last long, Winder's body hurled itself at Holgate. Both men crashed to the ground. Drake heard a yelp of pain.

He was alongside them in seconds.

'My arm, my fucking arm,' Holgate yelped.

'Luke Holgate, I'm arresting you on suspicion of murder. You do not have to say anything but anything you do say…'

Chapter 49

The urgent medical attention Luke Holgate needed to his broken arm meant an interview with him wouldn't begin until the following morning. Drake returned to the station building, accompanied by Mike Foulds and a CSI team.

Drake jerked his head at the locked door. 'We need to get inside.'

'No problem,' Foulds said.

Seconds later Drake stepped inside and clammy stale air filled his nostrils. Drake and Foulds used their mobiles to illuminate the darkness.

'I'll get one of the lads to set up a floodlight. We'll be able to get a better look then.'

Drake spotted two chairs, one had clothes piled on the seat. Using a latex-gloved hand Drake moved the fleece and jeans to one side. Underneath the chair were a pair of mud-caked boots. Had he discovered the clothes Holgate used to return to Isaac's home?

'Mike,' Drake bellowed.

Foulds appeared in the doorway.

'I want these items of clothes and boots checked first.'

'Sure thing.'

Drake left the CSIs to their work and he travelled to Holgate's home where he joined Sara and the search team as they dismantled his home. A space at the rear of the garage that stood alongside the property had been converted into a makeshift study. Several well-thumbed books that recorded the activity of healthcare serial killers filled a small bookcase. Concealed at the bottom of a small filing cabinet was a cardboard box containing several large syringes and a plastic contraption with small taps that looked like it connected to an intravenous cannula. It gave Drake more valuable evidence.

They called at the hospital to speak to Luned, but she was asleep and the doctor on duty explained that apart from bruising to her ankles and wrists she was unharmed. He prescribed a restorative night's sleep.

Annie was waiting up for Drake when he finally arrived home. A warm smile puckered her cheeks when he confirmed Luned was safe and well and fast asleep in hospital.

'Have you eaten?'

He thought about a reply, but he couldn't remember. Did he have a sandwich at lunchtime? He remembered Sara offering him a bottle of water sometime in the afternoon that he had drunk gratefully. Tiredness dragged at the back of his neck and burned his eyes. He finished a glass of water as Annie made him scrambled eggs. He cleared the plate hungrily.

'You need some time off after this case is over,' Annie said.

She was right of course but tomorrow he had Luke Holgate to interview.

He woke the following morning convinced he hadn't moved an inch all night. He glanced lazily at the clock. The custody time limits wouldn't wait so he dragged himself out of bed and showered. After a rushed breakfast he got to his car; a weekend always meant the traffic was light. Ordinary people, with straightforward lives, were at home with their families, enjoying breakfast in bed or a leisurely walk. But Drake was off to interrogate a murderer.

He called Sara. She excused her breathlessness with an explanation that she had just finished a five-mile run. It amazed him how anyone could be that energetic in the morning. They agreed a time to meet to plan for their interview and Drake called the area custody suite. The sergeant on duty confirmed Holgate had slept all night, eaten breakfast and was still complaining about the pain he suffered from his broken arm. The sergeant attempted humour. 'You can autograph the cast when you're here.'

Drake's final call was to Superintendent Hobbs confirming the arrangements for the interview. Holgate wouldn't be released. Charging him with abducting Luned would be more than enough to justify his remand in custody.

Drake reached his office – the important part of their work been completed, Holgate had been arrested. But they still had hundreds of hours of interviews ahead of them.

Winder arrived soon after. 'Morning, boss.' Relief tinged his greeting. 'I spoke to the hospital on the way in. Luned's better this morning. She was up, talking, having breakfast.' Now he sounded thrilled.

'I called too,' Drake smiled. 'It was good to hear she's okay.'

Once Sara arrived, they planned the outline of their interview.

As she sat down the telephone rang and he recognised Kings' number.

'Good morning, Lee.'

'The syringes you discovered are 50 ml versions and would let him inject fatal amounts of air into the patient's veins. And you also recovered a three-way tap used in hospital that Holgate had adapted to connect directly to an oxygen cylinder. I experimented this morning – quite macabre.'

'Thanks Lee.'

'Do you have the evidence you need?'

'I hope so.' Drake rang off and got to work with Sara.

By late morning Foulds announced his arrival with a greeting to the team in the Incident Room. Then he stood on the threshold of Drake's office. 'Good morning, Ian. The clothes in that old place came up trumps.'

Drake waved Foulds into his room.

'There were glass fragments in the trousers that match the glass in the windows at Isaac's home. And I'm guessing that the mud on the boots came from the field near Isaac's home or his garden.'

Drake wanted to punch the air, but he settled for a grateful nod. It was another piece of the jigsaw. Then

Winder appeared in the doorway to his office clutching pieces of paper.

'I printed out some notes Holgate had made on his mobile.' He handed it to the inspector. 'You were right, boss. It's Capon's and Isaac's dates of birth, and both correspond to their key safe codes.'

A smile broke over Drake's face.

'Looks like you've got him bang to rights,' Foulds said.

It was early afternoon by the time Drake and Sara reached the area custody suite and spoke to the sergeant. They collected the tapes and headed for the interview room.

Drake nodded to Pat Stokes, one of the regular solicitors, who represented clients being interviewed by the police. She gave Drake an uncertain look. Holgate sat by her side sharing a lazy and disinterested glance with Drake and Sara.

Drake said nothing although he could tell from Stokes' body language she was expecting some small talk. He fiddled with the cassettes, dropping each into the compartments in the machine sitting on the table. Looking over at Holgate who was checking the fingernails of his left hand Drake wondered how he'd respond. Then he glanced at Stokes and nodded.

Instead of starting with some preliminary questions Drake looked over at Stokes and proceeded to arrest Luke Holgate for the murder of six individuals he named slowly. He cautioned Holgate who only looked up once Drake had finished, shaking his head incredulously.

Drake placed six photographs on the table facing Holgate and Stokes and identified each in turn before pushing the image of Emyr Isaac an inch or so nearer to Holgate. 'Do you remember Emyr Isaac?'

Holgate stared at the image and then up at Drake raising a quizzical eyebrow. He said nothing.

'On the evening before he died you were one of the

paramedics called to his home. We have a statement from your colleague who confirms that once you had treated Emyr Isaac he left you alone with Mr Isaac whilst he returned to the ambulance. Is that correct?'

Holgate took in a breath and let it out slowly. He gave Drake a what-on-earth-are-you-talking-about look.

'The following morning Mr Isaac was found by a carer in a pool of blood. It appeared that he had fallen against the metal surround of the gas fire in his bedroom. Was Mr Isaac alive when you left him?'

Holgate gave an incredulous turn of his head.

'Bruising on Mr Isaac's arms and wrists suggest he struggled with someone.'

'That's not a question, inspector,' Stokes said.

'I believe you returned later that evening to stage a burglary to deflect attention away from you.'

'Another statement, Inspector.'

Drake kept looking straight at Holgate, sensing he was laughing at them, jeering.

'Did you smash the window at Mr Isaac's home after you'd returned at the end of you shift?'

Holgate shook his head pitifully.

Drake repositioned the photograph of Isaac alongside the others and then pushed David Morris's image towards Holgate.

'The evening before Mr Morris died you and a colleague went to his property. Did you speak to him?'

No reply.

'Mr Morris was quite well known and a well-liked character. But a combination of circumstances meant a full post-mortem became necessary and the CT scan revealed the initial post-mortem results of a heart attack was incorrect. Mr Morris had died from an embolism as a result of air being injected directly into a vein. And you visited Morris the evening he died.'

'And how are you suggesting my client could have been

responsible for that?'

Drake reached into the folder on the table. He produced a series of photographs of the various syringes recovered from Holgate's property. 'In order to inject someone with enough air to cause a fatal embolism a large syringe is needed.' Drake tapped the images he had placed on the desk. 'Like these removed from your home, Luke. And like the one you were about to use on the patient when Luned Thomas caught you in the act.'

Holgate chortled his amazement. 'This is mad. I'm a paramedic. I wouldn't kill anybody. I've never killed anybody. What you're saying is completely insane.'

At least he was responding, Drake thought.

It took Drake another three hours to go through the precise circumstances for the deaths of John Kerr, Michael Capon and William Longman.

Each time Holgate responded with body language suggesting disbelief mixed with shock. He held up his hands feigning blamelessness. He rolled his eyes. He squinted at Drake and Sara disbelievingly. He made convincing sounding pleas of innocence.

'But you have absolutely no evidence my client was directly responsible for any of these deaths.' Stokes announced. 'My client didn't attend at Capon's house the night he died so suggesting he killed him is preposterous.'

Drake ignored her but he couldn't ignore Holgate's convoluted explanation.

He was staring at a healthcare serial killer with a cold dark heart. But the face showed a different persona to the world. Behind the eyes was evil and Drake shivered.

He found the screen shots from Holgate's mobile. Let's have your explanation for the numbers, Drake thought.

'We discovered several notes on your mobile.' Drake looked up at Holgate. Nothing in his expression suggested he knew what was coming.

He pushed over printed copies of the notes.

'Please explain the entry CA followed by six numbers.'

Holgate gave it a puzzled look as though he was surprised.

'Why did you make this note and what does it relate to?'

Holgate blinked but said nothing.

'The note relates to Mr Capon and the numbers are his date of birth. Is it correct that when you receive a call the patient's date of birth is notified to you?'

Holgate looked over at his lawyer perplexed. Stokes said nothing.

'Because Mr Capon's date of birth was the security code to his key safe.'

Drake caught the slightest hint of a sinister veil crossing Holgate's face but it was gone in seconds.

'And you made a record of Mr Capon's details when you called at his home the week before his death. It was a precaution wasn't it – in case you didn't have the opportunity to kill when you were there on duty. Did you return later that day or during the small hours of the following morning to kill Mr Capon?'

Holgate clenched his jaw for a moment before shaking his head disbelievingly.

'Take a look at the other set of letters and numbers. Did you make this record?'

Holgate stared at the details of Isaac's date of birth, but again made no reply.

'It's Emyr Isaac's date of birth. Why did you make a record of his details on your mobile?

Holgate responded by pushing over the sheets dismissively at Drake.

From a folder on the desk Drake produced two photographs of Holgate's jeans and boots. He placed them in front of Holgate. Then he waited. Stokes was the first to look up.

'These are items of clothing recovered from the old

station building where you kept DC Thomas. Do they belong to you?'

'I don't know what this is about. There has been some terrible mistake.'

Drake ignored Holgate. 'We recovered glass fragments from the jeans that match the glass in Emyr Isaac's home. Can you explain that?'

Holgate puckered his cheeks and shook his head mournfully.

'And the boots we recovered are being forensically examined for any trace of a link to Mr Isaac's garden.'

A flash of hatred sparked across Holgate's eyes.

It was cold and dark and evil.

What would Grant Ibbott make of the video recording? It would probably be the stuff of academic research in the future.

Drake had left the footage from the A&E department when Victoria Rowlands had been admitted to the end of the interview. He nodded to Sara who opened the laptop sitting in front of her.

Drake pointed to the image of Victoria Rowlands. 'We'd like you to look at this video footage from the evening Victoria Rowlands was admitted to hospital.' He kept his gaze fixed on Luke Holgate as he and Stokes watched the monitor.

'Can you explain to us what you are doing with Mrs Rowlands?'

No reply.

'You had no connection with her. You hadn't brought her into the hospital, had you?'

Holgate glanced at the ceiling, letting out a long disbelieving lungful of air.

'We have a detailed account of Mrs Rowlands' care at the hospital once she was admitted. She died a few hours after you had injected her. Why did you do it, Luke?'

Now Holgate tut-tutted and shook his head, scolding

Drake as though the inspector were a mischievous schoolchild. Drake glanced over at Sara, she gave him a glance that shared his incredulity.

'We recovered several large syringes, a stash of Class A drugs from your property as well as several books relating to serial killers. Can you explain why you had these items?'

Holgate folded his arms together, drew them close to his chest and said nothing.

Drake finished the interview by asking him about the abduction of Luned.

Stokes interrupted Drake. 'Was this covert operation authorised properly?'

'Full disclosure of everything related to this inquiry will be made in due course.'

By the end of the afternoon Holgate had still refused to speak and was taken back to his cell. Stokes made comments about the difficulties the prosecution faced in proving evidentially that her client was responsible. 'He's going down for a very, very long time.' Drake said to her as she left the custody suite.

He enjoyed the catharsis of venting his spleen at Holgate's solicitor.

He had spent hours in an airless claustrophobic interview with a man who was utterly sick. He wanted to leave, get away from the custody suite, remind himself that humanity was better than this. He finished the paperwork with the custody sergeant and Sara joined him as they left.

'What did you make of them boss?' Sara said.

'I feel drained. That was one of the strangest, darkest interviews I have ever done. I never want to be involved with anything like that ever again.'

Chapter 50

Drake arrived at headquarters in good time for his meeting with Superintendent Hobbs and Andy Thorsen, the senior Crown prosecution lawyer. He wore his most sombre navy suit, a powder blue shirt and a silk tie with discrete burgundy stripes. Drake had spent hours earlier that week preparing all the paperwork, marshalling all the relevant arguments. A decision would be made that morning about the final charges Luke Holgate would face. Rachel and Peter Ackroyd had already appeared before the magistrates and had been lucky to receive a suspended sentence for the theft from Isaac's home. But without evidence against Mervyn Ostler there was nothing they could do and he escaped prosecution, for now. Drake had little doubt he would be back in trouble soon enough.

A senior manager at the Shropshire County hospital adopted a serious tone when he had explained that 'certain irregularities' had occurred in the assessments of death rates during Luke Holgate's shifts. It was going to take them hundreds of hours to make a proper assessment.

Drake had a similar conversation with a manager from a hospital in the north-east of England where Holgate had worked. 'I can't believe it,' the man had said in dire tones after he confirmed there would be a detailed analysis of Luke Holgate's employment.

If there was enough to justify an investigation into Holgate's employment history at both these hospitals it would be a job for the local police forces in Shropshire and Newcastle. Drake didn't think he could stomach the prospect of investigating another link to Luke Holgate. All he wanted to do was see Holgate charged, convicted for multiple murders and locked up.

But his fitness to stand trial was a concern. Drake arrived in the senior management suite in good time and Hannah showed him into Hobbs' room where the superintendent and Thorsen were sitting around the paper-strewn conference table.

'Let's start with the straightforward decision,' Andy Thorsen announced using his best businesslike voice.

The senior Crown prosecution lawyer usually managed a disinterested, deadpan delivery allowing Superintendent Price to inject emotion and what little humour was possible. But it was Superintendent Hobbs in charge now and consciously or not he had adopted a detached officious approach to the meeting.

Luke Holgate had been charged with the abduction and imprisonment of Luned. His initial appearance at the magistrates' court had created a melee with dozens of reporters jostling for the few slots available in the public seating area. Outside, the building had been bathed with lights from the television crews. Journalists from Canada and America had badgered Drake, firing questions incessantly at him when he had arrived and when he left.

Drake had watched the news that evening as journalists chased the van taking Holgate away from the court back to prison. Susan Howells from public relations had become more and more irritable, complaining about stress and demanding to be told when a decision was likely to be taken about the murders.

So the decisions made that morning were likely to gain real attention.

'We charge him with the attempted murder of Jean Jones. Detective Constable Luned Thomas is an eyewitness. He offered no reasonable explanation for having these large syringes secreted in a bag that wasn't standard issue.'

Thorsen looked over the table at Drake. 'Constable Thomas has to be complimented on her bravery. I appreciate why the decision was taken to launch this covert operation. I'm not going to pass judgement on its wisdom.' He gave Hobbs a glance and added solemnly. 'It will be for others to do that in due course.'

Hobbs said nothing, did nothing, not even a blink of an

eye.

Thorsen looked at Drake. 'What's happened to Elaine Boxford?'

'We established that another member of the surgery staff had been responsible for the traces of drugs. Boxford moved back to Merseyside though,' Drake said.

'Understandable.' Thorsen turned back to the papers in front of him. 'The straightforward decision must be to prosecute Holgate for the murders of John Kerr, William Longman and David Morris. We can place him at the scene, so to speak, for each of these deaths.'

Thorsen shuffled some papers around – it left Victoria Rowlands, Michael Capon and Emyr Isaac.

Isaac had no family but Capon had a daughter and Victoria Rowlands had daughters and grandchildren. Drake hoped they would see justice delivered.

'Everything about the circumstances of Victoria Rowlands's admission to hospital and the details of the care she received while in hospital makes prosecuting Holgate for her murder justified. I've looked at that video repeatedly.' Thorsen sounded disturbed. 'I kept thinking to myself what the hell was this man doing? He had no reason to be there.' Drake had never seen Thorsen so troubled. A healthcare serial killer on the loose in North Wales had clearly shaken him. 'I wonder what a jury will make of it?' Did it mean he had doubts about prosecuting?

He paused. 'On balance I've decided we charge this fourth murder.'

It energised Drake that all the work he and his team had put into the case had been rewarded with this decision. But sadness tinged his thoughts that a combination of circumstances had allowed this sick individual to wreak a reign of terror on the unsuspecting elderly patients of North Wales. Drake wanted to say 'Brilliant, that's fantastic!' – but good judgement got the better of him. He replied. 'Noted.'

'Which brings us to the death of Emyr Isaac.' Thorsen

let out a long breath. 'And Michael Capon.'

Isaac's death had been the beginning of the inquiry. The image of Holgate outside Isaac's home that morning came back to Drake's thoughts. The paramedic had been there the previous evening administering to Isaac, discharging his duties.

'We can link Holgate to all the other four deaths because he was present, and I think we can make the logical assumption he had a large syringe with him on every occasion. But Emyr Isaac didn't die of an embolism and the glass fragments prove Holgate returned to the house in the middle of the night to stage the burglary. And as for Capon…'

Disappointment gnawed at Drake's mind. Frustration mixed with anger at the prospect that Holgate might get away with two murders.

'The evidence of the key safe codes for Capon and Isaac is disturbing and compelling. I don't think that we can anticipate a successful outcome to prosecuting Holgate with murder.'

It wasn't unexpected.

'But I think we charge in any event. Let's see what a jury thinks.'

Chapter 51

Luke Holgate pleaded not guilty to every charge, even the abduction of Luned and her unlawful imprisonment. It made defending him a difficult exercise and Drake felt the occasional spasm of sympathy for his legal team. The trial was listed to last for a month and with all the additional preparation necessary Drake had focused on little else for several weeks.

He had given evidence early in the proceedings which meant he was able to sit in court whilst the rest of the testimony was presented against Luke Holgate. Listening to the cold, objective language the lawyers used to summarise the case only made Holgate's crimes seem worse, and at the end of each day Drake would return home feeling exhausted.

The defence barrister had done his best to discredit Grant Ibbott, describing his attempted profiling of Holgate as unproven and unscientific. Ibbott hadn't allowed the lawyer to annoy him, he had replied courteously and helpfully, pointing out that all he could do was offer an opinion based on his academic background. He reminded the barrister that it was a matter for the jury to decide on guilt or innocence. Drake had read the horror on the faces of the jury as the details of the offences were outlined.

The defence barrister's attempt to identify motive went around in circles. There hadn't been one. The prosecution didn't need to establish a motive. They presented the evidence and would allow the jury to determine Holgate's fate. That was how the system worked.

The defence barrister reserved his most aggressive cross-examination for Rachel Ackroyd who tearfully explained what had happened when Holgate had been present in John Kerr's house. He had torn into her, suggesting she had fabricated everything. She had been the one to come on to Holgate and he had rebuffed her overtures.

Drake wondered what the defence barrister really felt at

having to cross examine Luned on the basis she had been a willing participant to her incarceration and being tied to the bed had been part of a pseudosexual game she had enjoyed. An embarrassed tension filled the court and Drake could tell the defence barrister disbelieved every single part of his client's explanation. It must disgust him, Drake thought, having to follow his client's instructions knowing it was a lie.

Disbelief and disgust and horror filled the faces of the jury during Luned's cross-examination. Luned was calm and measured, replying to each question carefully, dismissing each without emotion. By the end her voice trembled, and the prosecuting barrister got to his feet, interrupting his colleague, inviting the judge to consider whether any further questioning was prudent. The defence barrister conceded nothing further could be achieved and sat down.

It was Friday afternoon, a little after two when the court ushers circulated around the court building announcing that the jury had completed its deliberations. Waiting for a jury to return with its verdict meant hours sitting around, drinking watery coffee, trying to make endless strands of small talk. The barristers had adjourned to the rooms set aside exclusively for them, quaintly called robing rooms, where Drake guessed they were working on their next cases.

Drake returned to the court building. He pushed open the door and walked down to the section reserved for police officers. Hobbs was already in place, Sara by his side and Drake joined them nodding over towards the prosecuting barrister.

The ranks of journalists who had attended throughout the trial was swollen now the verdicts were imminent. Drake had no doubt that whatever happened the news would make headlines all over the United Kingdom and further afield.

He glanced over his shoulder and saw Holgate emerge from the staircase that led to the cell area below the court. He made no eye contact, stared straight ahead as though he were an innocent, disinterested bystander. Drake had seen emotion in the eyes of killers who realised they were facing a lifetime incarcerated in prison.

Frequently darkness and always hatred.

Staring over at the jury as they streamed back into court Drake realised there were no guarantees. Holgate might be acquitted on all charges. Had they proved beyond reasonable doubt that he was guilty? The prospect, however slim, of Holgate walking the streets that evening sent an icy shiver through Drake.

The jury sat down.

The robed court clerk adjusted the tab of his wing collar and asked for silence.

The judge entered, everyone got to their feet.

Seated again, Drake listened to the court clerk addressing the foreman of the jury. 'Have you reached verdicts which you are all agreed?'

'Yes.'

Drake didn't move, neither did Sara or Hobbs or the barristers. He could hear his heart thumping against his rib cage.

'On the charge of the murder of David Morris how do you find the defendant?'

'Guilty.'

Until then Drake hadn't realised that he was clenching his fists tightly. He looked down at them and slowly let the tension escape.

It was the same verdict for John Kerr, Victoria Rowlands, Emyr Isaac and William Longman.

Drake's fists were now unfurled, placed firmly on the desk area in front of him. It meant multiple life sentences.

Finally, the court clerk asked for a verdict in relation to the attempted murder of Jean Jones. Another conviction. And they did the same when the charge of abducting Luned was read out. One left.

'And to the charge of murdering Michael Capon?'

The jury foreman cleared his throat. 'Not guilty.'

Then he sat down.

When the defence barrister was half-way through his plea in mitigation the judge glared at him, cutting short his pitiful advocacy. 'Your client has embarked on a disgraceful exercise to discredit a very courageous detective constable pursuing bravely a difficult inquiry. And he has sought to disparage a carer discharging her duty in caring for an elderly man that your client killed. I suggest you think most carefully about the comments you wish to make.'

Duly scolded, the barrister sat down.

The judge turned to Holgate, barking for him to stand up. 'Your offences are amongst the most heinous I have ever come across. I have no hesitation in sentencing you to five consecutive life sentences with a minimum term of thirty-five years.'

Drake stood up when the judge left and once Holgate had been taken to the cells he felt like dancing a jig in the aisle but his legs were too wobbly from the relief flooding through his body. He settled for shaking the hands of the prosecuting barrister and Andy Thorsen vigorously. 'He'll probably die in prison,' Thorsen said.

No better outcome, Drake thought.

Chapter 52

Drake returned to headquarters by late in the afternoon knowing he had to leave in good time to join Annie at her parents' new home, and had it not been for Hobbs insisting on speaking to his team he wouldn't have bothered. The board was still in place but there was a relaxed end-of-the-week feel to the Incident Room when Drake entered. Luned gave one of her serious nods before smiling but she didn't quite match Winder's grin. Sara joined Drake and shook his hand energetically.

'Thirty-five years,' Winder said.

'And once he's gone through the parole system it could be forty,' Luned added. 'He'll be into his seventies by then.'

'There's a chance he'll never be released,' Sara said.

Superintendent Hobbs was still in his uniform when he entered the Incident Room. 'I suppose you've all heard about the result this afternoon. It was disappointing the jury didn't convict him of the Capon murder but in the grand scheme of things I don't think we have to be concerned. I wanted to compliment you all on the dedication and thoroughness you've demonstrated throughout.' Hobbs turned to Drake. 'I'd like a word, Inspector.'

After carefully closing the door Hobbs sat down. 'I was notified this morning that the assistant chief constable wants to formally review the decision made to undertake the covert operation. It was implied to me it was likely to be a box-ticking exercise.' He gave Drake a let's-be-best-mates turn of his head. 'Somebody from headquarters will review our decision-making process. In view of the excellent work completed by your team and the satisfactory outcome to the case today I'm sure I can rely on you to cooperate fully with the inquiry.'

No reservations about the original decision to launch the covert operation were to be shared. Hobbs wanted to protect his reputation and would have been keen to point the finger of blame at anyone other than himself had the result been different. Fortunately for him that wasn't the case.

'Of course, sir. I shall be delighted to confirm how Luned's suggestion had been supported by you. It would be appropriate, I'm sure, if her name were to go forward for a commendation award.'

Hobbs gave him one of his usual inscrutable looks. Drake could tell he understood exactly what he meant.

'Excellent idea.' Hobbs got up and paused. 'I'm sure your team are looking forward to a good few days' rest. Tell them to get off for the weekend.'

Hobbs made his gesture sound like a grand allowance as though he were a feudal lord giving his serfs a meagre tip. Drake and his team wouldn't have needed Hobbs's consent: they would be out of headquarters as soon as he had left them. Drake spent a few moments rearranging his desk disposing of some redundant Post-it notes before deciding that for once he would be leaving early.

Annie's parents had been in their new home for a little over a week. Roland Jenkins' recent health scare was a thing of the past although his wife regularly fussed over him whenever Drake and Annie met them. The bungalow occupied an elevated position on the outskirts of Beaumaris looking out over the Menai Strait. Since Rebecca Jenkins had seen Annie's home, she had been determined that her next house would have a sea view.

'I understand the case is finished,' Roland said as he shook Drake's hand warmly by the front door before lowering his voice. 'I've got a lovely bottle of Bordeaux ready for tonight.'

Drake smiled. Roland's love of red wine would earn him a reprimand from his wife, but he had said to Drake often enough that life was too short to go without enjoying a decent bottle of wine. And that evening Mair Drake and Elfed Matthews were joining them. It was a sort of housewarming. Until her parents had made friends, joined various local clubs and societies they would have to rely on Drake and Annie and now Mair and Elfed to socialise.

'Thirty-five years is an awfully long time,' Roland said to Drake as he followed him through the hallway into the sitting room with the attached conservatory that enjoyed the view Rebecca valued.

Annie got up and kissed him and he curled a hand around her waist and drew her close. 'It's over,' he whispered in her ear.

His mother arrived soon afterwards with Elfed and they settled into a quiet evening of good food, Roland's excellent wine and some conversation about the Rowlands' new life on Anglesey. Drake smiled over at Annie, wondering what the future held but at that moment life felt good.

Printed in Great Britain
by Amazon